SAVING
Grace

SAVING Grace

SERVE AND PROTECT 2

NORAH WILSON

Saving Grace

Copyright © 2010 Norah Wilson

Published by Norah Wilson

This book is a work of fiction. References to real people, establishments, organizations, or locations are intended only to provide a sense of authenticity, and are used fictitiously. The characters and events portrayed in this book are fictitious, and are not to be construed as real. Any similarity to real persons, living or dead, is coincidental and not intended by the author.

This book contains content that may not be suitable for young readers (under 18).

Cover by Kim Killion, Hot Damn Designs

Book design by Michael Hale, Hale Author Services

ISBN: 978-0-9878037-3-3

Chapter 1

BEING DRUNK SLOWED RAY Morgan's reaction time. The telephone managed a full ring before he snatched the receiver.

"Grace?" To his own ears, his voice sounded like someone else's.

A second's silence, then a man's voice. "That you, Razor?"

Ray sagged back into the depths of the couch. John Quigley, from the station.

Not Grace after all. Never again Grace.

"Yeah, it's me." Ray dragged a hand over his face. "'Fraid I'm no good to you tonight, though, Quigg."

Another pause. "You okay, Ray?"

"Sure. Been keeping company with Jim Beam, is all." Ray's lips twisted at his own wit. Okay, so maybe he wasn't that witty, but it was either laugh or cry. "S'okay, though. I'm not catching tonight anyway. Hallett is."

"Just a sec, Ray."

Quigg must have covered the mouthpiece, because Ray could hear muffled conversation in the background.

"Okay, I'm back," Quigley said.

"I was sayin' to call Gord Hallett. He's your man tonight."

"I don't need a detective, Ray. I was looking for you."

"Huh? You're looking for me at, what…?" He squinted across the room at the glow of the VCR's digital clock. Grace's VCR. She hadn't slowed down long enough to take anything.

What had he been saying? Oh, yeah, the time. "…eleven o'clock at night?"

"It's Grace."

At the mention of his wife's name, Ray felt the hollowness in his gut open up again, wide and bottomless as ever. Guess the bourbon hadn't filled it after all.

Leave it to Grace to get stopped on her way out of town, in her red Mustang the boys in Patrol had come to know so well. Had she explained why her foot was so heavy tonight? His grip on the phone tightened. Had she told the uniform — a guy Ray would have to face every day for the next ten years — that she was rushing off to meet her lover and couldn't spare the horses?

Her *lover.*

"You got her downtown?" he asked evenly.

"Downtown? Hell, no. They took her to —"

"'Cause you can keep her. You hear me, Quigg? I don't care."

"Dammit, Ray, listen to me. She's been in an accident."

Ray shot to his feet, dragging the telephone off the table. It hit the floor with a crash, but the connection survived. "What happened?"

"She missed a bend on Route 7, rolled her vehicle."

He felt his stomach squeeze. "Is she hurt bad?"

"Hard to say. By the time I got there, they were already loading her into the bus. But she didn't look too bad, considering she rolled that puppy like the Marlboro man rolls a cigarette. Paramedic said he thought she might have lost consciousness for a bit, but she seemed pretty with-it to me."

Wait a minute, Quigg was off duty. Why'd they call Quigg?

Unless Grace was hurt so bad they thought his best friend should break the news.

Ray gripped the receiver so hard now his fingers hurt. "Why'd they call you?"

"Nobody called me. Suz and I were on our way home from visiting friends when we came on the scene. I stopped to see if our Mountie friends could use a hand. When I saw it was Grace, I offered to make the call."

Okay, relax, man. Breathe. Maybe it wasn't that bad. *But she'd rolled the car.*

Pressing a thumb and forefinger to his closed eyelids, he pushed back the images from every bad wreck he'd seen in his twelve years on the force.

"They taking her to the Regional?"

"She's probably there already."

"I'll be there in —" Ah, hell, the booze. *Morgan, you idiot.* "Quigg, I'm in no shape to drive. Can you send a car?"

"Way ahead of you, buddy. Stevie B will be there in about four minutes."

❧

Four hours later, Ray sat across the desk from Dr. Lawrence Green-field, the neurologist who'd just finished Grace's workup.

The six cups of coffee he'd downed had sobered him up, but his stomach lining felt like he'd been drinking battery acid.

"So she's going to be okay?" Ray had been through such a wild range of emotions in the five hours since Grace had dropped her bombshell, he didn't know how he felt about this news. Christ, he didn't even know how he was *supposed* to feel. He eyed the doctor, who looked way too young to be fooling around with anyone's grey matter. "She'll walk away with no real injury?"

"I wouldn't go that far. At least not yet. She did suffer a Grade Three concussion." Dr. Greenfield leaned forward in his chair, steepling his hands. "Brain injury is more of a process than an event, Detective. It can escalate over as much as seventy-two hours, so we'll have to wait and watch for the next little while. What I *can* tell you is she has no focal injury we can pinpoint with conventional imaging."

"Focal injury?"

"No concentrated damage in any one area. The scans were clean. On the other hand, any time a patient loses consciousness, we have to be suspicious."

"What do you mean, suspicious?"

"She could have a diffuse injury, where the pathology is spread throughout the brain, rather than focused in a specific spot. We'll have to follow her for a while to rule out more subtle brain injury."

Ray slouched back in his chair, kicking a leg out carelessly. "She's conscious now?"

"Yes. And anxious to see you."

Ray rubbed a hand over the back of his neck. "Then I think I'd go back and look at those scans again, Doc."

"I'm sorry?"

"She can't possibly want to see me." He congratulated himself on how matter-of-fact he sounded. "She left me tonight. She was on her way to join her lover when she had her accident."

Dr. Greenfield blinked. "She told me she was coming home from an interview with a man who raises miniature horses, and that you'd be worried that she was late."

The pony interview? "Doc, that interview was a week ago. The story ran on Monday."

"I see." Dr. Greenfield leaned back. "Well, this puts things in rather a different light."

"What are you saying?"

"I'm saying we could be looking at a retrograde amnesia."

Amnesia? Oh, Christ, he was in a bad novel now. "But you said she'd escaped injury."

"Amnesia can accompany any loss of consciousness, however brief, although I thought we'd ruled it out." Greenfield removed his glasses and polished them. "She identified the date and day."

"Couldn't she have picked that up from the EMTs or the hospital staff?"

"Absolutely. Amnesia victims can be very good at deducing such things from clues gleaned after the accident. But she correctly answered a whole host of other questions for me, including the results of Tuesday's municipal election."

Ray digested this information. "Is it possible she remembers some things, but not others?"

"Oh, yes. In fact, it's quite probable." Dr. Greenfield replaced his glasses. "Amnesia can leave holes in the memory, with no predicting where those holes will appear. The location of the gaps can be as random as the holes in Swiss cheese. In fact, we call it Swiss cheese memory."

Terrific. Freaking wonderful. "So she might remember the election results, but not the fact that she's taken a lover?"

"I suppose it's possible."

To his credit, Greenfield's gaze remained steady, but Ray could read his eyes. Faint embarrassment, carefully masked empathy for the cuckolded husband.

"Or she may not have forgotten Romeo at all, right, Doc?" he rasped. "Just the fact that she told me about him."

"That's also a possibility," the neurologist conceded. "Whatever the case, Detective, I can vouch for the fact that she seems genuinely anxious to see you. She's very much in need of some sympathy and support."

Ray made no comment, keeping his face carefully blank.

"I should add that new memories are especially vulnerable, since it takes a few days for your brain to move them into permanent memory." Dr. Greenfield hunched forward again. "Do you use a computer, Mr. Morgan?"

Ray struggled to follow. "Of course I do. Who doesn't?"

"Well, to make a very crude analogy, fresh events, whatever might have happened in the last couple of days, are to your brain what random-access memory, or RAM, is to your computer. If the computer unexpectedly loses power before a bit of data gets stored on the hard drive, it's lost. You can boot up again, but whatever was in the RAM has been wiped out. Thus, with any loss of consciousness, it's possible to lose memories that were in transition."

Great. She'd probably forgotten she'd dumped him.

Ray stood. "Well, no time like the present, is there, Doc? Let's go see my darling wife."

Dr. Greenfield's eyes widened. "Surely you don't plan to tell her ... I mean, you won't —"

"Won't what? Suggest she call her boyfriend so she can cry on his shoulder instead?" Ray drew himself up, growing in height and girth, and let his expression go flat in the way he knew inspired fear. *Bad cop to badder cop.* "Why shouldn't I? She chose *him.*"

Dr. Greenfield looked singularly unintimidated, no doubt because he'd already seen the raw edge of Ray's anguish.

Damn you, Grace, how could you do this to me?

"The fact remains that she seems to need *you* right now. She's quite distraught. The last thing she needs is to be upset any further. If a diagnosis of retrograde amnesia is confirmed, I'd like to give her a chance to recover her memories on her own." Dr. Greenfield's intense gaze bored into Ray. "Can I have your cooperation on that point?"

Ray stared back at the doctor, unblinking. "I hear you, Doc. Now, take me to her."

⁂

Grace Morgan felt like a dog's breakfast.

Despite the painkillers the nurse had given her, everything she owned seemed to hurt, albeit in a distant way, and her head ached with a dull persistence. But she hadn't cried.

In fact, she seemed unable to cry. Instead of tears, there was just a hot, heavy misery in her chest. If only Ray would come. If he were here with her, she could cry rivers.

She'd cry for her beloved Mustang, shockingly crumpled now, a red husk of twisted metal they'd had to open like a sardine can. How had she come out of it alive?

She'd cry for her carelessness.

She'd cry for scaring Ray, and for scaring herself.

Ray. He would gather her close and soothe her while the pain seeped out, soaking his shirt. He would lend her his strength, his toughness. He'd kiss her so carefully and sweetly ....

She could almost cry, just thinking about it. Almost.

Ray, where are you?

On cue, the door swung open to admit her husband. Her heart lightened at the sight of him, so strong, so solid. His shoulders seemed to fill even this institutional-size doorway.

If she felt bad, he looked worse. Haggard. And for the first time she could remember in the six years she'd known him, he looked positively rumpled, and his face was shadowed with stubble as though he'd missed his second shave of the day.

Poor pet. He must have been so worried.

"Ray." Her right arm hindered by IV lines, she reached across her body with her left arm. He took her hand, but there was something wrong. He looked ... funny. Guarded. Wrong.

Oh, Lord, was she dying after all? Was her brain irrevocably damaged and nobody wanted to tell her? She could be hemorrhaging right now, her brain swelling out of control. Maybe that's why her head hurt. Maybe ....

Then he touched her forehead, brushing aside the fringe of hair peeping out from under the bandage, his gentleness dispelling her crazy impression.

"You all right?"

She would be now. "Yeah, I'm all right. Unless you know something I don't."

That look was back on his face again. "What do you mean?"

"They didn't send you in here to tell me they mixed up the charts, by any chance? That my brain is Jell-O after all?"

He smiled, but it didn't reach his eyes. "No, your head is fine, as far as they can tell."

She drew his hand to her cheek, pressing it there with her own palm. Some of the pain abated. "That's what they told me, too, but you'd never know it from the way I feel."

"Do you remember what happened?"

She swallowed hard, her throat tight with the need to cry. "I rolled the Mustang."

"Like a cowboy's cigarette, to quote Quigg." Another ghost of a smile curved his lips. Lips he hadn't yet pressed to hers.

She smiled tremulously. "I guess I'm lucky, huh?"

"Very lucky."

The tears welled, scalding, ready to spill. "I really loved that car."

"Something tells me you could love another one."

Again that twisting of his lips. It wasn't humor that lit his eyes. What? A vague, formless anxiety rose in her breast.

"A newer model, with fewer miles on the odometer. Or maybe something faster, flashier."

She wasn't imagining things. His tone was … off. What was it she was hearing? Accusation? Grace blinked. "Are you very angry? About the car, I mean?"

He seemed to swallow with difficulty, and his hand tightened on her chin. "Grace, I don't give a damn about the car."

For the first time since he entered the room, she finally saw what she expected to see in his face. *To hell with the car. You're okay. You're safe*, his eyes said. Her sense of strangeness dissipated.

"I was so scared."

He pulled her into his arms. The dam broke and her tears spilled over at last.

⁂

They kept Grace overnight for observation.

Ray stayed, planting himself in the single chair by her bed. Once he dozed off, waking when the night nurse came in for yet another check. At eight o'clock, he left Grace to her breakfast and went down to the lobby to find a pay phone.

He was a fool, plain and simple. He knew it, but knowing didn't seem to help. He was going to take her home anyway.

Of course, it wasn't like he had a helluva lot of alternatives. He couldn't send her home to her mother, that frozen excuse for a human being, even supposing Elizabeth Dempsey would take her daughter in. Grace's father had died two years ago, completing the retreat from an imperious wife which Ray figured must have begun minutes after Grace's conception.

No, there was no place for Grace to go. Not in her current condition.

Ray dropped his quarter and punched in the number, kneading the tense muscles at the back of his neck as he waited for his Sergeant to answer. It was likely to be a short-lived arrangement anyway, having Grace back home. When she didn't show up for her rendezvous, no doubt lover boy would come looking —

"Quigley."

"Quigg, it's me."

"About time you checked in. How's it going?"

"Grace is good. Concussed and sore as hell, but okay."

"Yeah, I've been getting regular updates. But that's not what I meant."

Ray bit back a sigh. "Is this where I'm supposed to ask what you *did* mean?"

"Last night you were ready to let her rot in the lockup."

"What's wrong with that?" Pain shot up to the base of his skull, and Ray massaged his neck again. "Biggest favor I could do for the motoring public, with that lead foot of hers."

"Except you don't know how to be mean to Grace. Leastways, not before yesterday."

"Yeah, well." Ray rubbed at a scuff on the tiled floor with the toe of his Nikes. There was a pause at the other end of the line, no doubt so Quigg could digest that pithy comment.

"I think you should take some time off," Quigg said at last.

"That's actually why I'm calling. I'll need a day or so to get Grace settled."

"I was thinking more in terms of weeks."

"Weeks?" The idea of spending days at home with Grace as she recovered her mobility — and her memory — filled him with cold dread. Not that it would take long. Even if nature didn't cooperate, Grace's paramour was bound to show up to hurry the process. Ray had been counting on putting in long days on the job, both before and after Grace's veil of forgetfulness fell — or was ripped — away.

"I can't take time off. You'll be short-staffed."

"Not for long. Woods is three days away from rotating in."

"He'll need orientation . . . ."

"He's been here before," Quigg said. "Couple of days, it'll be like he's never been gone."

"But what about Landis?"

"I'm pretty sure our small-town bad guy will be here when you get back."

"There's nothing small-town about that bastard, and you know it." Ray knew he was letting the simmering fury of his domestic disaster leach into his voice, but he didn't care. That puke Viktor Landis was a worthy target for it. "He's got his fingers into every dirty deal that goes down in this town."

"And some day you'll catch him at it, but not this week. And not next week." Quigg's agreeable tone turned hard. "Compassionate leave, Razor. Two weeks, starting now. The work'll be here when you get back. It's not going anywhere."

"But I only need a few days, not weeks."

"Take 'em anyway."

A definite command. Ray gripped the receiver tightly. Dammit, how could his friend do this to him? He *needed* to work.

"Get away from the station house," Quigg said, his voice softer now. "Spend some time with Grace. Chrissakes, Ray, you haven't taken a real break since your honeymoon."

Quigg's words stopped the retort on Ray's tongue. Had it been that long since he'd taken a vacation? He was passionate about his job, but *four years?* Why hadn't Grace said something?

"What do you say, buddy? You gonna take the time or do I have to suspend you?"

Before his promotion last year, Quigg had worked right alongside Ray in the detective bureau. Hell, he was the best friend Ray had in the world. But it wasn't going to make any difference here. Quigg meant business.

Ray put his hand on the phone's switch hook, ready to break the connection. "A week."

"Two." Another command. "And Ray? I know you're not in the market for unsolicited advice, but I'm gonna give you some anyway. Whatever you need to do to get straight with Grace, do it. She's a keeper."

"You're right."

"Of course I'm right. She's a good —"

"I meant about the unsolicited advice." With that, he replaced the receiver.

He stood staring at the telephone for a few minutes. Then, feeling like a man condemned, he turned on his heel and went in search of the doctor to see about Grace's discharge.

⁂

Six days later, Grace sat in her bedroom, battling tears.

Her headaches had receded, and her bruises were resolving nicely. The total-body agony she'd come home with had faded to mere muscle pain, easily tamed by a couple of Ibuprofen. In fact, she had everything a recuperating patient could wish for.

Ray had taken time off to nurse her. He'd fixed her meals, bought her medication, ferried her to and from the doctor's office, and generally anticipated whatever she needed before she asked for it.

In those first days, he'd massaged her sore muscles and changed the bedding regularly. He'd helped her in and out of the bath until her soreness abated enough for her to manage by herself.

He rented videos for her, most of which they watched together.

He talked to her, too. Did she remember the bird-watching trip they'd taken to the Tantramar Marshes last year? The Christmas they spent in their first apartment, before they'd bought this house? He even pulled out the photo albums she'd lovingly constructed over the years, and which he'd largely ignored, and got her to narrate each snapshot.

Yes, her husband was the perfect companion.

And she was thoroughly, completely miserable.

Oh, he was the soul of kindness, but his kindness was platonic, his touch devoid of anything remotely sexual. Even with their heads bent together over the photo album, she hadn't managed to strike a spark off him. And she'd tried. Somewhere along the way, she seemed to have gained a care-giver and lost her lover. He even slept on the couch at night, claiming he didn't want to jar her sore body.

That last thought had her knuckling her eyes like a kid.

Oh, grow up. He just doesn't want to hurt you. It's up to you to show him you're better, that you're ready to be treated like a woman again, not an invalid.

Though she thought she'd been pretty eloquent on the subject last night when he'd given her the back rub she'd requested. Or at least as eloquent as she could be in a non-verbal way. She squirmed as she recalled the way she'd purred and stretched under his hands, but none of her signals had slowed his firm, clinical strokes or brought that fierce light to his brown eyes.

Why, oh why, couldn't he see how desperately she needed this connection with him, the reassurance of physical closeness?

She chewed at her lip. Maybe men really did need things spelled out. They were always complaining women expected them to read their mind. Maybe she had to be more direct about it.

Except he'd never had any trouble reading her body language before the accident. She'd never had to ask for *that*. The very idea made her face flame.

She'd come to Ray a shy virgin, and while he'd carefully and skillfully relieved her of that state, he'd seemed content for her to keep her demureness. More than content, she suspected. He'd grown up with a mother who prized ladylike decorum above all else. Grace grimaced, thinking how often her own nature fell short of that saintly mark, at least in thought if not in actual deed.

But in the five years they'd been married, Ray had never avoided their bed before. His disinterest *had* to stem from the accident, and his reaction to her injuries.

Her spirits revived as she warmed to the idea. Really, it made perfect sense. He'd always treated her gently, so careful not to frighten or hurt her. So much so that she sometimes wanted to scream. Obviously, he needed her to affirm her return to health more forcefully.

She'd do it, she decided. She'd do it tonight.

※

This was sheer, unmitigated hell.

Ray leaned against the cupboard as he waited for the kettle to boil. He'd been in some tight spots in his time. Hell, in the four years he'd put in on the Metropolitan Toronto force before coming to Fredericton, he'd seen some truly bad shit. But nothing had tested him quite like this.

Six days, and still she acted like everything was normal.

As far as he could tell, Grace's recall was perfect, except for the last day or two before the crash. Which meant she must remember the fact of her lover's existence. Much as he'd like to, he couldn't believe those random Swiss cheese 'memory holes' Dr. Greenfield alluded to could excise the bastard so neatly.

Clearly, though, she had no memory of telling him.

And equally clearly, she was in the mood for sex.

Sex.

The word brought down the cascade of visuals he alternately tortured himself with and ruthlessly suppressed. His wife, another man. Grace welcoming another man, opening her arms for him, parting her legs —

The shrill scream of the kettle dragged him back from the edge of madness. Cursing, he shut the burner off, forcing the images back into the dark place from which they'd escaped.

Back to the problem at hand. What to do about Grace's amorous urges? He threw two tea bags in the pot and added boiling water. He sure as hell wasn't going to oblige her. Thank God for that puritanical streak her mother had instilled in her. She wouldn't ask him to make love to her, at least not in so many words. As for her non-verbal invitations, he'd continue to let them sail over his head.

How long would it take for her memory to return? Greenfield had urged him not to force the matter, allowing Grace to remember by herself. But there was a limit to how much a man could take, a limit Ray feared he was rapidly approaching.

And where was this jerk? It'd been *six days*. What kind of man wouldn't come looking for a woman like Grace when she failed to show up?

The smart kind. The kind who fears the righteous wrath of a man who carries a gun for a living.

With a fierce oath, he drove the violent fantasy from his mind. Satisfying as it was, it was only fantasy. If Grace wanted to walk out that door with another man, he wouldn't detain her.

Grimly, he put the teapot on the tray, along with the weekly rag containing the story he knew she was going to hate. Willing his face blank, he lifted the tray and headed to the bedroom.

***

Where was he? She'd heard the kettle whistle minutes ago.

Grace lay on the bed pretending to read, wearing nothing but one of Ray's good white shirts.

Well, okay, Ray's shirt and a pair of bikini panties. She wasn't brave enough to dispense with that bit of covering. But it was literally a *bit*, a barely-there scrap of lace.

She flicked back her hair, lustrous from the oil treatment she'd used on it earlier. Smooth and touchable as silk, straight as a waterfall, it was her one vanity. She tossed it back again and drew one knee up, striving for a sexy pose.

Striving and failing. Shoot. She was far too jittery to pull this off. Ridiculous to get so twisted out of shape over the prospect of seducing her own husband. It's just that he'd been so ... distant. While he accepted her touch, she sometimes got the soul-shriveling impression he had to fight himself not to shake her off. And he sure as heck hadn't initiated any touching of his own, at least nothing that wasn't related to her care. Now that she was so much better, he hardly touched her at all.

Oh, God, what if his distance sprang from more than concern about her injuries? What if he didn't want her? What if he found her efforts at seduction crass? What if he turned her down?

Grace pressed a hand to her stomach. It felt like she'd swallowed a dozen Mexican jumping beans, like the ones her father had given her when she was six. Jumping beans her mother had discarded with the trash despite Grace's protests that the caterpillars inside would perish before they could emerge as butterflies.

She groaned. *Way to go, Gracie. When he comes in, you can be wearing that whipped puppy look you get when you think about Mama. That'd be real seductive.*

No, she needed to think positive thoughts. She needed to show Ray she was a well woman. Strong. Lustful.

Very lustful.

Abandoning the magazine, she rolled onto her back. Closing her eyes, she imagined Ray approaching the bed, looking down at her with those smoldering, hooded eyes. He'd bend down to kiss her with exquisite delicacy, and his hand would go to her waist, careful not to rush her. Then, as she grew ardent beneath him, he'd lift his hands to her breasts.

Her breathing grew short. With one hand, she cupped a tingling breast, using her other hand to skim her thigh where the hem of Ray's shirt left off. Next, he'd slowly unbutton the shirt —

Something — not noise, for Ray always moved soundlessly as a cat — made her open her eyes. He stood in the doorway, a tray clutched in his hands, looking like he'd been turned to stone.

Which, I guess, would make me the Medusa head.

Grace shook the dismal thought away. At least she'd captured his attention. Even as a blush warmed her face, she drew herself up on her elbows.

"There you are." Her shallow respirations made her sound breathless as a schoolgirl, but she couldn't help it. "I was going to come looking for you in another minute."

Her words had the effect of unfreezing him. His movements jerky, he approached the bed, putting the tray down on the night table.

"I brought you the weekly paper." Keeping his eyes firmly fixed on the tray, he poured the tea. "You better read it."

Grace's shaky confidence took a plunge. He hadn't even spared her a sideways look after that first eyeful. To counter her flagging assurance, she reminded herself how much he loved seeing her in his shirts. He'd said so dozens of times, proved it dozens of times.

She took a deep breath, drew herself up on her knees. "I can think of things I want more than the Tribune," she said, running her index finger along his bare forearm.

Ray sloshed the tea he was pouring. With a muffled oath, he put the teapot down and snatched the newspaper up before it could become totally saturated. Grace shrank back as he shook droplets off the newspaper.

"Here," he said gruffly, thrusting the paper at her while he mopped the tea up with a napkin. "Front page, bottom right."

Her face burning, she took the paper, more as a physical shield to hide her humiliation than anything else, but the photo at the bottom of the page drew her eye. The sight of her crumpled Mustang, its roof peeled back grotesquely, struck her hard. Without warning, her mind lurched backward.

She was in her car, hurtling through the night, the road black, unwinding in her headlights like a shiny snake. Her hands gripped the wheel, and her heart was heavy with misery. Oncoming cars, their headlights brilliant blobs through the prism of her tears. Tires catching the graveled shoulder. That sick feeling when she started to lose it. Then ... nothing.

"You okay?"

Grace lifted a hand to her head.

"It's not like you didn't expect this, right?" Ray swiped the bottom of her teacup with a cloth napkin and handed it to her. She accepted it automatically. "It's one thing for your own paper to give the story a pass, but you had to know this other rag would run with it."

She looked up at him, seeing black road, headlights. "My accident — what time was it?"

His gaze slid away. "Ten thirty. Ten forty-five."

Almost eleven o'clock! That couldn't be right. She'd been coming home from an interview with the horse guy. Garnet Soles.

The idea seemed somehow both right and wrong. She'd started home from that interview well before five o'clock. It just didn't add up. And what was she doing out that late?

"Ray, where was I going?"

He lifted his gaze to meet hers, his expression guarded. "I don't know."

She searched his face for long moments. He spoke the truth, she decided at last. But he also lied. If he didn't know *where* she was going, he most certainly knew *why*.

"I wasn't coming back from the horse interview."

She swallowed when he shook his head.

"I've forgotten something important, haven't I?"

He nodded.

"That's why Dr. Greenfield kept asking me those questions."

"Yes."

Her stomach took a plunge. That's why Ray had pored over the photo albums with her. Testing her memory, not reminiscing.

Ask him. Ask him why you were flying down that rain-wet highway after dark.

No! Whatever it was, she wasn't ready to hear it.

Something scalded her thigh. She looked down to find she'd spilled most of her tea on herself.

Ray swore, taking the china cup from her trembling hands.

"Your best shirt," she said.

He cursed. "It's my fault."

"It's the one I bought you for your birthday last year."

"Forget the shirt." He strode to the bathroom. She heard the splash of water, then he was back, wet cloth in hand.

"Egyptian cotton." She examined the brown splotch. She'd bought it at a men's luxury store, spending the better part of a paycheck on it. Ray appreciated a really fine shirt.

"Here, put this on your thigh."

Suddenly, it seemed imperative that she save the shirt. If she didn't deal with the stain immediately, it would set, and she couldn't use bleach on the fine fibers. "I'll wash it now."

Her fingers fumbled with the buttons, but he brushed her hands away.

"Forget the shirt, dammit. Just lie down and let me put this cold cloth on that burn."

She lay back. He was right; it was just a shirt.

Ray perched beside her on the edge of the bed and gently applied the cold cloth to the red flesh at the top of her thigh.

As he bent over his task, Grace studied his lean face, so infinitely dear to her. Deep grooves bracketed a sensual mouth, and sandy brown hair sprang back from a high, smooth forehead. His downcast lashes lay sooty against his dark skin, shielding warm brown eyes.

Oh, God, why did it feel like she was losing him? It made no sense. Nothing made sense.

He glanced up. "Better?"

"I'm scared."

A muscle leapt in his jaw and he lowered his gaze again. "It'll be okay," he said, his voice gruff as he flipped the cloth to the other, cooler side.

Would it really? Something terrifying loomed at the edge of memory, just beyond her grasp. Would it ever be okay again? A shudder racked her.

"Hold me, Ray." The words were out before she knew she was going to say them. His head came up again and she met his eyes, realizing with a shock that they were as pain-filled as hers must be. Her fear took another leap. "Please."

He groaned, pulling her into his arms. She pressed herself against him, seeking to obliterate the fear bleeding into her soul from that dark, shrouded corner in her mind. *Love me*, she begged silently, her hands roaming his back.

He crushed her against his chest, trapping her arms and burying her face against his neck. Oh, Lord, he was going to rock her like a baby. He planned to comfort her in that same sexless way he'd treated her all week.

No! She wouldn't let him do this. Her arms might be pinned by his embrace, but she still had options. She opened her mouth on his neck, tasting him with her lips and tongue.

"Grace."

Her name on his lips was a growl, a warning she was past heeding. She needed this, needed him. Wriggling on his lap, she inched higher, kissing the underside of his clenched jaw, inhaling the clean scent of the lemongrass soap he used.

"No, Grace." He grasped her upper arms. "Your leg."

"It's fine. *I'm* fine. I have been for days."

He eased her away, holding her at arm's length. A few days ago — shoot, maybe a few minutes ago — she'd have let him put her aside. But not now. She couldn't let him retreat to that place he'd been these past days.

She dipped her head as though giving up, and he slackened his grip. The instant he did, she leaned into him, using her full weight. Had he anticipated such a move, she never could have budged him, but as it was, she overbalanced him easily. The next instant she sprawled atop him. The look of astonishment on his face would have been funny, under other circumstances.

Oh, my God, I'm on top! What now?

Quickly, before he could recover his wits, or maybe before she recovered her own, she bent and kissed his slack mouth.

For a few heartbeats, he lay there, unresponsive. Fueled by equal parts of fear and need, she kissed him with renewed desperation. Then, just as she began to despair, she felt him catch fire beneath her. In a single heartbeat, he was right there with her. Trapping her head, tangling his fingers in her hair, he kissed her back.

Giddy, she slid her hands over him, glorying in the way he arched up into her. Could she take him like this, claim him as thoroughly as he'd claimed her so many times? The idea sent bolts of excitement zinging jaggedly along her nerve endings. Did she dare try?

Deciding she had nothing to lose, she broke the kiss and sat up so she could tackle his belt.

He groaned and pulled her back down. Wrapping an arm around her, he rolled her swiftly onto her back, pinning her beneath him. She wanted to protest, but then he was kissing her again, deep and hot and insistent, and she couldn't think of one single thing to complain about.

Besides, it was probably best this way. She needed him to take her with an authority that left no room for doubt.

"Love me, Ray," she urged against his ear. "Love me like you've never loved me before."

His body stilled. Cursing, he levered himself off her and strode out of the bedroom.

Grace was still trying to process what had happened when she heard the front door slam. A few seconds later, Ray's truck roared to life, reversed out of the driveway and accelerated off. As she listened to the sound of his engine growing fainter, she realized she'd felt this same black despair before.

At the wheel of her car as she sped away from her husband on a ribbon of wet blacktop.

Chapter 2

D AMMIT, HE REALLY SHOULDN'T have left Grace like that.
Ray wasn't a mile out of town before that sober second thought took root. Not that he let it stop him. He let a good twenty miles roll past before he finally pulled into a busy truck stop. Nosing his black Pathfinder in between an eighteen-wheeler and a gleaming RV, he killed the engine.

She was starting to remember. Not everything, but it was beginning to come. He'd seen the fear in those pale blue eyes.

He closed his own eyes, and instantly saw Grace's face. And God help him, her softly rounded body, draped in his shirt. He'd almost dropped the damned tray when he'd walked in to find her sprawled on their bed, touching herself.

It wasn't just dismay over her introducing sex when he so desperately needed to steer clear of that minefield. No, the shock was that she'd done it at all. Then she'd pinned him to the bed like a wrestler taking an opponent to the mat and kissed him senseless. Grace just didn't do those things.

At least, not with you, chump.

"Arrrgh!" Ray slammed out of the truck.

For a moment he stood there in the parking lot, his chest heaving. Yards away, oblivious to his distress, traffic whizzed by, disappearing into the August evening.

For a moment, he thought about getting back in his truck and driving straight into the deepening dusk. He could just drive and drive, stopping only for gas and to sleep. There'd be nothing and no one to stop him until he hit the Pacific Ocean, three thousand miles away. The idea was incredibly seductive.

Sighing, he turned on his heel and walked into the brightly-lit restaurant. Though he'd kicked the habit eight years ago, the urge for a cigarette was almost overpowering. But instead of buying a pack of Export 'A's, going outside and chain-smoking a half a pack, he sat down and drank three cups of truck-stop coffee.

Feeling both queasy and jittery from all that coffee, he left the tired-looking waitress a generous tip, climbed into his vehicle, and headed home.

Four miles down the road, at sixty miles per hour, the front tire on the driver's side blew out. The SUV veered sharply across the centerline.

Ray hit the brakes, fighting with the wheel. Oh, Lord, a row of transports in the oncoming lane!

Fear, sharp and acrid, lanced through him as he realized the vehicle wouldn't be strong-armed back into the right-hand lane. He was gonna be bug-splatter on the lead rig's grill!

Taking his foot off the brake, he wrenched the steering wheel hard to the left. He sucked in his breath, half expecting the SUV to topple with that sharp maneuver. By some miracle, it streaked across the highway, avoiding a head-on collision by mere yards.

The sound of an air horn echoing in his ears, he found himself on the paved shoulder. He struggled to keep the Pathfinder out of oncoming traffic and off the guardrail, which was all that stood between him and the Saint John River, glistening in the moonlight. Violent gusts from the rigs passing just inches away buffeted his vehicle. The guardrail suddenly looked about as tall as a street curb.

Even as he thought these things, part of him marveled that he could. But every second seemed to stretch out forever, every action and reaction seemed reduced to slow motion.

Had it been like this for Grace? When the Mustang careened out of control on that rainy highway, had she thought about the husband she'd left behind? Or had she thought only of her lover, grieving the fact that she might never reach him?

Suddenly, he had control again. Like an elastic band, time snapped back.

His heart hammering in his chest, he brought the SUV to a shuddering stop flush against the guardrail. Gripping the steering wheel, he sagged forward.

Dear God, that was close!

A moment later, the last of the trucks chugged past. When all was clear in both directions, he nudged his crippled vehicle across the lanes to the proper shoulder so he could change the blown tire.

Quite suddenly, he wanted to jump out and smash the vehicle's windows, its smooth, undented hood, its taillights. He wanted to scream. He wanted to run as hard as he could until the cool evening air turned to fire in his lungs.

Instead, he took a deep, steadying breath, flicked on his hazard lights and climbed out of the Pathfinder.

Retrieving the tire iron, jack and spare, he dropped them on the pavement. Grabbing the tire iron, he squatted. With hands that still shook, he felt for the lug nuts securing the tire.

"*Christ on a bike.*"

Couldn't be.

Ray shifted, letting the moonlight strike the tire's rim. His eyes confirmed what his fingers had told him.

The wheel was secured by a single nut. *One.* It was a miracle the thing hadn't fallen off!

In a mouth-drying flash, he imagined the wheel coming off, saw his truck pitching nose first into the pavement and flipping into the path of those rigs . . . .

Cursing, he shook the images away and bent to the shredded tire again. The wheel must have wobbled like hell, which explained why the sidewall had blown so catastrophically. Just wait until he got his hands on the people who'd rotated these tires!

Well, changing the tire was out of the question. One nut wasn't going to hold his spare on long enough to get him home.

Home. He sagged against the SUV's bumper.

Home used to be Grace's arms. Lord, he wished he could go there now. If only he could forget what she'd forgotten. He'd crawl into her arms, lose himself in her.

But he couldn't forget. Even if he could, sooner or later she'd remember, and despise him for his weakness.

Or maybe not.

What if the last few days before the accident were gone forever? To use Dr. Greenfield's 'RAM theory', what if those memories never made it to the ol' hard drive? Maybe he could win her back....

Oh, God, you're pitiful, Morgan.

Yanking the truck's door open, he grabbed his cell phone and called for a hook.

An hour later, he climbed out of the cab of the tow truck. He stood at the mouth of his driveway as the wrecker pulled away, his shiny SUV still on board.

Wishing he'd actually bought those cigarettes he'd only thought about at the truck stop, he watched the wrecker turn onto the next street and head east. He lost sight of it quickly, but still he stood there until he could no longer hear the deep roar of its engine. Sweet Jesus, he didn't want to go inside.

Reluctance was a band of steel squeezing his chest, making his breathing shallow and his pulse quicken. But he knew how to deal with fear. Ignore it, push through it. Scared, not scared — in the end, it didn't matter. You just had to do what needed doing.

Squaring his shoulders, he trudged toward the house. Three paces from the door, it opened. Grace stood there, silhouetted in warm, yellow light.

"Ray, what's wrong? Was that a tow truck?"

"It's nothing. I had some mechanical trouble."

Well, at least she was fully dressed. Armored, almost. She wore jeans and hugged a big, ratty sweater around herself. She stepped back to let him in.

As he shouldered past, he caught a whiff of the stuff she used in the bath. His relief evaporated. With that scent in his nostrils, she might as well be naked, or wearing that damned shirt of his.

Again, he thought how therapeutic a shot or two of hard stuff would be. Something with bite, something that would burn all the way down and anesthetize him for the exchange to come.

No, that was a bad idea. A very bad idea.

"I need coffee," he said.

She followed him to the kitchen, where he found a full carafe of coffee already on.

"We need to talk, Ray."

His hand was surprisingly steady as he poured himself some of the black brew. He inhaled. Regular dark Columbian, not the hazelnut half-caf stuff she usually sipped at night.

He held the pot out, cocking an inquiring eyebrow. "Refill?"

"No, thanks. I've already had more than enough."

"The high-test stuff, too." He replaced the carafe and turned, leaning against the counter.

"Ray, where was I going that night?"

Guess that was it for the small talk.

"Where, specifically?" He looked down at his mug. "I don't know. You wouldn't say."

"Then tell me why. I know you know." She hugged the bedraggled sweater close. "Why was I out there?"

Sorry, Doc. I can't dodge her questions any longer.

"You were leaving me."

Silence for a few heartbeats. "No."

A denial, but her voice was weak, her eyes glazing as though she were looking inward.

"You're remembering." He put the mug down, the coffee untasted.

"I think I remember needing to get away." She looked up at him, her blue eyes covered with a sheen of tears. "But that can't be right. Things were so good ...."

"Evidently not."

"What was it, then?" She straightened, obviously steeling herself to hear the worst. "What made me leave?"

How dare she look so tortured? He was the one who'd been screwed over, dammit. Ray gripped the counter top behind him until his fingernails screamed.

"You couldn't take a guess?"

"No. That's why I'm asking you."

He turned away. Picking up his mug, he dumped the coffee down the drain, rinsed his mug and put it on the draining board.

"Come on, Ray. For God's sake, just tell me!"

He turned to face her again, schooling his features into a bland mask. "Marital infidelity."

She took a step back at those two words.

"Infidelity?" She gaped at him with horrified eyes, as though he'd just slid a knife between her ribs. "You were having an affair?"

A harsh laugh escaped him. "Hardly."

"But you said infidelity …."

"Not mine, Gracie." He looked deep into those blue eyes and watched shock explode there. "*Yours.*"

⁂

Grace fought the panic rising in her chest. "No!"

"Yes." Ray's face was cold, implacable. "That's where you were going. You were leaving me to hook up with lover-boy."

"No. That's impossible."

"You stood right here and told me, in this very kitchen."

"No." She was repeating herself, but *no* was the only word her mind could form.

"*Yes.* I caught a home invasion just before end-of-shift, so I'd put in a couple of hours of OT and got home late. You were waiting for me here, about where you're standing right now. But you weren't keeping supper warm, were you Gracie?"

She pressed both hands to her temples, trying to push back the confusion. It couldn't have happened. She couldn't have left Ray. She'd never leave him. *Never.*

"That can't be right. I wouldn't do that."

"Ah, but you did. You said you'd met someone else, someone who meant more to you than I ever could. You said you were sorry, but there was no point in my trying to stop you." His voice grew stronger, louder with every accusation. "You said now that you knew what love was supposed to be like, you couldn't settle for less."

Grace covered her ears. "Stop! You're making this up."

He laughed, a harsh, ugly sound. "Funny, that's what I accused you of doing, making it up. But you convinced me."

She dropped her arms to her sides. "But there's no one. I mean, I don't remember —"

He shoved his hands into the pockets of his jeans. "Dr. Greenfield said you'd probably have random blanks. There'd be stuff you might not remember."

"Random blanks? But I don't remember anything ... any*one*."
God, she was losing her mind. Maybe she'd already lost it. "How
can you call it *random* if a whole thread is missing?"

Ray angled his face away, but she could see he was struggling
with his own emotions. "Maybe it's a new development. Greenfield
said new memories can be especially vulnerable."

Grace swallowed. "How new?"

"Three days."

She laughed, but it came out more like a sob. "You think I'd run
away with someone I'd had a relationship with for *three days*?"

"How should I know?" A muscle leapt in his jaw. "Until recently,
I'd wouldn't have believed it under any circumstances."

"But three days ... I wouldn't —"

"There's another possibility."

"What's that?" Hysteria welled in her chest, driving her voice
higher. "Insanity?"

"Psychological trauma."

"Psychological trauma?" she echoed. "Is this another thing Dr.
Greenfield neglected to tell me about?"

He looked away again. "No, Greenfield didn't mention it. But
I've seen it on the job. Sometimes people block memories selec-
tively."

"You think I *chose* to forget that I'd taken a lover and dumped
you?"

"It's not exactly a voluntary thing."

"But why?" she demanded. "What would make me do that?"

His head snapped back around. "How the hell would I know?"

His gaze blazed into her and she tried not to flinch. But dear
heaven, he looked as though he hated her. Grace wrapped her arms
around herself. "I'm sorry. This is so new."

"I haven't had too long to get used to it, either."

"When —" She choked, tried again. "When did I tell you?"

"The night of your accident."

Her mind wanted to shut down, stop processing, but she couldn't
let it. After a week of blundering around in the dark, she needed
the truth.

"I just told you? I mean, I just flat-out told you, then left?"

"Yep."

"I can't see myself doing that." She shrugged helplessly. "Doing *any* of it."

"I needed some convincing myself, but you persuaded me."

She searched his face. He was telling the truth. She read it in the hard glitter of his eyes, the ruthless set of his mouth. This was the root of the underlying coldness she'd sensed in him even as he'd nursed her so solicitously. This was why he'd rebuffed her clumsy seduction.

Oh, Grace, what have you done? And why can't you remember? A dozen different emotions tried to jam their way through a narrow bottleneck in her chest.

Stunned disbelief. *I can't possibly have done it.*

Hideous self-doubt. *Could I have done it, but the trauma of the betrayal made me forget?*

Mind-numbing fear. *Oh, Gracie, what if you did do it?*

Stomach-churning shame. *Sweet mother of God, what if I really did it?*

The tumult of emotions melded into a single one — hot, despairing, improbable anger.

"So, what's the story?" Her voice was brittle. "If I hadn't jumped you in there tonight," she indicated the direction of the bedroom with a jerk of her shoulder, "if I'd waited like a good little girl for you to touch me like I always do, how long would it have taken you to tell me this?"

His eyes narrowed. "The doctor said to give you a chance to remember it on your own."

"And what if that didn't happen? *Huh?* What then?" she demanded. "What if I never recover those memories? What did Dr. Greenfield say about that?"

"I don't think we have to worry about that."

"Why not? Why the *hell* not?"

She wanted to hit him. She wanted to pummel his chest, scratch him. Insanity. She had no right to this anger. She was the betrayer, he the betrayed. But knowing that didn't seem to stem the frightening rage.

"There's nothing there. Do you understand me, Ray?" she said. "*Nothing*. It feels like I'm never going to recover anything from that fog. How can you say that's not a concern?"

His eyes went flat. "I'm thinking you'll get a solid reminder any day now."

At his words, her anger peeled away, exposing its true face — fear. Her mouth went dry. "What do you mean?"

"Sweet thing like you? Sooner or later, he's gonna come for you, don't you think?"

Grace felt the blood drain from her face.

"I'll take the couch," said Ray, stepping around her.

❧

Ray came awake to the sound of casters rolling across hardwood flooring. He glanced at the clock on the VCR and stifled a groan. Three in the morning. Ignoring his stiff back, he swung his feet to the floor and levered himself off the couch.

She didn't hear him coming. For a moment, he leaned against the doorframe and watched her pore over the telephone book in the pool of light cast by the desk lamp. Beside her, the Pullman suitcase whose noisy wheels had woken him crouched next to two smaller bags.

His bags, he noted, recalling hers were still in the SUV where he'd shoved them after Quigg rescued them from the Mustang's wreckage.

"Going somewhere, Grace?"

She whirled, one hand going to her throat. "I didn't mean to wake you."

"Obviously not." He flicked on the overhead light. "So, where are you off to this time?"

The abject misery in her face made him wish he could pull back that flippant question. But in a matter of seconds, the look was gone, her expression carefully smoothed.

She shrugged. "I thought I'd go back home for a few weeks."

"Oh, Lord, not that."

She colored fiercely. "It's all right. I can handle Mama."

"You don't have to go back there, Grace. You don't have to go anywhere."

She dropped her gaze to the floor. "I can't stay."

"Why not? This is your home, too."

She caught her lower lip between her teeth. "I just can't."

Suddenly, he couldn't bear for her to leave. Not again. Not yet.

"If you leave now, Grace, you might lose your only chance of regaining those memories."

She looked up at him then, her beautiful eyes red-rimmed and brimming with more tears. "I don't want to remember."

Her unhappiness pierced him. "Don't worry about it tonight. Just go back to bed. Things'll look better in the morning."

"I can't sleep. I feel like I might never sleep again."

He almost smiled at that. "You will. Life has a way of going on. We'll figure something out. But right now, let's get you back to bed. I'll take these cases up."

She studied him for a moment. "You really want me to stay?"

What he wanted was for the last week not to have happened.

No, he wanted more than that. He wanted to go back in time to when Grace felt the first stirring of dissatisfaction, only this time he'd pay attention to what she needed, what she wanted.

But that was a child's wish. An impossibility. There was no going back. He'd settle for understanding what had happened.

Settle for it? Hell, he *needed* to know what had gone wrong. He didn't see how he could go on from here without that knowledge. And for that to happen, Grace had to remember.

"Yes, I want you to stay."

Her eyes lit, and Ray cursed himself. Hope was a luxury neither of them could afford. So he looked away and did what he had to. "What I mean is, it'd be better for both of us if you regain your memory, and this is the best place for you to do it."

"I see."

"I doubt it. Now go on up. I'll bring you a hot toddy."

"I'm scared, Ray."

The fear in her voice brought his head up. And, oh, damn, he shouldn't have looked into her eyes. He sighed. "Don't worry. It'll be okay."

"I think it's bad, the thing I can't remember. I think it could hurt us. It could hurt you."

"No." Ray couldn't have kept the bleakness out of his voice if he tried. "It can't get any worse. It can only get better from here. Trust me. I need you to do this for me, okay?"

"Okay," she said, then turned and climbed the stairs.

⁂

Grace listened to Ray's breathing, deep and even in the darkness, and knew he was asleep. He'd held himself stiffly for hours, until finally, *finally*, he succumbed some twenty minutes ago.

It was pity alone that kept her husband here on the bed with her, albeit on top of the covers. She knew it, but she didn't care. It was such a comfort to have him lie so close, to breathe the same air he breathed.

Dear God, she didn't want to remember. There was something there, something ugly just beyond her reach, and it was bad.

But Ray needed her to remember, so remember she would.

Even if it killed her.

Shivering, she drew the duvet closer, shut her eyes and let exhaustion claim her.

Chapter 3

SOME PEOPLE CLEANED COMPULSIVELY when anxiety rode them. Some threw themselves into their jobs. Others unplugged from life and plugged into the television. Grace cooked.

By the time Ray came downstairs the next morning, she'd amassed a small mountain of pancakes, cooked a half-pound of bacon, and set a dozen blueberry muffins on a rack to cool.

He cocked an eyebrow at the spread. "Expecting company?"

Grace blushed. "I thought I'd go back to work. I guess I felt in need of some fortifying."

He poured himself a coffee. "Are you sure you're ready for that?"

"Positive." She met his skeptical gaze. "I'm not going to remember anything as long as I'm closeted here, racking my brain. It'll come easier if I go back to my normal routine."

"Makes sense, but your boss'll be surprised." He heaped his plate full and headed for the table. "I left a message on her voice mail saying you'd be out for a couple of weeks."

"Yes, Katie will be surprised, but I expect she can use me."

She topped up her coffee and took the chair opposite him. For a moment she just watched him eat.

He looked so ... normal. Faded jeans hugged his legs, and his favorite black sweater, a little snug since that time she'd tossed it in the dryer, skimmed his torso. A week ago, she'd have found an excuse to lean across the table. He'd have caught her with a growl and pulled her onto his lap. She'd have laughed and brushed that lock of hair off his forehead, kissed his brow, his nose, his mouth ....

He glanced up to catch her watching him, and she dropped her hungry gaze.

31

"Not eating?"

"I ate already," she lied, knowing she couldn't choke down a morsel. She took a sip of her coffee to ease her throat.

"You must be anxious to get back to work, too, I suppose."

His fork stilled. "I won't be going back for another week."

Grace's stomach flipped. She put her cup down. "Because you want to hang around here, waiting for *him* to show up."

Ray pushed his plate away and threw his napkin down. "Because Quigg'll suspend me if I go back sooner."

"*What?*"

"I'm under orders to patch things up with you."

Her face burned. "John knows?"

"He knows something's not right." Ray drained his coffee and pushed his chair back. "I'm going to fetch the truck."

She blinked. "How will you get there? We have no car."

"I'll walk. I can use the exercise."

She followed him to the door.

"I'll take you to work when I get back. They're not expecting you anyway, so they shouldn't mind if you're late."

A week ago, she'd have been happy to fall in with his suggestion, but now she couldn't bear the idea of waiting around for him to come back and retrieve her. Maybe because her life felt so out-of-control, she needed to take charge of something.

"No, thanks, I'll call a taxi."

"Okay." He shrugged. "I'll see about a rental for you, until we settle with the insurance."

That lock of hair fell forward again, and she battled the urge to smooth it back. He'd only pull away and then she'd have to cry. The last thing she needed on her first day back was puffy, blood-shot eyes. Katie'd send her right back home.

"No, I'll take care of that, too," she said.

"It's no trouble. I have lots of time on my hands."

Out of nowhere, resentment boiled up. "It's my mess, Ray. *Mine.* For once, let me clean it up myself."

She turned and stalked back to the kitchen, knowing he was probably gaping after her. Grabbing his plate, she scraped the uneaten food into the garbage disposal then turned the unit on so she wouldn't have to hear the door close behind him.

⚜

Ray quickly realized that the day was too hot for the sweater he wore. It would have been fine had he been riding in his truck, but on foot, he'd already broken a sweat despite the relative coolness of the late August morning. Damned if he'd go back to change, though. Once he got clear of the close-set town houses, the breeze picked up, cooling him.

Too bad it couldn't cool the anger burning in his chest.

He turned onto a main thoroughfare and started the long walk up the hill to the car dealer.

Where the hell did Grace get off? All he'd done was offer to rent her a car so she wouldn't be stuck at home, but she'd rounded on him like a cat who'd had its hair ruffled the wrong way.

Well, if she wanted to take care of her damn mess, she was welcome to it.

Thirty minutes later, Ray stood, hot and irritable, in front of the dealership manager. "Mr. Melville, you got the message I left you on your voice mail?"

"I sure did, Detective."

"Then you know I came close to becoming a hood ornament for a Freightliner because of your service department's negligence."

The other man shifted. "I'm sorry about that, but before you say anything more, I'd like you to take a look at the vehicle."

"Let me guess." His words dripped sarcasm. "You're gonna show me something to suggest this wasn't your fault at all."

The manager colored but kept his composure. "The customer is always right, of course, and if you feel it was our negligence, we're quite prepared to replace the tire and the bent rim free of charge. But if you'd just take a look, sir."

He shrugged and started toward the garage bays.

"No, not in there," called Mr. Melville.

Ray looked around, then lifted an eyebrow. "Where, then?"

"Way over at the far corner of the lot. I had it moved this morning."

"Why?"

Mr. Melville cleared his throat. "Frankly, we're a little leery of it."

Ray's mouth fell open. "Come again?"

"We think it may have been sabotaged."

"You shittin' me?"

"Please, Detective, let's just have a look."

Three minutes later, Ray toed the shredded tire. "Okay, what am I looking for?"

"Not the tire. The door, over here on this side."

Ray moved to the passenger side. "What about it?"

"See those scratches? It looks like someone used a car-breaking tool on it, the kind the tow-truck driver uses after you've locked your keys in."

"Slim Jim?"

"Right. And it looks like it was used with some haste."

Ray examined the scratches and grunted noncommittally. "Maybe. Or maybe they've been there for months. Who'd notice a few scratches like that?"

"Would you notice if your glove compartment was broken?"

"Definitely. I always keep it locked."

"Not anymore. It's busted."

Ray peered through the window. Sure enough, the door of the glove compartment hung open.

"Okay, so someone broke into my vehicle. I don't see how that advances your case for sabotage. In fact, it probably happened last night, right here on your lot. I'd have noticed last night if the glove compartment were broken."

"Maybe, maybe not. Someone went to the trouble of sticking it shut with electrical tape."

Before Ray could express his skepticism, the manager took his arm and urged him back a step or two from the vehicle.

"See the nut covers on those rims?" He pointed to the rear wheel.

"Yeah."

"You have to use a special adapter to remove those covers."

"I wouldn't know. I've never had to change a tire on this vehicle."

"Guess it's supposed to deter opportunists from stripping the wheels right out from under you. It's a small little do-hickey, about so big around and so long." The older man used his fingers to approximate the size. "We generally put them in the glove compartment so they don't get lost."

In the glove compartment. The *broken* glove compartment.

"Let me guess — mine's gone."

"Gone," he confirmed.

"Maybe your man forgot to put it back, like he forgot to put all the lug nuts on."

The older man snorted. "Yeah, and maybe we broke into your car and busted your glove compartment to shift the blame away from ourselves. But we didn't, Detective. I've already told you, we're prepared to pay for the tire and the bent rim, even the tow charges. What do we stand to gain by lying about this?"

"How about so I don't sue your ass?"

"You won't sue." Melville's response was immediate. "Even if you could prove negligence, you'd also have to prove damages. This incident might have given you some grey hairs, but the courts don't take judicial notice of that."

Ray arched an eyebrow. "What, you studying law in your spare time?"

Melville returned his stare.

Ray rubbed his neck. The man had a point. Maybe there had been tampering.

"Come on over here, Detective."

Ray followed the other man around the car.

"Okay, we've taken all but one of the nut covers and nuts off the front tire on this side, just so you can see what it looks like."

"Pretty noticeable," he conceded.

"I'll say! Stands out like a missing hubcap. If we hadn't put 'em back on that left front wheel when we rotated your tires two weeks ago, you couldn't help but notice it. You'da had a gander at it every time you approached the vehicle."

Dammit, he was right. No way could he have overlooked that. Noticing details was second nature.

"Look, you probably think I've been watching too many movies, but all of these things —"

"Actually, I think you might be onto something."

"You do?"

"I do. Can I use your phone? I need to get a team up here to go over this vehicle."

⁂

Four hours later, Ray guided the thoroughly-inspected Pathfinder into his driveway.

Ident had dusted for prints, but Ray wasn't hopeful. Whoever did this would have worn gloves, or wiped the surfaces clean. Then the bomb squad guys swept the vehicle. Lastly, the dealer's mechanics had given it an exhaustive mechanical inspection. It was clean. There was even a replacement adapter thingy for tire changes nestled in the newly-repaired glove box.

He'd felt a little dumb summoning the guys, and fully expected to take a ribbing for it, especially when the vehicle came up clean. There were, of course, a few cracks about going to any lengths to escape paying for a safety inspection, but once they'd heard about his near miss on the highway, they'd turned deadly serious.

Ray guided the SUV into the garage, then closed and locked the metal overhead door. If someone really was out to get him, no point making it easy. Still, he'd feel better when he got an alarm system installed, on both the truck and the house.

At least he didn't have to face Grace yet. She'd be at work. When he'd called earlier to tell her he'd be delayed, she'd already left the house. Ray selected his house key, inserted it in the lock and twisted. It didn't turn. *What the hell?*

With his left hand, he twisted the knob and the door swung inward. Unlocked. Grace never left the house without locking it.

His hand went automatically to where his shoulder holster should have been. Damn.

Call the cops. Isn't that what he preached in this situation? *Never investigate yourself.*

Except he *was* a cop, albeit an unarmed one. And no way was he going to call in the cavalry twice in one day. Besides, he wouldn't be unarmed for long.

Ray pushed the door open and risked a quick glance. The foyer was clear. He eased inside, scanning the room. Leaving the door ajar, he glided to the stairs.

His heart pounding, he held his breath, listening.

Nothing.

Moving stealthily, he climbed the stairs, taking care to avoid the squeaky tread three steps down from the top. The hallway was clear, too. A few more steps and he'd be in his bedroom where his gun sat in a locked strongbox in the closet.

The bedroom door was ajar, but there was nothing unusual in that. Careful not to hug the wall too closely — an excellent way to catch a ricochet — he crept the few steps to the bedroom door. Taking a deep breath, he peered around the doorjamb. The room was empty, though he could still smell Grace's perfume. He exhaled, drew another deep breath.

Still in stealth mode, battling adrenaline, he entered the bedroom. He moved to the night table, feet soundless on the carpet. The drawer pulled out silently. Grabbing the clip for the 9mm, he moved quickly to the closet where he eased the bi-fold door open, grimacing at the small noise it made.

As quietly as he could, he drew his keys from his pocket and knelt to open the strongbox.

Then he heard a muffled thump from the en suite bathroom. Abandoning stealth for speed, he jammed the key into the lock, twisted it and flipped the box open. Snatching his weapon, he jammed the clip home, slid a round in the chamber and whirled.

"Ray!"

Grace. It was only Grace.

"Ray, what are you doing?"

Christ, he'd pointed a loaded gun at Grace. Was *still* pointing a loaded gun at her. Hastily, he dropped his arm.

"Dammit, you scared me."

"*I* scared *you?*" She pressed a hand to her chest as though to keep her heart from leaping out.

"I found the door unlocked." His heart still pounding, he unloaded the automatic and returned the clip to the drawer.

She sank on the end of the bed, shaking visibly.

"I thought you'd gone to work," he said. "You never leave the door unlocked when you go. I thought there must be an intruder."

"For a second, I thought—" She broke off abruptly, clasping her hands together in her lap.

"Thought what?"

"It doesn't matter."

Suddenly, he knew it *did* matter. A lot. He moved to the end of the bed to better see her face. "I think it does, Grace. What did you think?"

"Nothing. I .... Nothing."

"You're shaking like a leaf. Tell me."

"For a split second ...." She dropped her gaze to her clasped hands.

"For a split second you thought ... ?"

She looked up at him again, her pupils still dilated with shock. "I mean, I know you'd never do anything like that, but just for a second ...."

His heart stumbled, then lurched on with a painful thudding. "You thought I was going to shoot you?"

She said nothing, but he saw the answer in her eyes.

She really thought he'd been going to shoot her!

Him, a cop, sworn to uphold the law. Her own husband.

He waited for the anger to come, but all he felt was a stunned, sinking despair.

Dear Lord, what did he look like through her eyes that she could think such a thing, even for a second? No wonder she'd looked for something else.

Some*one* else.

"Oh, Grace."

He sank onto the bed beside her. Her gaze dropped and he followed it to his service weapon, now unloaded, which he still cradled in his hand, its weight familiar and comforting. Suddenly, he saw it as she might see it — an obscene extension of his arm. A tool to amplify male aggression.

He jumped up, shoved the gun back into its box and locked it. He'd been so goddamn careful with her, tried so hard to always show her gentleness, never let her see the hard face of his soul. But she must have sensed it anyway. Sensed it and magnified it to reach some chilling conclusions.

He put the strongbox back in the closet and turned back to her. His face must have shown something of his thoughts, for hers creased with remorse.

"I didn't mean it," she said, moving closer. "I didn't really think you'd hurt me."

"Yes, you did."

"No."

He just returned her gaze.

"If I did, it was my own guilt talking." She stood, laid a hand on his arm. "Why wouldn't you hate me? I betrayed you."

His arm muscles flexed involuntarily, and she dropped her hand. She closed her arms around herself, her whole posture a picture of misery. He looked away. "I don't hate you."

"Well, that's something, at least. Now, if *I* could just stop hating me."

Her tone drew his gaze back. Damn. He wanted to put his arm around her shoulder, pull her close, comfort her. "Don't," he said instead. "Don't torture yourself."

"If I could just remember." She'd unclasped her arms and began to worry a frayed cuticle on her thumb. "You'd think I could remember something that life-altering, a relationship so important that I chose to throw my marriage away ...."

Her voice broke and this time, Ray did lift an awkward hand to rub her back.

"You'll remember," he said. "I think you were right about going back to work, getting back to routine. Once you take the pressure off yourself, it'll come."

"Ah, yes, work." She cleared her throat. "Actually, there's a problem there."

"Yeah?"

Grace turned to him, her blue eyes swimming with unshed tears. "I no longer have a job."

Ray's jaw dropped. "They *fired* you while you were recuperating from a car accident?"

"No. I quit."

"But why?" He blinked. She *loved* that damned newspaper. "I thought you were keen to go back."

"Apparently I quit the day of my accident. I told them they could keep my accumulated vacation pay in lieu of notice, emptied my desk and left."

Ray tried to keep the shock from his face. "You don't remember any of that?"

"Nothing. Apparently I was pretty vehement about it. Katie wanted me to work out my notice, but I refused. I guess that's why she didn't visit me in hospital."

She managed a smile, but the expression held so much pain it made his heart squeeze.

"You don't remember thinking about giving your notice?"

"No." She shrugged helplessly. "I know I used to complain sometimes that they didn't take me seriously, but I really thought I'd be there forever, eventually move up the ladder . . . ."

She'd quit the paper. The knowledge twisted his gut. She really had planned to leave.

"What am I going to do?"

She sounded so damned desolate. All he could do was shrug. "Ask for your job back."

She shook her head, blinking rapidly.

"Katie might be pissed, but she'll take you back. Want me to talk to her?"

"No!"

He stiffened. "Right. I forgot. This is your mess. You don't want my help." He turned to leave but she gripped his arm.

"They've already replaced me."

Her voice broke again. He looked down at her upturned face and knew he couldn't leave her like this. Her eyes, so wide and blue, were filled with unanswerable misery.

"What's happening to me?" she asked. "How could I do these things and not remember?"

"It's okay." He did slide a comforting arm around her this time. She felt smaller and more fragile than he remembered. "You'll see, Gracie. It'll be okay."

She clung to him hard, and for a moment, he thought she was finally going to have a good cry. Instead she surprised him by pulling away after only a few seconds, drawing herself up. He could almost see her pulling her pain inward.

"I've been thinking." She sniffed and swiped at her eyes. "We should retrieve my bags from the trunk of the Mustang. Maybe if I could look at what I'd packed, it might trigger —"

"Damn, I forgot. Quigg recovered that stuff. He gave it to me the night of the accident."

"You've got my bags?"

"In the back seat of my truck. I'll fetch them."

A moment later, he popped the hatch on the SUV and hauled out the bags. As he did so, he remembered the look Tommy Godsoe had sent him this morning when he'd searched the overnight bag, after his canine partner had pronounced it explosives-free.

"This yours, Razor?" Tommy'd held the bag up by its handle.

"Grace's," Ray had replied. "I forgot it was in there."

Tommy had given him an odd look over the roof of the Pathfinder. "Grace's, eh? Well, old buddy, I wouldn't waste any time getting it back to her, if I were you," he'd said, then zipped the bag closed again and resumed his search.

Ray's face burned again as it had then, imagining only too well what was in the bag.

Grace had a passion for underwear. Nothing tacky, but she loved color. Funky orange and lime green and deep purple, in silk and lace and velvet. Bras that cupped her lush breasts and high-cut panties that made her legs look miles long.

Cursing, Ray slammed the hatch and went back inside.

Grace hovered just inside the door.

"Where do you want 'em?"

"The bedroom, I guess."

He carried his burden upstairs, with Grace on his heels. Briskly, he flopped the suitcase on the bed and dropped the leather satchel beside it.

"There you go."

He turned to leave, but she called his name. He stopped in the doorway but didn't turn.

"You're not going to stay while I go through them?"

He turned his head to the side. "So I can see what you packed to start your new life? No, Grace, I think I'll give that a pass."

The distressed little sound she made echoing in his ears, he went downstairs, where he lay down on the couch and draped an arm over his eyes.

⁂

Grace turned back to the bed, looking at the suitcases through a film of tears.

She lifted her gaze to the mirror above the dresser. "Don't you dare cry," she told her reflection. "You brought this down on your own head. Deal with it."

Except dealing with it was easier said than done. She'd never had to suffer Ray's contempt before. She let her breath out on a sob. How was she going to bear it?

The same way he's had to bear what you did to him.

This time, she tried not to flinch from that truth. She'd ditched him in the most brutal way imaginable. Then she'd proceeded to leave her employer in the lurch, pack her bags and leave town. And for what? A man she couldn't even remember.

Couldn't remember, for pity's sake.

And not for lack of trying. When she'd come back from the office, she'd lain on the couch, numb from shock. As her mind floated, she'd tried to bring this man's features together. She'd closed her eyes and tried to hear her lover's voice, feel his touch, taste his kiss. But no matter how the features she conjured started out, they always shaped themselves into Ray's dark face. The only voice she could imagine whispering sweet words in her ear was Ray's. The only smell, only taste, only touch — his.

She wanted to cry. She wanted to scream, *No, I didn't do it!* She wouldn't have done it. Couldn't have done it.

Yet she must have done it. The evidence was damning.

Her gaze fell on the suitcases. Ray was right. She needed to unearth those memories. There must be an explanation for her behavior. She had to believe it. For all that people were inclined to dismiss her as a lightweight, she wasn't flighty. And she certainly wasn't given to mad impulse.

Of course, she would also have qualified herself as loyal as a Labrador Retriever, and look what she'd done.

Tears started to well again. *The suitcase,* she reminded herself. She wiped damp palms on her jeans, then opened the big suitcase.

Oh, thank God. The top layer was all familiar stuff. She actually smiled. What had she expected? A black leather bustier? Edible underwear? Crazy to be so relieved.

Or maybe not so crazy. Her small smile faded. If she could cheat on Ray, she obviously didn't know herself very well.

Forcing her attention back to the task, she started removing garments one by one, piling them on the bed.

Two pairs of jeans, two pairs of khakis, a half-dozen t-shirts, a few blouses, two sweaters, a pair of low-heeled pumps, her Puma runners, and her most serviceable underwear. Some of the items she'd known she'd find because she'd noticed them missing. Other items, she hadn't yet missed. But there was nothing remarkable in the whole lot.

Her brow furrowed as her initial relief that the bag wasn't jammed with crotchless panties gave way to puzzlement. Why hadn't she packed better underwear?

Because you wouldn't wear anything for another man that you'd worn for Ray.

Okay, but surely she'd have bought new stuff. Underwear was too important to her. She wouldn't pitch an idea for a feature to Katie without wearing her best underwear, let alone run off to meet a man who was actually going to *see* it.

She picked up the perfectly nice but unexceptional underwear and slid the pieces into her dresser drawer with their finer cousins. Obviously, the decision to leave had been made in haste.

Or in a fit of despair.

On that thought, she stowed the rest of the clothes back in the drawers and closets, then turned her attention to the other bag.

If the suitcase told her little, the overnight case would tell her less. She already knew what it contained. Hair dryer, cosmetics, skin-care products, and all those other little items that were missing from the bathroom vanity, dresser top and jewelry box.

Suddenly, the idea of unpacking and putting away all the accouterments of her life with Ray made her throat hurt. How long before she'd be packing it all up again?

Don't, Grace. Just don't.

Jumping up, she snagged the handle of the satchel and pulled it closer to the edge of the bed. A tug of the zipper, a wrench of the wrists and the bag lay open.

Grace leapt back. Holy cow! Guess she hadn't remembered *everything* she'd packed.

"Ray?"

His name emerged as little more than a croak, probably because of the fear bleeding the strength from her limbs and making her tongue cleave to the roof of her mouth. She swallowed, then turned and walked carefully out of the bedroom to the head of the stairs. She called Ray's name again, louder this time. He materialized below a second later.

"What is it?" he asked, his expression politely inquiring.

"I think you'd better come up here and take a look."

Chapter 4

OH, LORD, DIDN'T SHE get it? He didn't want to know if she'd packed that mocha-colored lace number or her silk kimono or her diaphragm.

He was just about to tell her so when he noticed how white she'd suddenly gone. Then she swayed. Ray took the stairs two at a time, catching her before she could fall.

"What is it? Is it your head? Are you dizzy?"

She sagged against him as he pulled her back from the top of the stairs.

"In there ...."

"In the bedroom?"

She backed away far enough to look up at him, blue eyes wide in her fear-pinched face. "I don't know where it came from, Ray."

Her fear leapt to him like a wildfire jumping a fire break. "Grace, what are you talking about?"

"In the suitcase ...."

"What's in the suitcase?"

"Maybe it's in my head. Maybe I'm hallucinating." Her fingers dug into his biceps, eyes pleading. "Please tell me I imagined it."

"Okay, let's just go have a look."

Keeping one arm around her shoulders, Ray urged her toward the bedroom. Her steps dragged with reluctance, so he left her standing on the threshold and strode into the room himself.

The larger suitcase lay open on the bed, empty, and the leather satchel sat there beside it. It was unzipped, but the soft sides had fallen together again, shielding its contents. He felt sweat break out on his forehead.

Logic told him there couldn't be anything dangerous in the bag; Tom Godsoe and his dog had gone over both suitcases. But whatever was in there, it scared Grace so bad she couldn't say it aloud. Whatever it was, it made her prefer to think she was delusional.

And whatever it was, it was going to change his life. Again.

Shaking the last thought away, he yanked the bag open.

"Jesus, Mary and Joseph!" Money. Cash money. Lots of it.

Grace, from the doorway: "I didn't imagine it, did I?"

Ray lifted one of the bundles, fanning the bills. "There must be ..." - he paused to do a mental calculation - "... nine or ten thousand dollars here. Where the hell'd you get this wad?"

She stepped into the room. "I told you, I don't know."

"But so much ... how can you not remember where you got it?"

She stiffened. "Ray, I threw my marriage away, quit my job, and tried to leave my life behind." She marched over to the bed, snatched up a bundle of twenties and shook it under his face. "If I can't remember why I did those things, why should I remember *this*?"

Stupid thing to say. "Of course. I'm sorry."

The fight seemed to drain out of her at his apology. She looked down at the money in her hand for a moment, and when she lifted her gaze again, her eyes looked tortured.

"I'd shred every last one of these notes, then burn the scraps, if I could just have my life back."

Her words caught him fair in the heart. "Aw, Grace." She looked so miserable he just couldn't bear it. Lifting his right hand, he cupped her face, and for a moment she leaned into his palm, closing her eyes. Then, abruptly, she pulled back.

"Okay, we'd better figure this out," she said, her voice brisk if a little tremulous. She tossed the money down on the bed. "I don't think I could have embezzled it from the paper. No access or opportunity."

Embezzled? Gracie? "I don't think you have to worry about that. You're not a thief."

"I didn't think I was an adulterer or a liar, either." Her lips twisted in the kind of bitter smile he never imagined her wearing. "I think we have to consider all the possibilities, however improbable they sound."

A spark of admiration ignited in his chest. The old Grace would have fallen apart. She'd have cried on his shoulder, borrowed his strength and accepted his comfort. But this new Grace seemed determined to face the situation squarely.

"I'll start with the bank."

"The bank?" Ray lifted an eyebrow. "We don't have that kind of money laying around."

"Unless I cashed in my RRSPs."

His heart contracted at the bleak expression on her face, but he knew better than to show it. She was holding herself together by force of will.

"You're right. We have to think outside the box, here. Okay, you check on the RRSPs. I'll call the insurance company to see if the equity in our policies is still there."

"God, yes, the policies. You check them out."

Grace used the phone by the bed while Ray used his cell phone. As he waited on hold for the agent to check on the policies, he listened to Grace's one-sided conversation. By the time the insurance agent came back on the line, Ray already knew the RRSPs were intact. So was the equity in the policies.

"Well, there's a small mercy. At least I didn't clean us out." Grace sat on the bed and pushed her hair behind her ears.

Ray almost wished she *had* cleaned them out. At least then they'd know where the money had come from. He sat down beside her.

"So, where does that leave us?" she asked. "Should I stash it in our safety deposit box until my memory comes back?"

"Dammit."

"What?"

"Tommy Godsoe."

"What about Tommy Godsoe?"

"He saw the cash in my truck."

She blinked. "What was Tommy doing going through my bag?"

"It's a long story."

"I think I can spare the time."

Damn, he'd hoped not to have to tell her about this. On the other hand, maybe it was just as well. If he really was a target for Viktor Landis's thugs or some crackhead with a grudge, she could be caught in the crossfire. If she knew about the danger, it'd be easier to persuade her to lie low.

Besides, he pretty much had to spill the story if he hoped to get her to go along with what he was going to suggest.

"The mechanical trouble I had the other night?" She nodded that she remembered. "The garage thought there may have been some tampering."

"What kind of tampering?"

"Removing all but one of the nuts on the left front wheel."

She sucked in her breath on a hiss. "Did the wheel come off?"

"No. Tire blew before it could work its way off."

"So you called Tommy and Max to go over the truck?"

Cripes, she could dredge up the police dog's name when she couldn't remember where she'd picked up that shitload of cash?

"Ray, is that what happened?" she prompted.

He gave himself a mental shake. "Yeah. Truck came up clean, but Tommy tossed the bags in the course of his search."

Her forehead puckered. "I don't understand. You *knew* the money was in there and you didn't forewarn me?"

"No, I didn't know. Tommy didn't mention the cash. He just gave me a funny look and asked me if the bag was mine. I told him it was yours."

"You didn't go see for yourself when he gave you that funny look?"

He bristled at her tone of disbelief. "Dammit, Grace, I thought he was sifting through your skivvies."

Grace jumped up, her face flushing. "Yeah, well, that's the other thing. I didn't pack any."

"You didn't pack any what?"

"Nice underwear. Just the basic stuff."

The news loosened the fist clenching his heart, but as soon as he recognized his relief, a taunting voice rose up. *So she had qualms about wearing the same lingerie for another man. So what?*

"That's neither here nor there, is it?" he said, his voice gruff. "We need to make a decision about this money."

"What do you think we should do?"

"How do you feel about taking it down to the Station and getting them to stash it in Evidence?"

"*Evidence?* You think it's dirty?"

"I don't know what to think." He stood, shoving a hand through his hair.

"Maybe *he* gave it to me."

Ray didn't have to ask for clarification of who "he" was. "Maybe. But all we know for sure is that it's a helluva lot of cash, and we can't say where it came from. Factor in that Tommy knows about it. Tommy and probably the rest of the guys who were there this morning."

"You think we should turn it in? Explain my amnesia?"

"It's your decision. They'd give us a voucher so you could reclaim it when your memory comes back, if it was legally gotten."

"And if it's ill-gotten?"

She bit her lower lip as she waited for his reply.

"Depends how it falls out." He rubbed the back of his neck. "It could work to your advantage. Or we could be digging you a hole a lawyer might have a hard time getting you out of. That's why it has to be your decision."

She tortured her lower lip some more. "But in the circumstances, it would look better for you if we turn it in?"

"Probably. But if it's dirty —"

"Ray, if I committed some kind of crime to get this money, I'd just as soon face the music."

Despite her assertion, she looked scared as a schoolgirl. Ray gave a curt nod, struggling to conceal his internal battle.

Half of him admired her courage.

The other half was offended, dammit.

She actually thought he'd hand her over, complete with a big, fat ribbon tying up the case for the prosecution? Hell, if he thought for a minute she'd come by the money in some shady fashion, he'd sit on it until he figured something out.

But the way he saw it, the money had to have come from lover-boy. There could be no other explanation. A token of his affection, or maybe just to reassure her as she left the security of her marriage. Frankly, he didn't give a damn which it was. He just wanted a look at the bastard.

When she'd left him, she'd refused to name the other man. Now, as long as her amnesia persisted, she *couldn't* name him. By convincing her to lodge the money with Evidence, Ray figured he could pretty much count on meeting the S.O.B. sooner or later. Surely he'd come looking for a refund if he thought Grace had stiffed him.

Plus he'd be able to banish the inevitable questions that must have arisen in Tommy Godsoe's mind and the minds of the other guys.

"Okay," Grace said. "Let's take it in."

Ray nodded.

"Can we do it this afternoon? It makes me nervous having it here."

"Sure." He grabbed an empty shaving kit from the closet. "Stuff the cash in this and I'll call Quigg to set it up."

Grace started filling the kit, handling the bundles as though they carried some contagion, and Ray reached for the phone. Before he could lift the receiver from its cradle, the phone rang.

"Hello?"

"Razor, Tom Godsoe."

"Tommy." Ray lifted a hand to pinch the bridge of his nose. "Ah, about this morning, what you saw in my truck —"

"That's why I'm calling, about this morning."

"I can explain the money."

"That's good, buddy, cuz it looks like you're gonna have to."

Ray's pulse gave a kick. "What do you mean?"

"Hell, I'm sorry, Razor, but I kinda told the guys."

Dammit. "And?"

"And somebody blabbed to Creighton."

Ah, hell. Geoffrey Creighton. Not what he needed right now. But he could handle it. "It's okay, Tommy."

"No, man, it ain't okay."

"I can handle Creighton. He's had a hard-on for me since his wife tried to stick her tongue down my ...." Ray suddenly became aware Grace had zipped the bulging kit shut and was watching him. He picked up the phone and crossed the room. "Well, ever since that Christmas party."

"Creighton's not the only one has a hard-on for you, Razor."

Ray's heart took another leap. "What are you saying?"

"IAD."

Internal Affairs. "Holy hell, Tommy, what'd you tell them?"

"Hey, I mighta told the guys, but I'm no stinking rat. It musta been one of the others."

"Dammit." Ray did a mental inventory — Davis, Mailer, Ketch, Isaacs .... "Okay, who do you like? Danny?"

"Can we talk about this in person? Meet somewhere, maybe? I'm feeling a little squirrelly talking about it on the phone."

"Okay." Grace had moved closer so she could read his face. He resisted the urge to turn away again. Balancing the phone on his hip, he asked, "Why don't you come on over?"

"How about some place more discreet? Some place we can just roll our windows down?"

Jesus, Tommy really *was* spooked. Not only did he want an over-the-door conference, he wanted a clandestine one. Ray racked his brain for an appropriate site.

"How about the parking lot of the new high school in thirty?" he suggested. He could almost hear Tommy weighing the merits of the location — it was damned near in the middle of the woods, at the end of a cul-de-sac. This being summer break, the school parking lot could be counted on to be deserted. Nothing at the top of that lonely hill but mosquitoes.

"Okay, you got it. Thirty minutes," Tommy agreed.

Ray replaced the receiver.

"What's going on, Ray?"

"Just a little wrinkle." He carried the phone back to the night stand. "Tommy mentioned that wad of cash to the guys, who mentioned it to some other guys, who mentioned it to Internal Affairs."

"Internal Affairs?" Grace sank down on the edge of the bed. "My God, you're in trouble. This is all my fault."

"Trouble?" Ray rolled his shoulders, then lifted a hand to massage the back of his neck. "Nah, we'll just explain."

"Explain what? That I don't know where it came from?" *Oh, God, please don't make him pay for whatever it was I did. Bad enough to hurt him, but this — the job, his reputation....*

"Your memory will come back. We'll just lodge the money with Evidence like we planned. In the meantime, I haven't done anything to raise any eyebrows, so there's nothing to worry about."

Grace wished she could share his confidence. "It sounded like you were arranging to meet Tommy."

"He wants to talk face-to-face." He looked at his watch. "Speaking of which, we'd better get a move on. I told him we'd meet him in half an hour."

She jumped up, sudden tears stinging the backs of her eyes. She was so damned tired. Her self-concept battered by guilt and shame, she didn't even know who she was anymore. And in the background, hovering just out of reach, was that white hum of almost-memory. It was like that name that eluded you, yet you knew it was right there, almost on the tip of your tongue.

"This is all my fault. If I could just remember ...."

"You will."

She gazed at the carpet, blinked rapidly. What she'd give to go into his arms right now, until her world shrank to just the feel and smell of him.

Then she felt his hand settle on her shoulder, warm but awkward, the way a man might comfort another man. She felt the burn of tears collecting again, congesting her nasal passages and tightening her throat. Lifting her gaze to his, she saw his eyes had softened, but there was still that distance.

You put it there, she reminded herself brutally.

Though her heart ached, she swallowed the neediness and straightened her spine. "If anything bad comes of this, I'll never forgive myself."

He dropped his hand from her back. "Trust me, Grace, this isn't anything I can't handle."

"Then why'd you agree to meet Tommy?"

"For his sake, not mine." Ray went to the closet and retrieved a fresh shirt. "He feels bad for his part in this. Like I told you, there's nothing IAD can nail me for."

She averted her eyes as he changed shirts, busying herself by running a brush through her hair. Though she thirsted to see him, she knew her gaze would be as unwelcome as her touch. By the time she turned back to him, he had strapped on his shoulder holster. Force of habit, she supposed, as she watched him retrieve his service weapon. Going to the station without it probably felt like going shirtless.

"We ready?"

"Ready," she said, grabbing the overstuffed shaving kit before he could. Suddenly, she wished he hadn't touched even one of the bundles. Despite his faith that he had nothing to fear from an internal investigation, she had a bad feeling about the money. A very bad feeling.

⁂

Ray took his eyes off the road long enough to cast a sidelong glance at Grace. She sat with her head stiffly angled toward the passenger window, intent on the vegetation in the ditches.

Not that he could blame her. The fifteen-minute trip had been accomplished in near-total silence, and not the comfortable kind. Maybe he should have tried to strike up some kind of conversation. Back there at the house, she'd looked for a moment like she might fly apart if he so much as breathed on her. She sure didn't need the added strain of this awkwardness. Unfortunately, they seemed incapable of chitchat. It was either this silence or the heavy-duty stuff. Nothing in between.

And if they got into a real conversation, he might ask the questions that never left his head, the ones he'd sworn not to let pass his lips. *Why? What'd I do wrong? Where'd I lose you? Did you ever think of him when I held you?* The questions that burned into his soul. The ones he didn't think he could bear having answered, even if she could, or would, answer them.

He turned into the school's long sweeping driveway, spotting Tommy's black Camaro immediately.

"That's Tommy's car," he told her.

He parked the SUV far enough from the other vehicle so Grace wouldn't have to hear everything Tommy said. No point feeding her anxiety.

As he crossed the asphalt, he felt twitchy between the shoulder blades. Grace must be watching him.

When Ray was still ten yards from the other car, the Camaro's door swung open. Before Tommy could put both feet on the asphalt to climb out, the car's rear window on the driver's side exploded. Both men froze. Then two quick *pa-ting, pa-tings*, and two neat holes appeared in the car's fender over the rear wheel well.

Sniper! Unholstering his weapon, Ray hit the deck, but not before seeing the expression on Tommy's face, a mixture of shock and accusation. *Christ, he thinks I arranged this!* A split-second later, Tommy hit the accelerator and shot off, his door swinging shut with the forward momentum.

Another two or three bullets skipped off the asphalt a few feet away, sending fragments of blacktop flying. Rolling quickly to the left, Ray came up running, zigging and zagging. Behind him, he heard bullets whine off the pavement.

"Ray!"

Grace! Would she even know what was happening? The shooter was using a silencer. Would she understand what was unfolding?

"Get out of here!" he shouted. "There's a sniper in the school."

Another *phut* sound signaled another bullet digging into the asphalt, entirely too close to his feet. He took three more strides and dove behind a long, low cement planter, one of those commercial jobs the landscapers liked to fill. This time, the bullets made a completely different sound as they sent shards of cement scattering.

Pressing himself close against the low architecture, he heard the Pathfinder's engine kick to life. Thank God he'd left the keys in the ignition. And thank God he'd left it pointed toward the parking lot's only exit. Presuming there was only one sniper, she should be able to get away. Just to make sure, he'd give her some cover.

Using every inch of the planter to conceal himself, he searched for the suspect. There! Rooftop. He squeezed off a couple of rounds. It was a hard shot, shooting up like that, but he must have come close because the shooter pulled back.

Ray heard the SUV's tires squeal. *Atta girl. Go Grace. Go now.* Except when he glanced her way, he saw she'd pulled a U-turn and was barreling towards him. Christ, what was she thinking?

A bullet pinged off the sidewalk close enough to send a shard of concrete slicing into his cheek like a hot knife. Swearing, he fired back twice. Then Grace was there, the back door on the driver's side already opened for him. He rolled out onto the sidewalk and squeezed off three more rounds. Then, launching himself from his knees, he dove into the SUV's back seat.

"Go!" he shouted, but Grace didn't need his instruction. She'd already popped the clutch. The vehicle lunged forward, throwing him against the back of the seat. Seconds later, she pulled another U-turn and sped out the driveway. Tires squealing in protest, she rounded the turn onto the broad avenue and shot off down the hill.

Chapter 5

Grace's heart crashed against her ribs and her knuckles ached from gripping the steering wheel.

"Okay, don't slack off until we're clear of this street." Ray clambered into the front passenger seat. "We need to get out of here before the cops come."

She shot him an incredulous look. "Someone shot at you back there! I'd think you'd be glad to see them."

"I'm not so sure about that."

New fear sliced into her. "What do you mean?" She glanced at him, and her heart took another bump when she saw him eject the spent clip from his gun and jam another one into place. "I thought we were going to go to the cops."

"Circumstances have changed." He holstered his gun and fastened his seatbelt.

"Yeah, we're in *immediate* danger now. Which is all the more reason to go in."

"Take this right coming up."

She obeyed automatically, and he guided her through another series of turns until she found herself on the approach to the Merrill Bridge.

"I thought you just said we weren't going in."

"We're not. Stay on this street, then turn down King."

She did, but as they passed the police station, several cars, their lights flashing and sirens wailing, spilled out of the parking lot and sped north across the bridge. Grace fought down panic. Why was Ray avoiding the police?

He reached to steady the wheel as the Pathfinder wandered too close to the right lane. "Careful."

Okay, Grace, focus. One thing at a time. She pulled up at the red light. "Okay, this might work better if I know where we're going."

"The Crowne Plaza."

Not four minutes later, she turned into the hotel's parking lot. Ray directed her to a spot in the center of the lot. She nosed the vehicle into the space and killed the engine. Exhaling, she released the wheel and rolled shoulders gone stiff with tension.

"Okay, why aren't we at the station right now?"

"Because Tommy's already there."

She blinked. "I should hope so. But what's that got to do with anything?"

"He thinks I tried to get him killed."

"No!"

"I saw his face, Grace. Those bullets had to be meant for me, the way they came over my shoulder, but Tommy couldn't tell that from where he sat. He thinks they were meant for him, that I set him up."

"But you could explain —"

"I can guarantee he won't be in a listening mood. At least not right away. Nor will anyone else, not with an internal investigation going on."

The damned money again. This was all her fault .... "Why are you so certain the shooter was after you? Maybe he was after Tommy."

"I'm the one who just had my vehicle sabotaged. I'm the one who's been stepping on some nasty guys' toes."

She chewed her lip a moment. "I still think you could explain what happened."

"Explain?" He ran a hand through his hair, making it stand up. "Hell, I don't even *know* what happened. We've got all this money we can't explain. IAD's breathing down my neck. And now I've got somebody trying to shoot me, and a friend who thinks I tried to get him killed."

"Wait a minute, how did the shooter know where you'd be? He couldn't have followed us, or he wouldn't have had time to get set up."

He looked at her. "Hell if I know."

Grace held his gaze. "Maybe Tommy set *you* up."

"No way." He rejected the idea forcefully. "I'm the one picked the meeting spot. Besides, I saw his face. The shock .... No, he really thought I'd betrayed *him*."

"Then how?"

He swore. "Wiretap."

She gasped. "You think your own shop would tap our phones?"

"The same department that's apparently been investigating me? Oh, yeah. And I can think of any number of judges would be happy to sign the wiretap order, too. But who's to say it's a legal tap? It's more likely the handiwork of whoever sabotaged my truck, whoever just *shot* at me. Hell, they could have the whole house wired."

"You think someone has been listening in on us?"

"On our telephone conversations, at least. Whoever was on that roof had to have known in advance. Which means they knew where I was going, who I was meeting, even why we were meeting."

She sucked in a breath as a thought occurred to her. "What about...?" She held her hands up to indicate the interior of the car.

"No. It's clean. The boys swept it this morning."

For a few minutes, they were both silent, thinking. Grace took a deep breath. "I think we should go in anyway. You didn't do anything, so the money can't hurt you, right? And sooner or later, I'll remember where it came from, or they'll figure it out for me. Either way, you'll be in the clear, and in the meantime, we'll be safe."

"No. These people I've pissed off ...." He rubbed the back of his neck. "I just don't want to take any chances."

"Chances?" She blinked at him incredulously. "How could going in be riskier than sitting out here in the open?"

"If we go in under the circumstances, they're gonna want to detain us while they check out our story. Which means we'd be sitting ducks for whoever *did* try to fill me full of lead."

She sat silent a moment, absorbing his words. "You think they could reach us inside the station?"

"On our way into the station, inside the station, in transit to another location .... Yeah, these guys, I think they could reach us almost anywhere, if they want to bad enough."

She'd thought she'd reached the limits of fear when the gunman opened fire from the school's rooftop, but Ray's words showed her otherwise. They flooded her nervous system with new dread, leaving an acrid taste it in her mouth.

With sudden clarity, she knew she'd felt this way once before. Desperately, she grasped at the wisp of memory, but it was gone before she could trap it.

"What kind of people are they, Ray?"

"Connected people."

"The mob? Here in New Brunswick?"

"Organized crime is everywhere, and Canada is fast becoming a prime location. Borders are porous, manpower's stretched thin, and our banking laws are laxer than American laws."

Another silence. Grace turned to watch a man in a suit cross the parking lot, throw his bags in the trunk of his Saab and drive away. She turned back to Ray.

"We can't go home, can we?"

Something of her desolation must have shown on her face, because his mouth softened.

"I like our chances better if we stay on the move."

Grace digested that. "Is that why we're here, to ditch the car in a parking lot that never empties?"

"That's right. With any luck, they won't find it for a few days, or even weeks."

Weeks. "And now we beg, borrow or steal another vehicle and slip out of town?"

"Bingo." Ray flipped the glove compartment open and dug around inside, extracting a flashlight, some maps and a first aid kit. "Though borrowing is out. We don't wanna lead men with guns to anyone's doorstep. And we don't have to steal. Not as long as we have this."

He lifted the shaving kit from the floor and dropped it on his lap with the other stuff he'd dug out of the glove box.

The money! For the first time, Grace was grateful for the tremendous wad of bills. They could pay their way without leaving a credit card trail.

Of course, if it weren't for the damned money, they wouldn't be in this fix.

"So, what now? Do we rent a car?"

"Buy one. To rent, we'd have to produce ID, credit cards, that kind of stuff. So we'll buy a clunker. Something cheap but mechanically sound enough to get us around."

She frowned. "Won't you have to register it, insure it and all that stuff before you drive it off the lot?"

"With the right incentive, on top of no arguments on the grossly inflated sticker price, I expect a used-car dealer could be persuaded to delay the paperwork a while."

Grace blinked thoughtfully. "Half of this incentive now, half later, to make sure he doesn't change his mind?"

"Yep."

"And in the meantime, it'll look dealer-owned. We're just test-driving a used car."

"You're pretty good at this," he said. "Seems like your talents were wasted at that paper."

His praise caught her off guard. She ducked her head and laughed. "Yeah, well, that's what I've been telling them for years, but nobody's been listening."

Grace started as he put two fingers under her chin and tipped her head up to meet his gaze. His eyes were soft and liquid enough to drown in.

"Well, maybe you'll get a story out of this, hmmm?"

Don't, she thought. *Don't touch me. It hurts too much when you stop. Which you'll do in about a millisecond when you remember what I did.*

Keeping her face carefully blank, she said, "Story? I'll be happy if we can just get out of this without getting shot at again."

He pulled back, his eyes hardening. "You're right. It's time to move."

He climbed out of the car and she followed suit, grabbing her purse. From the back seat, he retrieved his gym bag. Removing his racquetball gear, he replaced it with the money, the things he'd scavenged from the glove box, and an emergency road kit from the back of the truck.

"Got a pen in your purse and something to write on?"

Grace dredged up a smile. "You might catch me without a lipstick or coffee money, but you'd never catch me without pen and paper." She produced a coiled notebook and handed it to him.

"What do you need it for?"

"To make a shopping list."

Already his hand was racing across the page. She leaned closer to read what he'd written. *Hair dye, self-tanning lotion, barbering kit* .... The stuff of disguises.

"Hey, I don't see 'car' there. Shouldn't that be at the top of our list?"

"That's because *I'm* shopping for the car. You've gotta get this stuff."

"We're going to split up?"

"It'd be a lot quicker." He looked up from his list. "Unless you'd rather wait here? I can do both."

Don't leave me alone. "Why can't we go together?"

"Because if someone takes another shot at me, I don't want you at my side."

"Oh." Her mouth went dry at the thought of more gunfire. Yet the idea of being separated from him brought its own brand of panic. What if she got picked up by the police? What if *he* got picked up? There was no point arguing, though. "Okay."

"You should be able to get everything at the mall we just passed." He scrawled a few more things on the list and handed the note pad back to her. "If you can't get a barbering kit, just get some good scissors. Oh, and buy lots of other unrelated stuff, and spread your purchases around. You don't want to stick in some clerk's mind like you just robbed a bank and need a disguise."

"Do we meet back here?"

"No." He pulled his cell phone from his coat pocket. "I'll call you on this when I'm ready to roll, and you can meet me at the mall's north exit."

She looked down at the cell phone in her palm. "Can they trace this?"

"They can *locate* it, once they get organized to look for it. The cops, that is. I don't know about this other crowd. In any case, we'll ditch the phone before we leave town." He picked up the Adidas bag and slung it over his shoulder. "We'd better get moving."

"Wait, Ray."

He turned back toward her.

"You've cut a small cut on your face." She pointed to her own right cheek to help him locate it. "Better clean the blood up before you go car shopping."

He lifted a hand to the nick. "Right."

An hour later, Grace entered the ladies' restroom near the north exit of the mall. With supper hour approaching, the mall was emptying out and she found herself alone in the washroom. Alone wasn't good enough, though. Not after the feeling of exposure she'd endured since entering this mall.

She slipped into a stall, placed her bags on the floor, perched on the toilet and tried to stop shaking.

God, she was such a coward. Everything had gone better than she could have hoped, yet here she was trembling.

No one had challenged her. Heck, the clerks had pushed her purchases over their scanners and made change without even glancing up. But she'd still felt as though a thousand eyes were watching her.

The phone shrilled in her purse, making her jump. Ray!

Or maybe not Ray. Maybe someone phoning for Ray, someone who could track her to this very washroom, this very stall ....

Oh, stop it! She fumbled for the phone, pulled it out.

"Hello?"

"You ready?"

She sagged against the stall's wall. "I'm ready."

Five minutes later, she stepped outside and scanned the street. There he was, in a battered old blue Toyota Corolla. As she approached, he reached back and popped the rear passenger door open. She deposited her bags on the back seat, then climbed into the front. They pulled away from the curb smoothly.

Inside, the car's upholstery was worn. A crack in the dashboard had been mended with duct tape. She laughed.

He glanced at her. "What?"

"Nice ride."

"Isn't it just?" Ray merged with traffic, then stopped behind a black sedan at a red light. "Two-hundred-sixty-thousand klicks, but there's a new motor under the hood. It shouldn't die on us."

"How much?"

"Fifteen hundred."

She smiled. "I think you got ripped off."

His mouth turned up at the corners. "That was the plan, remember?"

Grace's smile faded. "Did you have any trouble?"

He shook his head. "It's amazing what service an extra five hundred'll buy you."

"Cash transaction, too. He'll probably pocket another five hundred and claim you beat him down on the sticker price."

"Naturally."

Traffic was moving again. She glanced at the street signs. "We don't seem to be headed toward the highway."

"I've got a stop to make first."

"Where?"

"Right here." He signaled and turned into the bus station.

"Ray, are you crazy? If the police are looking for us, they'll be all over this place."

"Relax. I won't even have to get out of the car. I just need to find a … look, here comes our man."

She whipped her head around, scanning frantically for anyone they might know, but there was no one. Just a thin, tough-looking teen in baggy khakis and a hooded jacket crossing the parking lot, duffel bag slung over his shoulder.

"Quick, Grace, the cell phone."

She dug the phone out of her purse and slapped it into his open palm as he rolled his window down.

"Hey, kid," he called.

The young man, who Grace could now see was probably no older than seventeen or eighteen, turned toward Ray's voice.

"How'd you like to make a quick twenty bucks?"

The young man snorted. "In your dreams, old man."

Ray swore, drawing Grace's attention. To her surprise, a blush stained her husband's face.

"I'm not looking for *that*."

"Yeah?" The teen stepped closer, his lean face wary but interested. "What *are* you looking for, then?"

"See this phone?"

The young man nodded.

"It belongs to my soon-to-be-ex-wife."

"So?"

"So, I'd like you to take it with you on the bus."

"To Manitoba?"

"Far as you're going. As long as you promise to run the phone bill up. Hell, call 1-900 sex lines, if you want to. Just so long as you use it at least once a day."

The kid stepped closer to the vehicle, and Grace had to lean toward Ray to keep his lean face in view.

"Won't it stop working when I get out of the province?"

Ray bared his teeth in vindictive smile. "It's got roaming."

"You're not jokin', are you? I can really call sex lines?"

"You can call anywhere you like."

"You look like a cop."

"No kidding? You think cops don't have messy divorces?"

Grace could almost see the kid's thoughts.

"No one'll come after me?"

"Not if you dump it at the end of the line."

The kid inclined his head. "Twenty bucks, too?"

Ray folded a bill, clamped it to the phone with his thumb and offered both to the kid.

"Deal." The young man took the phone and money, slipping them into his coat pocket. "Way to stick it to her," he said approvingly.

"Shut up, kid. There's nothing admirable about this."

Grace sucked in her breath at the ferocity of Ray's tone. Even the young tough took a step back.

"Then why you doin' it?"

"'Cuz I'm an asshole." Ray sighed. "Just make the daily calls, okay?"

"She musta done you pretty bad, huh?"

Ray looked straight ahead. "I'll live."

Grace watched the skinny teen in his oversized clothes disappear into the bus terminal, the echo of that last exchange reverberating in her head.

She musta done you pretty bad, huh?

I'll live.

Grace blinked fiercely. *Oh, Ray, I'm so sorry.* Because she couldn't say that, she adjusted her seatbelt and said instead, "So, if the cops try to find you through the cell phone, they'll think you're headed west to Manitoba?"

"Let's hope," he said, pulling back into traffic.

She swallowed to ease the ache in her throat. "Where to now?"

"I think we should stay right here in town."

"Here? When everyone is looking for us?"

"*Because* everyone is looking for us. It'll be safer to travel in disguise, so we need to check into a motel and transform ourselves."

"But I thought switching cars —"

"A different car won't help us if they've already thrown up roadblocks. There's not a cop in town wouldn't recognize me at a checkpoint."

They chose a no-tell motel just inside the city limits. A row of dingy-looking units hunkered on one side of the small office building, and a handful of cabins squatted on the other side. Ray pulled up in front of the office, the Toyota stuttering a few times after he shut the engine off. When he made a move to get out, Grace grabbed his arm.

"Wait. Shouldn't I do this? Your face is bound to be more familiar than mine."

He sat back. "You're right. Okay, let's get you some cash." He reached into the back seat and retrieved the shaving kit. He passed her a wad of bills. "That should do it."

She was tucking them into her purse when Ray cursed.

"What?" Heart thudding, she scanned the parking lot, expecting to see cops, but it was deserted.

"In the window. The desk clerk is watching us."

She glanced up to see a slender man watching them from behind the registration desk. For a moment, she had a flash of Norman Bates from *Psycho*.

Grace, get a grip. "So?"

"So he knows there's two of us, and the guy always does this part. It's the man's job to protect the woman's reputation, even in a place like this. *Especially* in a place like this. If you go in there alone and ask to pay cash, he'll figure you're trying to protect my identity. Then he'll figure you've got our happily-married mayor out here, or maybe a councilman at the very least. If we arouse his curiosity, I can guarantee you he won't rest until he gets a glimpse of me."

She nibbled her lip. "We could pick another motel."

"No, this is the best location."

"So what do we do?"

He thought for a moment. "Give him that glimpse he wants."

She tried to read his face in the light cast by the motel's flickering sign, but half of it was in darkness. "What if he recognizes you?"

"He won't."

"How can you be sure?"

"Because he's a man and we're gonna give him something else to look at."

Grace's pulse jumped. "What do you mean?"

"As soon as you tell him you want to pay cash, he's gonna jump to some conclusions. We might as well play into his presumption, act hot for each other."

Her heart seemed to stop, then leapt to thudding life again. "I don't see how that's going to keep him from recognizing you."

"Let me worry about that, okay? You just play along, act like you can't wait to get horizontal."

Could she do it? Could she let him lay hands on her when he so clearly loathed touching her? And could she bear it when he dropped the pretense, once they were safely inside?

"What?" he demanded. "Think that kind of performance is beyond you?" He twisted toward her, but she didn't need to see his face to read his anger. It was there in his voice.

"It's not that —"

"Hell, Grace, just pretend I'm *him*. That should do it for you."

Pain lanced her to the bone. Pain for him, for her. She turned away, scrabbling at the unfamiliar door until she found the handle. The door popped open and the dome light came on, but before she could get out of the car, he restrained her by grabbing her arm.

"Are you forgetting our audience?"

She glanced up to see the clerk had come out from behind the desk and was standing in the window watching openly now. Then Ray's head blotted out her view as his mouth closed on hers.

She sat motionless for a few stunned seconds as his lips moved over hers, hard and angry. There was anger, too, in the hand that came up to hold her head prisoner. But heaven help her, this was Ray, and she missed him so badly.

She opened her mouth to the demand of his.

Instantly, he deepened the kiss, his tongue invading her mouth, demanding a response. For a few heartbeats, shock prevented her from providing it. He'd never kissed her like this before. The hot insistence of the invasion swept her up.

She'd braced a hand against his chest when he'd grabbed her, but now she curled her fingers into his shirt and pulled him closer. Oh, God, the taste of him! And the smell. She didn't care if she ever breathed anything else again. The clean cotton smell of his shirt mixed with the lemongrass soap he used, and all of it underlain by his own unique musk.

She lifted her arms to encircle his neck, straining closer. In that instant, the kiss changed. There was nothing left but desire, his anger burned away in its cleansing fire. No longer needing to hold her head prisoner, he dropped his hands to her waist. She felt a draft of air as his hands slipped under the thin shell she wore, then the bliss of his palms on her midriff, the undersides of her breasts.

She wrenched her mouth from his. "Oh, yes, Ray, touch me."

His fingers flexed on her breasts, drawing a moan from her. Suddenly, she needed to touch him like this, too, feel the warmth of his skin beneath her palms. She slid her hands down his chest and pulled his shirt free of his jeans. Her fingers found the hair-roughened skin of his abdomen, but before she could explore further, he drew back, putting a layer of cooling air between them again.

She opened her eyes. "Ray?"

"I think we've convinced junior in there that we need a room. Guess we're better actors than I thought."

The words would have cut her, had she not heard the tremor in his voice or seen the way his skin was so tightly drawn over his face. He'd been no more acting than she was. The knowledge helped her fight off the despair that hovered so close.

"Ready for act two?" he asked.

"What do I do?"

"Just register us as Mr. and Mrs. Smith. Tell him we'll want to get a fast start tomorrow, so you'd like to pay cash right now."

"He's not going to believe that."

"He's not meant to."

Of course. His register was probably full of John Smiths.

"Remind me again, why is he not going to recognize you?"

"If he's hetero, which I think we can safely say from the way he's watching us, he'll be too busy checking you out."

Ray jumped out of the car and came around just as she closed her own door. To Grace's surprise, he pulled her into an embrace. This time, his kiss was controlled, purely for show. Still, a little tremor raced through her as he released her.

"Lead on," he said, "and make it look good."

She closed her eyes for a second. *Pretend. That's all you have to do. Pretend it's for real.*

Taking his hand, she tugged him toward the office, doing her best to look like a woman embarking on a sexual adventure. The clerk, who'd retreated hastily behind his desk, glanced up as they burst through the door. Grace felt Ray's hands settle on her waist. She approached the desk, keeping Ray behind her.

"Can I help you folks?"

"We'd like a cabin," she said. Behind her, Ray lifted her hair off her nape and began nibbling the side of her neck.

The clerk's eyes widened. "Reservation?"

"No, it's kind of a spur-of-the-moment thing." Grace tilted her head to let Ray have access to her ear.

The clerk's eyes dropped to Ray's hands, which were now splayed on her belly. "The name?"

"Um ... Smith. Robert and Evelyn Smith."

His eyes flicked up to meet hers at that. "I can give you Cabin Three, at the end."

"That'd be great," she breathed, dropping a hand to cover one of Ray's, threading her fingers through his. Obligingly, the clerk's gaze dropped to their linked hands. "I'd like to pay for it now, if that's okay. We'll need to leave early tomorrow."

"Certainly, ma'am. Credit card?"

"Cash."

"Of course." He reached for a key from the pegboard behind him.

Grace inhaled sharply as Ray's hands snaked up under the hem of her sweater. She didn't need the draft on her belly to tell her Ray had exposed a significant amount of her skin. The clerk's expression told her as much.

"That'll be fifty-four dollars, including tax," he said to her mid-section.

She pulled three twenties from her purse.

"Keep the change," she said, snatching the key he'd placed on the counter. They whirled and made a speedy exit. Grace felt the clerk's gaze on her all the way out.

They'd done it!

Outside, in the flickering light of the motel's sign, Ray pulled her into his arms again. Grace lifted her face eagerly, ready to put her elation into another searing kiss, but he merely leaned close.

Of course. She thudded back to earth. This was just acting. From the clerk's perspective, he would assume they were kissing, and that's all that mattered.

"Good job," he said into her ear. "Now, you run along and unlock and I'll bring the car around. No need for him to see us drag the shopping bags in." He pulled back slightly, as though lifting his head after a kiss. "We've got a lot of work to do before morning."

His words brought the gravity of their situation home again. She'd been distracted while they'd performed for Norman Bates, but it all came flooding back now. Someone was trying to kill Ray. Possibly her, too, since she'd witnessed the sniper attack. And if Ray was right, they couldn't turn to the cops. At least, not yet.

Beneath those worries was a groundswell of more generalized anxiety about the memories she'd lost and the unexplained money. Dr. Greenfield had mentioned that paranoia was common in amnesia sufferers, but was she being paranoid to suspect the events she'd forgotten might tie into their current peril? She thought not.

Pulling away from her husband's mock embrace, she crossed the parking lot to the third cabin, trying to look like a woman eager for illicit sex instead of one ready to crack under the strain of fear and unhappiness.

Chapter 6

A s RAY UNPACKED THE contents of the shopping bags onto the coffee table, he was supremely conscious of Grace.

Of course, after that clinch in the car and the groping in the motel office, he'd be conscious of her if she were in the next cabin. But as it happened, she was moving around *this* cabin, checking the locks, plucking at the ugly green curtains he'd closed for privacy. Her scent swirled all around him.

Dammit, couldn't she just light somewhere?

A moment later, she emerged from the tiny bathroom and sat on the edge of the bed. He continued with the sorting, gaze down. Too bad he couldn't tune the sound of her out, too. He knew precisely where she was and what she was doing. He heard the small squeak as she sat on the edge of the bed, heard her soft sigh, the louder protest of the bed's frame when she flopped backward on the mattress.

Irritated with himself but unable to resist, he glanced at her. Just as he'd pictured in his mind's eye, she lay sprawled, arms outflung, contemplating the ceiling. Her hair was fanned out on the floral bedspread and her breasts jutted invitingly against the thin fabric of her top. The ache in his groin was back just like that. Suddenly, fiercely, he wished she'd get up and roam again.

He dropped his gaze. "I wouldn't do that if I were you," he said, focusing on the box of hair dye he'd fished from the bag. *Lightest Blond*. Was that for him or for her?

She lifted her head. "Do what?"

He pulled out another box of dye. *Dark Auburn*. "Get too cozy with that bedspread. It could probably be classified as a bio-hazard."

She rolled off the bed like it had caught fire.

"Just take the throw off," he advised without looking up. "I'm pretty sure they *do* launder the sheets."

He stuck his hand in the bag and came up with some headache medication and a bottle of vitamin C, which he added to the growing pile of irrelevant stuff she'd bought to camouflage the purpose of her shopping spree. Razor, barbering kit. Those he put in another pile.

"Yuck!"

He glanced up to see her peeling back the coverlet fastidiously, using the very tips of her fingernails. She let the fabric fall in a heap on the once-blue carpet.

She wiped her hands on her jeans. "I just didn't think."

No, he didn't suppose she had. The sugar daddy who'd landed all that cash on her certainly wouldn't have exposed her to a sleazy room like this.

The muscles of his jaw tightened, but he forced himself to relax as Grace came over to perch on the room's other chair, a Naugahyde-covered relic from another era.

He reached for the next bag, this one emblazoned with a department store logo and spilled the contents onto his lap. More good stuff, he decided as he rifled through it. Costume jewelry, self-tanning lotion, condoms ....

He shot a look at Grace, who blushed to the roots of her hair.

She leapt up. "What did you expect me to buy to go with the body jewelry and fake tattoos? A Little Mermaid night light?"

Ray made no reply, just put the package in the pile with the other unnecessary purchases.

She paced again while he emptied the rest of the bags, which contained clothes, mostly.

"I can see you had a particular look in mind," he said, after examining the last article of clothing, a hooded jacket much like the one the kid at the bus station had worn.

"You hate it. I knew you would." She'd stopped pacing and was now worrying at the cuticle of her thumb. "It's just that I couldn't think of anything else. I figured we could either dress up or down, and down seemed easier. And there was this store with all this hip young stuff ...."

"No, it's brilliant. No one who knows me will look twice when I get this stuff on."

She looked so grateful for his assurance, he felt like a real jerk. She must be scared witless. And it was his damn fault she was in this position.

Well, mostly his. The bag full of money in his truck hadn't helped. If it weren't for the money, there'd be no internal investigation, no friend who thought Ray had tried to whack him.

On the other hand, if he hadn't been rattling Landis's chains, he'd have no worries. The prospect of an internal investigation didn't scare him. Like he'd told Grace, he hadn't done anything wrong. But after that sniper attempt, he *was* scared to sit downtown while they sorted out the confusion.

He'd heard the rumors about Viktor Landis. Hell, everyone had. Back in Brighton Beach, they'd never been able to prosecute him. Cases fell apart, people disappeared. Frankly, Ray had taken the whole thing with a very generous dash of salt. It seemed exactly like the kind of rep that might attach itself to any Russian who'd spent time in that infamous Brooklyn neighborhood. Landis was dirty, all right. Real dirty. But Ray hadn't given much credence to the murmurs.

Until now.

Since his vehicle had been sabotaged and the high school's grounds left littered with shell casings, credence came much easier. Now, he could readily believe that if he turned himself in, he'd make an excellent cadaver by morning. And what would happen to Grace then? She'd been there in the car with him when the shooter tried to take him out. They'd go after her, too.

Grace. She was still punishing her poor thumb. "Yeah, this is perfect," he reiterated, gesturing to the baggy pants and the skater shoes. "You did great."

"Really?"

"Really. Next time I go on the lam, you'll be the first one I call."

She blinked rapidly, as though she might be fighting tears, but she still managed a smile. "Yeah? I bet you say that to all your fellow fugitives."

He laughed. Damn, but she kept surprising him. He knew plenty of guys who'd crack under this kind of pressure, but here was Gracie, holding up like a rock. The old Gracie would have buckled. Never mind that the new Gracie had a huge hole in her memory. Never mind that life as she knew it had been torn away this afternoon by a sniper's bullets.

Ray hauled himself up. What about life as *you* knew it? It had been ripped away the day she'd told him she couldn't bear to spend another night apart from the man she loved.

He picked up a box of hair dye. "Okay, let's get this done. What comes first? The cut or the color?"

"The color."

"Do I get to be red or blond?"

The corners of her mouth lifted. "Definitely blond."

Ten minutes later, he sat with his hair spiked up in wet tufts.

It had been torture to have her stand close enough to smell her scent, torture to feel her run her fingers through his hair as she applied the hair coloring. He'd sat stiffly, trying not to inhale too deeply, longing for it to be done.

"There," she announced eventually. "Done."

She stepped back and peeled off the latex gloves. Perversely, he felt a stab of disappointment at her retreat. Ignoring it, he pushed up off the chair.

"Geez, my scalp is starting to itch already," he complained. "I have to leave this on *how* long?"

"Wimp," she said mildly. "Think you can do mine, now?"

He accepted the box from her. "Sure. Nothing to it."

Except there was. It was damned complicated. Once he got all the goop on her head, a hideous thought occurred to him. "This'll wash out, right? It's not *permanent* permanent?"

She smiled without opening her eyes. "I can dye it back later. Why?"

"I like your hair the way it was."

She opened her eyes, her smile fading. "I think it's time to rinse yours off."

"Thank God. How do I do that?"

"Just shampoo it off in the shower. Oh, and use this on your head rather than the motel towel." She plucked a navy hand towel from the pile of purchases he'd pegged as superfluous. "Some of the dye always comes off on the towel. If we don't want the motel operators to know what we've been up to, we better use our own. And remove our own garbage."

He shot her a look. "Hey, you *are* pretty good at this. I'm definitely calling you next time." Of course, the need to remove their garbage had already occurred to him, but he wouldn't have thought to buy towels. He'd have just taken the motel's stained ones with him.

By the time he'd finished with the shower and pulled his jeans back on, Grace declared her own color ready to come off. He busied himself laying out the barbering stuff, but there was no shutting out the sound of the shower through the paper-thin walls. No shutting out the mental image of Grace standing under the spray, rivulets of water streaming down her body.

At last, the shower stopped. The plumbing made a loud hammering as she shut off the taps. Minutes later, she emerged from the bathroom in a cloud of steam, her hair wrapped in a dark towel.

"That bad, eh?"

She looked at him questioningly and he gestured toward the towel.

"Oh." She lifted a hand to it as though she'd forgotten it. "No, not that bad. Though I gave myself a start when I first looked in the mirror."

"Tell me about it," he said dryly, running a hand through his own nearly dry hair. It was so ... *yellow*. "So, am I gonna get a look at it?"

Grace unwound the little towel and shook her hair out. She combed her fingers through the tangles. "What do you think?"

He'd been prepared for fire engine red. "It doesn't look a lot different. Darker, maybe."

"Hah! Just wait'll it dries, or until you get a look at it under a better light source than that grimy sixty-watt bulb."

"You sound like you know what you're talking about."

She shrugged. "My mother had red hair for a while. A little goes a long way."

Ray wasn't sure whether Grace's last observation pertained to red dye or her mother. Both, he suspected.

"I don't suppose you have any hair-cutting experience?"

She smiled. "Actually, I do."

"You do?" How the hell had she come by that?

"Well, sort of. Dog clipping."

"You were a *dog groomer*? How come I didn't know that?"

She picked up the scissors and tested them, seemingly satisfied by the rasp of the sharp carbon blades. "Just for Mama. I learned to clip the poodles to save the grooming fees."

Right. Ostentation on a budget. That was Elizabeth Dempsey's style. And usually at her daughter's expense. He'd long ago given up voicing those thoughts. Grace always rushed to defend her mother, a woman who wouldn't return the favor.

"Poodles, eh?" He eyed the scissors in her hand with exaggerated wariness. Frankly, he wasn't too concerned, but he didn't mind pretending if it would take that look off Grace's face, the one she always got when she talked about her mother.

She laughed. "Don't worry, I won't make you look like Fi-Fi. Now, go wet your hair a little so we can get on with this."

A minute later he sat astride a chair, arms resting on its back, while Grace cut his hair. If having her color it had been bad, this was worse.

At the first touch of her fingers in his hair, he closed his eyes, only to find it intensified the sensations skating over his skin. He opened his eyes to find her breasts at eye level, just inches away. With both arms elevated, her hands busy in his hair, her bosom looked lusher than ever. He dropped his gaze, which settled on the leather belt cinched at her waist. She'd changed into a fresh t-shirt, which was tucked into her soft faded jeans.

Damnation. Why did she look so … perfect?

Not literally perfect. Hell, just look at her hips. They were way too narrow, almost boyish, and her waist didn't dip in that classically feminine hourglass shape. Her breasts, on the other hand, were improbably generous for her slim frame, creating an imbalance that he knew made her self-conscious.

And her face. He didn't need to look at her to picture the flaws. Her forehead was a little too high for true beauty, her nose too broad, and she had that very slight overbite. No, she was far from perfect.

But she was perfect for *him*. She always had been. And when she smiled, she lit up from within.

He shifted, cleared his throat. "We about through?"

"Through? Ray, I just got started. Now, sit still, would you?"

He dropped his hands to grip the back of the chair, but complied with her order to hold still. Thankfully, she moved to the side, taking the full-frontal view with her. He breathed a little easier, until her breast brushed his shoulder as she leaned in close to comb his hair straight up so she could grasp a lock between two fingers. He tightened his grip on the chair.

Snip, snip. Another clump of hair, yellow and startling, fell to the newspaper they'd spread on the floor.

That's it, Morgan. Just keep watching the floor.

Except now that he wasn't looking at her, he became more aware of her scent. It teased at his senses, the motel soap combining with her skin to produce a new fragrance, familiar but different. Lord, she smelled good. Warm, clean, his.

No, not his. Not any more.

Except he kept remembering the way she'd responded to him in the car. His palms remembered her breasts peaking inside her bra, and he heard again the way her breath had hitched and roughened.

He'd intended to punish her with those hard kisses that cared nothing for her comfort or pleasure, but she'd opened up to him, inviting him to take and take, then take some more. Only the knowledge that they were being watched had given him the presence of mind to put her away.

But no one was watching now.

What would she do if he grabbed her hips, pulled her close, buried his face in her breasts?

She'd go up like dry tinder. And so would he.

For a moment, he balanced on the knife edge of temptation. Why not? It sure as hell wouldn't mean anything, and afterward they could write it off to the dangerous situation they found themselves in. A mindless, adrenaline-driven tumble.

God, when was the last time he'd done *that?* Years.

Used to be that after a hair-raising shift, he'd go to the bar to tip a few with his buddies. Then he'd tip one of the ever-present badge bunnies into bed, working off his excess energy with athletic, no-holds-barred sex.

Of course, he'd long since learned to work it off more safely and responsibly, usually by thrashing Quigg at racquet ball, or alone in the weight room. Even after Grace came into his life, he still made routine use of the gym after a wild day.

Grace was such a sensitive thing. He'd always been careful to come to her with his control intact so he could show her the tenderness she deserved.

Though she hadn't seemed to need tenderness earlier tonight, in the car. Desire, hot and urgent, flashed through him at the memory.

She'd clipped her way around to his left side, her breast nudging his other shoulder as she leaned into him. The only thing that kept his butt glued to the chair was the fear of what he might do, what he might say.

Why wasn't I enough? How could you just stop loving me and start loving someone else? The questions rose up inside him, but he'd be damned if he'd ask them.

She'd put the scissors down and moved in front of him. She lifted his hair, comparing the length of the left side against the right, her face the picture of concentration. Suddenly, preserving his pride didn't seem so important. He felt the questions welling up again, threatening to spill out.

Quickly, before he could succumb to weakness, he summoned the images guaranteed to cool him off. Grace's limbs tangled with another man's. Grace moving under ....

"Done," she announced.

He leapt up, knocking the chair over.

"Whoa!" She sprang back as the chair crashed to the floor. "Careful."

He righted the chair, muttering an apology.

She picked up the scissors, handed them to him, then sat down in the chair. "My turn."

He looked at the scissors in his hand, appalled. "You want me to cut your hair?"

"I imagine you can do a better job on it than I can."

Panic flared in his gut. "You don't really need to cut it. It's a different color and everything. Just tie it back or stick it under a baseball cap or something."

She shook her head. "We shouldn't take any chances. Besides, if you think I'd let you sacrifice your hair while keeping my own, you've got another think coming."

He dragged a hand through his newly shorn hair. "That's different. It wasn't much of a sacrifice."

She arched a brow. "You haven't looked in the mirror yet."

"But, Grace, I'll make a mess of it. You love your hair. It's your ... *thing*."

Something flickered in her eyes, sadness or regret or maybe just wistfulness, but her voice was clear and determined: "I've made up my mind. If you don't do it, I'll do it myself."

He studied her for a few seconds. Dammit, she meant it. She'd take the scissors to it herself if he didn't do it.

He sighed. "Fine. You win."

She smiled at him, but it didn't reach the sadness in her eyes. He wished he could believe her melancholy had to do with the crime he was about to perpetrate on her hair.

"Why do you want to do this, Grace? Really?"

She lifted her chin. "I just have to."

He sighed. "Okay, but remember, you asked for it. I'll have you know my mother had a hairless Chihuahua when I was a kid, not poodles."

The lie came easily. He'd never had so much as a goldfish or a hamster in that lousy, poorly-heated walk-up he'd inhabited with his mother, but it brought a laugh to Grace's lips.

Ray was right, Grace thought, as she clutched the towel around her shoulders. Her hair had always been her "thing". A full, rich sable, it fell perfectly straight with the lightest encouragement with a brush and blow dryer. Everything else about her might be forgettable, but people noticed her hair.

It seemed only right somehow that she should sacrifice it.

"Okay, give me some guidance, here."

Poor Ray. He'd dodged bullets back there in that parking lot without breaking a sweat, but his hands were shaking now. She pretended not to notice.

"Just comb out a small section, then pull it tight between your fingers."

"Like this?"

"Closer."

"Forget it, Grace. I'm not cutting it that short. There'd be nothing left for the hairdresser to fix."

"But that's hardly short enough to make any difference."

They compromised, agreeing on a mid-length.

"Okay, what now?"

"Just angle your fingers like so." She used her own fingers to demonstrate.

"Like this?"

"Perfect. Now snip away."

He muttered something that sounded like "Hail Mary," and snipped.

The coppery lock fell onto her denim-covered knee. No going back now. For a moment, panic assailed her.

"Grace?"

She cleared her throat. "That's good. Keep going."

The second lock fell, this one hitting the newspapers, joining Ray's impossibly blond hairs. She blinked rapidly. It was just hair. An external manifestation of her stupid vanity. She would not cry.

Besides, her old precision haircut was fine for the woman she'd been before this nightmare started. The new Grace needed something different. It was going to take all the courage she could scrape together to get through this. Just as her smooth coif had given her poise and polish, maybe a sassier color and a rough-and-ready cut would lend her the edge she needed.

Image was everything, right? Fake it until you can make it.

"What do I do with the front?"

She glanced up at Ray. His mouth was set in that way that made his jawbones stand out, the grooves bracketing his mouth deeper than ever. He looked like a man completely out of his depth and hating it.

"Leave it fairly long, about so." She indicated a spot at the level of her cheekbone.

"Christ, I'm probably making a mess of this."

"Don't worry about it," she assured him. "With all the mousse and hair spray I bought at that drug store, I could probably make it look like the CN Tower, if I wanted to."

That earned a laugh, but when he made the next snip, his jaw had again taken on that grim line. The chair wasn't high enough, she noticed. He had to bend to do the job, which must be killing his back.

And that's not all she noticed, now that her panic had passed. His hands were clumsy in her hair, compared to the brisk competence of her stylist. But they were gentler, too. He separated the next section delicately, easing the comb through a snarl. She shivered.

"Sorry."

"It's okay. It doesn't hurt."

But it did hurt. Quite suddenly, it hurt a lot. It hurt that this was the first time he'd voluntarily touched her for so long, apart from that display they put on for the clerk.

And, oh, that scene in the office! She dropped her eyelids, her face heating at the memory. The way he'd touched her ....

She clamped down on the warmth flooding her belly. Nothing had changed. Their performance had been necessary to divert the clerk's attention.

Still, awareness shimmered through her when he pushed his fingers through her hair again.

"Almost done. Then you can get that cold towel off your shoulders," he said, obviously mistaking her shiver.

True to his word, he was soon finished. Grace didn't know whether to be relieved or disappointed when he pronounced her done. Removing the towel from around her neck, she strode to the closet-sized bathroom to inspect her new appearance. She flipped the switch for the overhead light and froze.

Yikes! Was that really her? Her eyes looked huge, her chin more pointed. Lord, it even seemed to lift her cheekbones.

Ray's reflection appeared behind her in the mirror. "What's the verdict?"

"Wow."

"Sorry," he said gruffly. "I told you it was a mistake."

"No, it's good. You did a better job on me than I did on you."

"Yeah, right."

"Really. A little mousse and a blow dryer and it'll kick butt."

He just regarded her in the mirror, unspeaking, a yellow-haired stranger.

She pushed a tendril of hair behind her ear and sighed. "I suppose I should style it now, so we can hit the road."

"No, let's get a few hours sleep first. We can finish our transformations in the morning."

She met his gaze in the mirror. "I thought we were going to sneak away under cover of night?"

He shook his head. "Better to blend in with rush hour traffic tomorrow morning than travel tonight. I just wanted to pay for the room in advance so we wouldn't have to show ourselves to the clerk after we'd morphed."

"We actually get to grab some sleep?"

The corners of his mouth turned up at her obvious relief, his eyes crinkling the way she loved. She smiled back into the mirror. For a few seconds, despite their altered appearances, they were the old Ray and Grace, but then his face sobered again.

"You take the bed; I'll sleep in the chair."

He turned and left the bathroom, leaving her staring into the mirror at the empty spot where he'd stood. She drew a deep breath, then followed him.

"That's not going to work, Ray. You'll insist on driving tomorrow, which is fine, but that means you're the one who needs the rest. I'll take the chair tonight, then doze in the car tomorrow."

"I can sleep anywhere, Grace. It's part of the training. You, on the other hand, would sit awake all night, and we can't have that. We're both gonna have to be sharp."

And you'd rather wake up with a cricked neck, a sore back and a killer headache than share that bed with me.

She felt like crying again, which was really stupid. He'd slept on the couch every night since she'd come home from the hospital. Why should it hurt that he sleep elsewhere again?

She shrugged and turned away. "Suit yourself," she said, picking up a t-shirt and disappearing back into the bathroom.

❧

An hour later, Ray sat slumped in the room's lumpy chair, listening to Grace's regular breathing. She'd fallen asleep almost immediately, as though her mind had just shut down.

Poor Grace. She wasn't used to this, hadn't asked for it.

He shifted in the chair, trying to ease himself into a more comfortable position. Trouble was, every time he shifted, his jeans dragged against his tender knees. He must have skinned them on the asphalt when he'd dived for cover. He shifted again. Finding a semi-tolerable posture, he willed his own mind to shut down. The minutes ticked by, evidenced by the glowing display on the clock radio every time he opened his eyes.

Dammit!

Standing, he shucked his jeans, then pulled his shirt off for good measure. Scooping up the dubious bedspread he'd warned Grace about earlier, he flopped on the chair again, covering himself. There.

But he couldn't stop his brain from whirling. The scene in the school parking lot kept running on an endless loop. The itch between his shoulder blades as he'd approached Tommy's car — he'd thought it was Grace's gaze following him, but it must have been the sniper. The car window exploding, Ray standing there frozen as he'd tried to process it, the thunk-thunk of slugs slamming into metal, the look on Tommy's face before he'd nailed the accelerator ....

Had they found anything at the scene? He knew better than to imagine they'd have apprehended the shooter. If it was Landis's man, he'd be no bumbling idiot. Of course, he was no sharpshooter with a rifle, either. If he had been, Ray'd be dead right now. Probably Grace and Tommy, too.

He thrust the thought away, turning his mind back to the shooter. No, the triggerman was no trained sniper, but he wouldn't be a total amateur, either. Even someone handy with a gun might have trouble with a roof shot. For sure he'd be GOA by the time the cops landed, having provided for a quick getaway. But would he have had time to clean up the scene?

Lord, he hoped not. If the shooter left spent shell casings, they could establish his position, reconstruct the attack. Tommy'd soon figure out the bullets that hit his car had whizzed past their real target.

Which, he realized, wouldn't alter much. If they thought he'd tried to set up Tommy to be whacked, they'd try to bring him in on a warrant. But if they figured out that the hit had been intended for him not Tommy, then they'd still want to bring him in, for protection. Grace, too. And Ray still wasn't ready to take the chance, not with an internal investigation hanging fire. God knew how long that could bung things up, especially with that dickwad Creighton howling for blood.

The money. Damn, it always came back to that, didn't it? They had to find out where it'd come from. Until he could explain that away, quickly and convincingly, they were screwed.

Grace cried out, dragging Ray's attention back to the here and now. Beneath the covers, she twisted in the throes of a dream. He closed his eyes, gritting his teeth against the desire to comfort her. After a moment, the thrashing stopped. Thank God. He felt some of the tension in his muscles drain.

He waited for her to settle again, but instead of smoothing out, her breathing became more ragged. In the dark, he realized she was crying. They weren't big, harsh sobs. In fact, her weeping was almost soundless. Somehow, that was so much sadder. It tore the heart right out of him.

He flipped the throw off, pushed himself out of the chair and crossed to the bed. Knowing it was foolhardy but unable to do anything else, he peeled the covers back and climbed in with her. She went stiff at first, but then she melted into his arms, clinging and crying in earnest.

When the storm of weeping had passed, she murmured against his chest, "I'm so scared."

"Sleep, Grace," he said. "I'll keep you safe."

She relaxed against him. Within a few minutes, she'd drifted back into sleep. Wondering whether he could keep his promise, Ray followed at last.

Chapter 7

HE WOKE UP IN a state of unbearable arousal. Grace's warm body curved into his, her head resting on his shoulder. Her lush breasts, confined only by the t-shirt she wore, pressed flat against his side. His left arm had gone numb from the weight of her, but he was only vaguely aware of that. More insistent was the drumbeat of physical need pulsing through his blood, pooling in his loins.

She was still asleep, her moist breath feathering the hairs on his chest. At some point in the night, they'd thrown the covers back. Now, her left arm lay across his belly, innocent in sleep but wildly arousing. Her hair, which had been wet last night when she'd crawled into bed, was now a tangle of shocking auburn.

For long minutes, he battled the urge to roll her over and take her, warm and half asleep, this flame-haired woman who was Grace, but not Grace.

Sweet Jesus, what was he thinking? Had he no pride? She'd made her choice, and it wasn't him. No way would he stand in for the man she really wanted. No way would he let his heart be ripped out again when she finally remembered where the hell she wanted to be and who she wanted to be there with.

Yeah, he had to get out of this bed.

In just a minute.

Then she opened her eyes. From a distance of six inches, he watched the fog of sleep give way to joy.

"Ray." She lifted a hand to touch his jaw.

Too late, he thought in the seconds before he covered her mouth with his. Hell, it had been too late last night when he'd climbed into this bed.

He kissed her softly and it was like coming home. All the anger and the pain seemed to have leached out of him in the night. She responded with a matching reverence.

As their lips and tongues mated, desire swelled, demanding more than soft kisses. Her hands found him, freeing him from the confinement of his boxers, pushing them down over his hips. Growling deep in his throat, he kicked free of their confinement. Then, lightning-quick, he rolled her onto her back. That fast, he was poised to enter her, his need pressing urgently against her most intimate flesh. He gritted his teeth. One thrust and he'd be home, if she'd just open her legs a little wider, tilt her hips the tiniest bit ....

Damn, was she trying to drive him crazy with all that wriggling? He grasped her hips to still her and would have thrust into her but for the cry that broke from her lips. Belatedly, he realized she was trying to struggle free. As soon as that fact registered, he turned her loose.

She leapt up, nearly inflicting some damage on him in her haste, and streaked to the bathroom. Seconds later, he heard her retching.

What the hell?

He sat up, nausea roiling in his own stomach.

Had she remembered the sonofabitch at last? Had recollection occurred at that critical moment, making her stomach revolt at the idea of making love with someone else?

Someone else. Dammit, he was her *husband.* The rest of the male population was supposed to fall into the category of *someone else*, not him.

He heard her retch again. Dragging a hand over his face, he pulled himself together and rolled out of bed. He yanked the bed sheet loose, wrapped it around his waist and went to investigate.

⚜

Grace sank down on the edge of the tub and applied a cold facecloth to her face with trembling fingers. Oh, God, what horrible timing. One minute Ray was making love to her and the next minute she'd been sick as a new sailor on a heavy sea.

"You okay?"

She dropped the cloth to see Ray standing in the doorway, looking rumpled and sexy as sin with the sheet bunched at his hip. But any hope she might have cherished that they could pick up where she so hastily left off died a quick death when she looked at his face. He looked like a stranger, and it had very little to do with the shocking blond hair and artificial tan.

"Yeah, I'm okay now. I don't know what came over me."

His face bore no expression, but a muscle ticked below his eye. "Then you didn't ... remember anything?"

Her eyebrows drew together. "Like what?"

"Like who you really wanted in that bed with you."

"No!" She felt the blood drain from her face, only to rush back in a painful flush. That's what he thought had sent her racing for the bathroom? *Oh, Ray.* Her heart felt like it would crack open.

She looked down at her bare feet, at the cigarette burn in the dull cushion floor, at the rust stain in the tub, anywhere but at Ray.

"No, I haven't remembered anything." She pushed the words past a lump in her throat. "My blood sugar must be out of whack or something. Now that I think of it, I'm starving. I guess I missed one too many meals."

"You sure?"

She risked a glance at him to find him watching her closely. "I'm sure," she said. Her stomach gave a loud rumble in support and she managed a smile. "See?"

"I'll go out and find us some breakfast."

The thought made her stomach lurch queasily again. What if something happened to him while he was out there?

"No need to do that. We've got some meal replacement bars here somewhere in all that stuff I bought yesterday. Why don't we have one of them? We can stop later for a proper breakfast after we've finished transforming ourselves."

After a few seconds' pause, he nodded his assent, then glanced at his watch. "We should get a move on if we want to slip out of town in morning traffic."

She stood, catching a glimpse of herself in the vanity mirror, all pale skin and tangled red hair. *Get used to it, Grace. It's the new you.* "Do you want to shower first or shall I?"

"You go ahead. I'm gonna turn on the radio news."

To see if there was any mention of their possible fugitive status. He didn't say it, but he didn't have to. She turned to the shower, drawing the cheap plastic curtain back so she could turn the taps on.

"Grace?"

Water temperature adjusted, she turned back to him, lifting an eyebrow.

"About what happened out there?" He jerked his head in the direction of the bedroom. "I'm sorry."

Her first instinct was to crawl under a rock or any ready hiding place. But that was the old Grace, she reminded herself. The new Grace, the Grace whose life could be ended by an assassin's bullet at any time, couldn't afford to take refuge behind a blush while vital things went unsaid.

So she looked him squarely in the eye and said, "I'm not."

"Huh?"

"I'm not sorry."

Heart pounding, stomach feeling a little sick again, she reached for the knob that tripped the shower. Then she pulled the t-shirt over her head, stepped naked into the tub and pulled the curtain on Ray's astonished face.

Half an hour later, after making use of the styling products she'd bought and the bathroom's puny built-in 1200-watt hair dryer, she emerged, dressed again in the t-shirt.

"Omigod."

She started to lift a hand to her hair but aborted the nervous gesture, reaching instead for one of the department store bags. "Omigod good, or omigod awful?"

"Grace, you look ... wow."

She buried her nose in the bag to hide the pleasure his words brought her. "The look's way too young for me, but I guess that's the point, right? To look different."

"Yeah."

Grace dug some costume jewelry out of the department store bag and a small cache of cosmetics from the drug store bag. When she looked up, Ray's gaze was still fixed on her hair. She'd created a crooked part, using pomade to texture it into uneven chunks. She grinned at his expression, succumbing to the need to touch a hand to her hair. "Weird, huh?"

"I can't believe you made it look so good after the butcher job I did on it."

She shrugged. "You can do anything with this stuff. I'll do yours, if you like."

He pulled back at her offer. "No need. I'll just wear a ball cap." He cleared his throat. "So, what am I supposed to wear?"

She crossed to the small pile of clothing, pulled some stuff out and handed it to him. "Did we make the radio?"

He shook his head.

"That's good, isn't it?"

"I didn't really expect they'd go public. Too unsettling for the community, the idea of a rogue cop out there."

He headed for the bathroom.

Grace turned the small TV on, flipping to the music channel to drown out the sound of Ray in the shower. Grimacing, she donned yesterday's underwear, still damp from last night's rinsing. Their first stop after breakfast would have to be for lingerie. She pulled on black athletic pants. Next came a tiny, bellybutton-baring cropped top that hugged her curves.

Makeup was next. Normally, her toilette was pretty minimal: moisturizer, a sheer foundation to even out her pale skin, a little blusher and she was out the door. That wasn't going do it here, though.

She closed her eyes and tried to picture the punked-up girls who hung out with their skater boyfriends downtown. Eyes and lips, lots of black. With that idea in mind, she tackled her makeup. The shower had stopped by the time she'd finished. Eyeing her reflection, she tugged her pants down until they rode on her hips like the girls she'd seen. Not bad. Still, she needed something else.

From the cache of costume jewelry, she chose a silver heart on a leather loop that fell to her cleavage, then added a plain braided choker, and finally a beaded hemp job that hung somewhere in the middle. To complete the picture, she slid an ear cuff onto her right ear and swapped her studs for a pair of dangly earrings made from tortoiseshell guitar picks.

In the bathroom, the hair dryer started up. Pushing her feet into new running shoes, she laced them up, then went to stand in front of the mirror.

Holy emo-punk Lolitas, Batman! She looked about fifteen.

The bathroom door opened and she forgot her own appearance as Ray stepped into the room. Grace dragged in a breath.

The big baggy jeans hung just right. Over the oversized white t-shirt she'd given him, he wore the short-sleeved plaid Sean John hombre shirt. He'd put on the skater shoes she'd given him and pulled the Cleveland Indians baseball cap over his hair. One hand was shoved into the pocket of his low-riding pants while the other rested on his hip, and the corners of his mouth were turned down. Even the small cut on his cheekbone seemed to lend him a measure of menace.

"Ray! You look ...."

He scowled. "I know exactly how I look. Like a punk. A thug." He pulled the cap lower over his forehead. "I couldn't go back now even if I wanted to. Look at me!" He gestured to the voluminous material of the wide-legged pants.

"You look great." She grinned.

"I look like walking proof evolution has hit a brick wall."

Grace's smile broadened. "Not yet, you don't. But you will when I'm finished with you." She held up several small packets.

"What's that?"

"Fake tats. Even with those clothes and that scowl, you look way too clean. You need some ink."

Fifteen minutes later, Grace steered him in front of the mirror. Barbed-wire tattoos marred both biceps and a snake crawled up his left forearm. He glowered at his reflection, which now included a heavy silver chain lying on his t-shirt. "Okay, *now* I look like a thug."

She laughed. "You look perfect. Not over-the-top into banger territory or anything. You still look like a citizen, but no one is going to get in your way."

He grunted. "Well, one thing's for sure. No one looking for me will look twice."

"Same here." She pulled on a transparent black shirt, eyeing her own tattoos through the fabric. "I look like a hooker."

"No," he said, his voice flat, "you don't."

Something about his expression made her glance up to meet his gaze in the mirror, but she couldn't read his expression.

"You don't look anything like a hooker," he reiterated, "But if you did, it'd be only fitting." He glared at himself in the mirror. "I look like your pimp."

She looked away. "The main thing is we don't look anything like we used to. That's all that matters, right?"

"That's right," he echoed.

⁂

They stopped for breakfast at a pancake house. Ray watched Grace attack a short stack as soon as the waitress delivered it. Cripes, she wasn't kidding about being starved. He pushed his plate toward her when she'd cleaned her own.

"Guess I ate too many of those bars," he lied.

"You don't want anymore?"

He almost smiled at her hopeful tone. "I'm done."

She speared his last pancake, plopped it on her plate and added syrup. When had she eaten last? He'd have to keep an eye on her, make sure she had regular meals. What had she said? Something about blood sugar? That's all they'd need, to find out she was borderline diabetic or something.

As Grace finished his meal, Ray noticed the cashier, a young man, eyeing them nervously. He scowled. What was *his* problem? Unless . . . his heart rate took a jump. Was the manhunt on? Had the cashier made them and called the cops?

"Ray, what is it?"

His gaze flicked to Grace, who'd cleaned her plate again, then back to the cashier.

"Nothing. We'd better go."

"If it's nothing, then why are you glaring at that kid?"

"I'm not glaring."

"Yes, you are. And you're scaring him to death."

He blinked. "Huh?"

"Ray, you don't look like you stepped out of GQ anymore. You look ... scary. And the way you're scowling, he's probably wondering if we're going to hold him up on the way out, then shoot him just for kicks."

Aw, hell. He forced his brow to smooth. "Told you I looked like a thug."

"Only when you glare like that," she said. "But maybe it's not such a bad thing. People will leave us alone."

People did leave them alone. Later, when Ray stopped to gas up the Toyota, he felt wary eyes on him as he stood at the pumps. When he went inside to pay, no one looked him squarely in the eye. He could almost hear the thoughts of the middle-aged man behind the counter. *We don't want no trouble, son.*

"What are you gawking at?" he wanted to shout. "It's only clothes, just a friggin' haircut." Instead, he gritted his teeth and asked for the washroom key for Grace.

While she freshened up, he leaned against the car's rusting fender. No wonder so many of the young punks he'd hauled up over the years had such a chip on their shoulder. When he got back to work — hell, *if* he got back to work — he'd try harder to give the pierced-and-tattooed toughs the benefit of a doubt.

He straightened as Grace emerged from the washroom. When she stepped clear of the building's shadow, the sun struck her hair, setting it aflame. As she crossed the parking lot toward him, his pulse jerked.

The morning was cool and she still wore the tiny jean jacket she'd bought, but it hung open, giving him a glimpse of skin between the short top and the low-riding workout pants. Normally, he didn't go for that get-up, but on Grace's body, there was nothing school-girlish about it. Her hips swayed, her stride confident as she approached him. She looked, he realized with another jolt, like a woman who knew exactly what she wanted sexually and how to get it.

That was one helluva transformation she'd pulled off!

Or maybe not such a big one. For all he knew, maybe she was a tigress in lover-boy's bed.

Grimly, he moved to her side of the car, opening the door.

"Ray, you're going to have to stop doing that stuff."

"What stuff?"

"Opening doors. Guys who look like you don't open doors for women who look like me."

"This one does." He closed her door, walked around the Toyota and climbed in.

Five minutes later, they were on the highway. He could feel Grace's confusion before she spoke.

"Saint John? That's where we're going?"

"Yup." He felt her gaze on him, but didn't take his eyes off the road.

"Wouldn't we be boxing ourselves in?"

He shot her a look this time, an appreciative one. She was right, of course. If the manhunt was on, it'd be hard to slip across the border into Maine. There'd be heavy scrutiny if they tried to board a ferry or bus, and a plane was out of question. They'd be hard up against the ocean with precious few options.

"What'd you have in mind?" she continued. "Stow away on a container ship bound for Cuba?"

"They'll expect us to go west to keep our options open."

"So we do what they'd least expect?"

"Right." He cast her a sideways look. "Besides, I don't want to get so far away that I can't monitor what's happening in Fredericton. Saint John's just an hour away. Plus it's urban enough that we'll blend in without raising any eyebrows. Can you imagine the looks we'd get in rural New Brunswick, decked out like this?"

He took his eyes off the road to glance at her again. Instead of the amusement he expected to see, her profile was set in stark lines.

"I came this way the night of my accident, didn't I?"

A green Subaru chose that moment to overtake them. Ray swore and clapped his gaze back on the road. He should have noticed the other car preparing to pass. He'd better pay attention or there'd be another accident on this highway.

"Ray? I was going to Saint John, wasn't I?"

"You were on this highway, yes, so you must have had Saint John in mind. Or maybe St. Andrews."

"No. Saint John."

The speedometer needle jumped. Ray eased up on the accelerator. "You said that like you remembered."

"Kind of." She chewed at her lip. "I think I planned to go to the airport there, catch a flight."

She'd been going to board a plane, fly away from him.

His speed dipped. She'd planned to put miles — maybe oceans — between them. "Do you remember buying a ticket?"

"No."

She might have disappeared forever. His stomach clutched. "Any idea where you were planning to go?"

She dipped her head. "I don't remember. And why would I fly out of Saint John when there's an airport in Fredericton?"

The misery of her tone penetrated his own reaction to the news. "It's okay," he said, placing a reassuring hand on her knee. "You did good. That gives us something to check out, at least. We can call the airlines, see if you'd booked anything."

She looked pitifully grateful for his words. Suddenly she seemed like the old Grace despite the sassy hairdo and youthful get-up. Ray wasn't prepared for the wave of fierce ambivalence that swept over him at the thought.

A glint of something in his rearview mirror caught his attention. Cripes! A transport truck, hard on his tail. He glanced at his speedometer. *Damn.* He'd let his speed drop. If they weren't on an upgrade, the big rig would have passed him.

Okay, no more conversation. And no more picking at the tangled knot of emotions his mind had become. He tramped the accelerator, then reached over to flick the radio on. He should be listening for news bulletins anyway.

Chapter 8

IT WAS TOO EARLY to check into a motel when they hit Saint John, which was fine with Grace. A motel room meant close quarters and nowhere to retreat to but into her head. Right now, her head was the last place she wanted to spend any time. After that tantalizing fragment from the night of her accident, she'd spent the rest of the trip trying to coax more memories out of the shadows. Her brain had refused to release its secrets, however.

Needing diversion, she roped Ray into going shopping. He grumbled that one pair of baggy-assed pants was one pair too many, but he went along. Two hours later, laden with bags, they made their way to the motel. This one wasn't as seedy as the one they'd picked in Fredericton, but it was no Holiday Inn either. It did, however, have two double beds.

As soon as they dragged their bags in, Ray picked up the telephone and called Air Canada. She listened to the one-sided conversation as she unpacked their purchases. By the time he'd struck out with the last of the airlines, she'd finished settling them in by installing their toiletries in the bathroom. Ray was sitting on the edge of one of the beds, his shoulders slumped, when she came back into the room.

"No luck?"

He straightened, putting the phone back on the night table. "Nothing."

She swallowed to ease her dry throat. "Maybe I planned to buy a ticket on the spot."

"Maybe."

Except she wasn't the impulsive type. She planned everything, down to the last detail. At least she used to.

She sank down on the other bed, toeing off the heavy athletic shoes without unlacing them. Frustration rose in her chest. She had to clamp down on the desire to kick the damned shoes across the room. "If I could just remember . . . ."

"You will. You just have to give it time. The memories are already starting to come," he reminded her.

She glanced quickly at him, then back at the floor. After a moment's silence, she gave voice to the fear that had been growing all afternoon. "What if it's not real?"

"What if what's not real?"

"Maybe I imagined it, that I was going to the airport." She contemplated her stockinged feet. "It's all fuzzy now."

Ray stood and walked to the window. Grace's gaze rested on him as he flipped the curtain back and scanned the lot outside. Then he turned back to face her. "You think you were wrong?"

She dropped her gaze again. "I don't know. It felt like the truth, when I said it. But now . . . I just don't know."

He came to stand beside her, close enough that she could feel his body warmth. Then he slid a finger under her chin and tipped her face up to his. "You're tired now. You'll feel different when you're rested."

"Will I?" She desperately wanted to believe him.

"Absolutely. We're safe now. We've got cash enough to lie around here for weeks, if we need to. Just concentrate on getting rested and don't press too hard. The memories will come."

"That's what Dr. Greenwood said."

"See? It's good advice."

She wanted to grasp his hand, to turn her cheek into his open palm. To prevent herself from succumbing to that weakness, she pulled back. She'd put him through enough.

His hand fell away immediately and he stepped back.

"Why don't you have a hot shower?" he suggested. "I can go out and rustle us up some food."

Her stomach rumbled at the mention of food. "I've got a better idea. You grab a shower first, then I'll have a soak in that sparkling tub while you forage for supper."

He nodded, heading for the bathroom. A moment later, she heard the shower running. Grace picked up the remote control and turned the television on, cranking the volume to compensate for the sound of running water. Flipping through the channels, she found a local news station. With the anchor's familiar voice in the background, she turned to unpack her purchases.

Not a bad day's shopping. Most of it was done at the city's hippest shops, but a lot of the stuff she'd found at the Salvation Army thrift store. Too bad she hadn't thought to start there. She wouldn't have thought of it at all but for Ray's incredulous reaction to the prices. She grinned at the memory of his words: "Grace, there are *holes* in these pants. I could get better at the Sally Ann, for chrissakes."

"In local news, here's a story that has police in Fredericton scrambling."

Grace glanced at the TV automatically at the mention of Fredericton. There on the screen was her house, but the front door was blown off. She stood there, feet rooted to the floor.

"Ray!" she called, but the water kept running. Obviously he couldn't hear her.

"A would-be burglar got a rude surprise when he tried to break into this Fredericton home," intoned the announcer. *"This and other stories after the break."*

As the program went to commercial, Grace raced to the bathroom. The door was unlocked and she threw it open. She would have yanked the shower curtain back, too, but Ray did that himself, almost colliding with her as he stepped naked from the shower.

"What is it?"

Grace just stared. His hair, sudsy with shampoo, stood straight up and water streamed off his body. But what riveted her attention was the gun he gripped in his fist. How had he gotten to it so quickly? Then she spied the towel on the floor of the tub, growing wetter by the second. He must have perched his gun on the edge of the tub, she realized, probably inside the towel.

"Grace!" He gave her shoulder a shake. "What's wrong?"

She blinked, her gaze lifting to his face. "On the TV. The news. Our house ...."

"What about it?"

"There's been an explosion. I don't know ... something about a burglar."

Gun now dangling at his side, he pushed past her and strode dripping into the bedroom. She trailed behind him. An ad-man's pitch for disposable diapers was running.

He shot her a look. "It's over?"

"No. I just saw the teaser. The story's coming up."

He returned his gaze to the television, seemingly oblivious of his nakedness. She went back to the bathroom and retrieved a dry towel, which she handed to him. He used it to wipe dripping trails of shampoo from his forehead and the back of his neck before finally wrapping it around his narrow hips.

Then the news anchor was back again. "A twenty-seven-year-old man is in serious condition tonight as a result of injuries sustained in what looks like a housebreaking gone bizarrely wrong."

The anchor's serious face was replaced by a shot of their house. She heard Ray's intake of breath as he took in the image of the smoke-blackened door of their home hanging ajar from one hinge. A black smudge of fire damage ran up to the roof, and debris from the explosion lay strewn on the lawn. Seeing the degree of damage shocked her, but it wasn't until the camera panned the front lawn and she saw that her favorite Hosta had been crushed that it really sank in.

"The home belongs to Fredericton Police detective Raymond Morgan and his wife, Grace Morgan." The camera cut to the newscaster again. "From what we've pieced together, it appears the injured man triggered an explosion when he tried to break into the house. The Morgans are said to be on vacation and unavailable for comment. Beyond that, police in Fredericton are being very tight-lipped. We will keep you informed of developments in this case, and of course will update you on the blast victim's condition."

The camera backed off to encompass the female co-anchor. "Wow, wouldn't that be some kind of welcome home present for the absentee owners if it hadn't been triggered by the attempted break-in?" Her partner agreed, and she segued into the next story about bed closures at the local hospital. Ray reached out and hit the power button on the TV, killing the picture.

"Damnation." His soft oath broke the silence.

Shaken, Grace looked from the black television screen to her husband's expressionless face. "Someone tried to kill us," she said numbly.

"Again."

That's right. Two attempts so far. And the thing with his truck! That was three. The choking fear she'd felt after the sniper attack came rushing back.

Slow breaths, Grace. It'll pass.

"Guess we did the right thing getting out of town," Ray said.

"Are you sure? Maybe we should turn ourselves in." Panic drove her voice higher. "They'll listen to you this time. Someone tried to kill you! They'll believe you now when you tell them the sniper was trying to kill *you*, not Tommy."

"They'll have figured that out already."

He was clothed only in a towel and his face bore no expression, but he somehow looked more menacing than he had earlier today with his fierce scowls and the hood's clothing.

"Then why don't we go in?"

"We talked about this before. I think we're better off right where we are, at least for the moment."

She looked away. "What are we going to do now?"

"Stick with our plan."

"Which is?"

"Lay low, wait it out."

"Wait it out?" She laughed, a harsh, breathless sound. She turned away, finding herself in front of the room's only window. "Wait for my memory to come back, you mean."

He didn't sigh, but he might as well have. She could hear it in his voice. "Grace, nothing's changed. Our situation is just the same as it was before you saw that broadcast. Yes, we've got to figure out where that money came from. And yes, it looks like the only way that's going to happen is if you remember." He came to stand behind her. "You've just got to put it out of your mind, relax. The memories will come."

Relax? How could she relax?

No, she wouldn't give in to panic. She lifted a hand, pressing a thumb and forefinger against her closed eyelids, pushing back the terror. She'd put them in this position with that God-forsaken money. Now she had to get them out.

Swallowing the lump of self-pity that had risen in her throat, she turned to Ray, only to find him much closer than she'd thought. Her heart took a leap.

Part of her wanted to take a step back, beyond the reach of his forceful aura. Another, bigger part wanted to move closer, to press her face to his chest and let the tears come. If she did that, she knew he wouldn't turn her away. She knew, too, that it would take very little encouragement for that comforting contact to ignite into passion.

The temptation to take that half step was agonizing. She knew she could forget her fear in his arms. The terror could be banished in a molten rush, leaving room for nothing but sensation. A hot tendril of need unfurled in her belly at the thought.

Why not press her advantage? It wasn't as if it wouldn't be therapeutic for him, too.

Because it wouldn't be fair to Ray. He'd made it more than clear he didn't want to resume a physical relationship with her.

She stepped back. "You're right," she said crisply. "You're absolutely right. Rest and relaxation." She smiled to show him she was okay. "Now, why don't you finish your shower? If I'm going to relax, I'll need my hot bath and a hot meal."

Surprise widened his eyes, followed by something that looked like admiration, and her spirits lifted.

He turned and followed his wet footprints back to the bathroom.

Fifteen minutes later, Ray left in search of supper. Within a few more minutes, Grace sank into a steaming tub. Lord, what a day. Closing her eyes, she slid lower to let the warm water lap at her breasts. Breasts that still ached from wanting Ray.

She'd made the right decision, though. She would have Ray back in her bed, but not that way.

Grace sat up, sloshing water over the edge of the tub. Wow! When had she made that decision?

Slowly, she sank back into the water's embrace, her heart pounding.

Could she do it? She thought about how close he'd come to taking her with such swift authority this morning when she'd woken up sick. *Absolutely.*

Should she? She gnawed the inside of her lip. *Under the right circumstances.*

Did she dare? *She had to.* Intimidating as the idea was, it was a whole lot less scary than letting him go without a fight.

It would have to be a conscious choice on his part, she decided. Not through the back door on some comfort-the-female thing. Not on the crest of an adrenaline wave when any willing woman would do. When she seduced Ray, he was going to know what was happening.

Smiling, she picked up the bar of soap Ray had opened and lathered the facecloth.

❧

There was something different about Grace. Ray couldn't put his finger on it, but he knew it was there. He watched her face carefully as she dug into her breakfast of poached eggs on whole-wheat toast.

Maybe it was as simple as coming to accept that she couldn't force the memories. She announced that she would treat them like flighty horses — pretend she didn't notice them getting closer and closer until she could slip a rope around one's neck.

"Are you going to eat your orange slice?"

At her question, he looked down at the bit of garnish lying on his now empty plate. "No."

She speared it with her fork, then transferred it to her fingers. Peeling the fruit away from the rind, she popped it into her mouth and sighed happily.

"I know." She grinned when she caught him staring at her. "All I do these days is eat. It's the absence of routine. I'm used to working from coffee break to lunch to coffee break to dinner. It's been *years* since I've had this much time on my hands, which is a good thing for my waistline."

"I'm sorry about that. You know, Quigg reminded me that we haven't taken a real vacation in four years."

She shrugged. "You've been busy. I've been busy."

He cradled his coffee cup in his hands. Too busy to look after his marriage?

"Hey," she said, "what are we gonna do today?"

It had been two days since they'd seen the newscast. They'd spent the first day seeing the sights of the Loyalists' city. One of the oldest cities in North America, Saint John boasted a colorful past, one that Ray was ashamed to say he'd never explored. But they hadn't indulged their curiosity too much. As Grace pointed out, like opening doors for women, it really didn't go with the personas they'd created.

The second day they'd spent poking around the malls, drinking tall lattes at an Internet café while they surfed for news and browsed the newspapers.

"Could we go to Fundy?"

Ray set his coffee down. "The National Park?"

"Doesn't have to be the park." She popped the last crust of her toast into her mouth and washed it down with coffee. "I just want to walk on the beach."

"It'd be cold," he warned.

"Oh, come on, Ray. We can dress for it. You're not scared of a little wind, are you?"

He snorted. No, he wasn't scared of a little wind. And it would be nice for a change not to worry about being made. Their disguises were good. Hell, they were damn good, but he still worried.

"Sure, why not?"

An hour and a half later, a picnic lunch packed in a cheap Styrofoam cooler in the trunk of the old Toyota, they hit the beach. The tide was retreating, so there were miles of packed sand to walk and hours to enjoy it. With gulls wheeling and crying overhead and smaller shore birds darting at their feet, they strolled. Sometimes they talked, sometimes they walked in silence, and occasionally they stopped to explore a sun-warmed tidal pool teeming with tiny sea creatures. With the wind tugging at their hair and the sharp tang of the seaweed in their nostrils, Ray found it both invigorating and restorative.

Every once in a while, he threw a question at her out of the blue to try to lasso an unwary memory. For the most part, it didn't work, but once, when he asked her where the plane she planned to board that night might be headed, she answered immediately: *Mexico.*

After that, they walked for a long time without talking.

Eventually, the tide turned.

"We'd better get back," he said, mindful of the speed with which these, the highest tides in the world, moved.

They retraced their path along the strip of sand, theirs the only footprints on this blustery, overcast day. When they reached the high water mark, they found a perch among some rocks to watch the tide come in. They sat for another half hour, listening to the rush and retreat of the surf. Finally, when a sliver of weak sun broke through around noon, Ray figured he'd better fetch their lunch.

"Wait here," he instructed. "I'll bring the cooler and we can have our lunch here."

A short while later, he began picking his way back across the rocks, the Styrofoam cooler squeaking with his every step. Given the uneven footing on the rough rocks, he had to keep a close eye on the ground, glancing up frequently to make sure he was still on course for the large rock where Grace sat with her arms wrapped around her drawn up legs.

Clearing the roughest part of the terrain, he looked up to check his course again and stopped dead.

Grace was right there where he'd left her, but she'd rolled back to lie on the rock, her face turned up to the sun's warmth. He felt sweat break out on his back. She'd locked her hands behind her head as a cushion against the unyielding stone, with the result that her breasts jutted invitingly, even beneath her thick sweater. She'd drawn one leg up, too, probably to ease the strain on her lower back imposed by the curve of the rock.

With anyone but Gracie, he'd suspect she'd choreographed the pose deliberately for maximum seductive effect. But she had no interest in enticing him. If she wanted to, she'd have done it two nights ago.

Yeah, he'd seen it in her eyes, the knowledge that she could pull him into that vortex of need that swirled dangerously beneath them. And she'd been so scared. He'd have obliged if she hadn't pulled away. He wouldn't have been able to turn her away.

If she hadn't seized that opportunity, she sure as hell wouldn't be trying to beguile him now. Unfortunately, knowing that didn't make the picture any less provocative.

She lifted her head to search for him, no doubt alerted to his abrupt halt by the cessation of the cooler's squeaking.

"Ray?"

She curled up to brace herself on her elbows. That posture did something completely different, but no less remarkable, for her breasts. Silently cursing, he started forward again, the cooler resuming its rhythmic *squeak, squeak.*

"Heavy?" She sat up as he deposited the cooler at her feet. "You looked like you had to stop for a breather there."

"Just gawking at how far the tide came up in the few minutes I was gone." He flipped the lid off the cooler, fished out two colas and handed one to her.

She glanced out at the water, which had advanced markedly. "Amazing, isn't it?"

He grunted in agreement, unpacking their dinner of fried chicken, cold salads and crusty rolls which they'd bought at the supermarket. As he passed takeout containers to Grace, she opened them and arranged them on the rock beside her. When the cooler was empty, he boosted himself up to join her.

"Napkins?"

He patted his pocket. "I figured the wind would take them. Let me know when you're ready for one."

"Good thinking." She bit into a piece of chicken, closing her eyes to savor the taste.

Ray dropped his gaze to the takeout box. Selecting a drumstick, he concentrated on picking it clean.

"Ummm, this is so good."

He glanced up to see her licking her fingers, and his mouth went dry. The last bite of chicken he'd swallowed seemed to lodge in his throat. Reaching for his cola, he popped the tab and downed half of it in one swig. Better.

Grace went on to sample the pasta salad, the potato salad and the bean salad, pronouncing them all wonderful. She then ate another piece of chicken and polished off a roll. Ray watched her, taking pleasure in the gusto with which she attacked the meal. It must the fresh sea air, he decided. He managed three more pieces of chicken himself, not to mention a generous helping of the salads and two of the rolls.

By the time they finished their meal, they'd attracted a small legion of seagulls. For the next twenty minutes, they tossed food-stuffs for the gulls until the advancing tide stole the last of the beach.

They sat a while longer in silence, contemplating the water which now lapped at the rocks below them. Twice a day, the ocean ebbed, then rushed back. Forty-five feet, it rose, compared to a world average of two-and-a-half feet. That's what the brochure at the motel said. Something like a hundred billion tons of salt water. A remarkable thing, yet it happened again and again, day in and day out. The constancy was somehow comforting.

Ray dragged a hand through his hair. They really should leave, he supposed, glancing at Grace. Her face was windburned and she must be tired. But it was so damned nice to be here with her, both of them relaxed, replete with food. How easy it would be to forget their shared nightmare and pretend that this was a real vacation, the one he hadn't taken time for.

Which was precisely why they needed to leave. Now.

He levered himself up and off the rock and started gathering up their garbage.

Grace stirred. "Time to go?"

"'Fraid so."

"Here, let me help you with the cleanup."

She got to her feet, bending to pick up the empty soda cans from where he'd jammed them between the rocks to keep the wind from carrying them over the cliff. Afterward, Ray didn't know what made his gaze follow her. As she stood up again, she wobbled. With no more warning than that, she pitched toward the water.

He didn't think; he just lunged. Catching a handful of her sweater, he hauled her back. She fell into him and he lost his balance, going down on the rocks. He landed hard, using his arms to cushion Grace's fall.

"Dammit, Grace! Do you have any idea how cold that water is? How strong the current? Christ, how would I have pulled you out of there if you'd fallen in?"

But she didn't hear his angry outburst, nor did she feel the little shake he gave her. She'd fainted!

Chapter 9

GRACE GAZED UP INTO Ray's anxious face, framed by a faint halo. The sun, she realized.

"What happened?"

"You fainted."

She tried to sit up. He grasped her arms and eased her up, doing all the work for her.

"How do you feel now?"

She took a mental inventory. Her elbow hurt. She must have banged it going down. No need to mention that, though. Ray looked ready to blow a gasket. "Fine."

His lips, already pressed together in a grim line, thinned and he stood. "We're going to the hospital."

Panic leapt. "The hospital? Are you crazy?"

"Crazy, all right. Crazy not to have thought of it before. The vomiting, and now the fainting …."

She blinked. "What do you mean?"

"Dr. Greenwood said these things can take a long time to resolve."

Huh? "What things?"

"Your head injury. He called it a process, not an event, something that needs monitoring. With your symptoms, we need to check it out."

"My head's fine, Ray."

"Great, then we won't keep the doctor long."

He turned to finish picking up the last of their garbage, stuffing it into the grocery-store bag.

The idea of going to the hospital terrified her, maybe because she feared Ray might be right.

"We can't go to the hospital," she argued. "We're supposed to be hiding out. I can't just whip out my Medicare card."

"You won't have to. We'll tell them we're American tourists. They won't have any objection to taking our cash."

"But there's nothing wrong with me. The vomiting … I was just hungry. I told you, I hadn't eaten. My blood sugar was low, that's all."

"Well, it sure as hell wasn't low blood sugar this time, after that meal."

"I just got up too fast," she said, ignoring his fiercely beetled eyebrows.

"We're going to get you checked out and that's that. Now wait here while I dump this stuff. I'll come back for you."

"I can walk!" she protested.

"Stay put, Grace. I mean it."

She stayed put, fuming. She wasn't an invalid, dammit. There was nothing wrong with her! And the last thing she wanted was for Ray to carry her.

Okay, letting him carry her was the *second last* thing she wanted to do. Making him any angrier was the last thing she should do.

Minutes later, he came back and gathered her into his arms and started picking his way back across the rocks. As they traversed the rocky beach, she held herself stiff, but midway, her pique gave way to concern. Was he limping?

"Ray, this is ridiculous. I'm too heavy, and I really *can* walk."

"Forget it. The ground is too uneven."

She chewed her lip. Yes, he was definitely limping. She could feel it. "Why are you limping?"

"Because somebody fell on me."

Guilt lanced her. "I landed on you?"

"You would have landed in the Bay of Fundy if I hadn't grabbed you. Now be quiet."

Her heart rate took another leap. Had she really been in danger of falling into the frigid bay? She squeezed her eyes shut, not wanting to think about it. Instead, she focused on Ray. He must have sacrificed his own body to break her fall. Her throat tightened painfully. Time to think about something else.

She cleared her throat. "Wouldn't piggyback be easier?"

He snorted. "I think I can manage."

"Fireman's lift?"

"Shut up, Grace. I need to save my breath."

They spent the rest of their afternoon in the waiting room of the ER at the Saint John Regional Hospital. To Ray's obvious disgust, the triage nurse didn't rank Grace's condition as terribly urgent. It was two hours later, therefore, before she got into an examining cubicle, and another half hour before the attending physician got around to her.

After asking her a few questions, the short, dark-eyed doctor said, "Before we order up any pictures, I'd like to do a full exam." He handed her a blue Johnny shirt emblazoned with the hospital's name and glanced at Ray. "Your husband is welcome to stay, or he can come back afterward."

"I'll wait outside," Ray muttered, then beat a retreat.

Great, she thought, as the doctor drew the privacy curtain to allow her to change into the gown. Ray brings her here against her objections, then leaves her to face the doctor with a pack of lies about being from Vermont.

"When was your last period, Mrs. Graham?"

Grace's heart skipped a beat. She told herself it was the use of Ray's mother's maiden name that made it thump so hard, not the question.

"I'm not sure I remember, what with the concussion," she said, fumbling to tie the gown at her neck. "The last one I can be really positive about was quite a while ago. A couple of months, maybe."

"Is there any possibility you might be pregnant?"

This time, her heart jumped into overdrive. "Pregnant?"

"Yeah, pregnant. By the way, just climb onto that gurney when you're ready and pull the drape over yourself."

"I don't …." Her voice cracked and she tried again. "I don't think that's very likely."

"But not out of the question?"

Out of the question? She felt the sudden desire to laugh and clamped down hard on it. Nothing was out of the question as long as she had this humongous void in her memory.

"I take it that silence means it's at least a possibility?"

"I guess."

"Ready back there?"

"Sorry, yes."

He completed the exam in a matter of minutes, his manner professional and proficient. Afterward, he snapped the latex gloves off, picked up his clipboard and made a quick notation.

"Well? What do you think?"

He glanced up, his brown eyes serious. "I think, Mrs. Graham, that you're probably pregnant."

At his words, her hands went to her abdomen. Ray's baby? She was carrying Ray's child? "Really?"

"The thickening of your uterus is certainly consistent with, say, a seven- or eight-week pregnancy, as are the changes in your breasts."

Her mind struggled to process the information, but her body, *her heart*, knew the truth.

A baby, hers and Ray's, in her womb right now. A tiny fetus drifting in a warm sea of amniotic fluid, dreaming. No, too young to dream yet. Probably no bigger than her thumbnail. But she could dream for it ....

The doctor was speaking again, cutting into her thoughts.

"If you want to shell out for it, we can get a blood sample right now and give you an official result within an hour or two. Or you can go to the drug store and pick up an over-the-counter urine test kit. They're very reliable these days, and you can do it at any time of the day. As an uninsured patient, it's certainly the more economical option."

"Yes, thanks, we'll go the drug store route," she said, thinking Ray wouldn't want to hang around so public a place for too many more hours.

Ray. He was going to be a dad.

Or maybe not. The thought blasted through her mind like an Arctic wind. *Maybe it's not Ray's.* Anxiety squeezed her stomach, leaving her battling a sudden surge of nausea.

"Is this going to be a problem with Mr. Graham?"

She forced her attention back to the doctor. "Sorry?"

"Do you have any concerns about how your husband is going to take the news? You looked a little upset just now."

Grace flushed as she realized how closely he'd been watching her reaction. "Oh, no, nothing like that."

"Are you sure?" he probed. "He looks like he could be … intimidating."

"He's not like that. He'd never hurt me," she blurted, sure her face must match her hair by now.

"Then you think he'll be pleased?"

Looking into this stranger's concerned eyes, she wanted to spill it all. She wanted to tell him she couldn't remember and that she was so tired. Instead, she uttered a husky, "Yes," and averted her head.

"Would you like me to be there when you tell him?"

That brought her head up. "Oh, no! I mean, no, thank you, Doctor. I'd prefer to tell him in my own way, in my own time."

"You know you have options?"

In the middle of her misery, the doctor's kindness to a transient patient touched her. *Bloody hormones.* She had to redirect him before she started crying.

"I know," she said, smiling. "It's okay, really."

He searched her face and nodded once. "Okay. Now, I know you're on vacation, but I suggest you make an appointment with your family doctor when you get back to Vermont."

She glanced at him sharply, a new anxiety flooding her system. "Is there any particular reason I should see my doctor? I mean, do you think there's something wrong? The fainting …."

"Not at all. Dizziness and fainting are common in the first trimester. It's your body's reset switch when you have a drop in blood pressure. And no, it's not harmful in and of itself, but you could injure yourself falling. Just use a little common sense. Eat regularly, don't stand up too quickly, and avoid getting overheated.

If you do get dizzy, lie down, put your feet up. Maybe even have a carbohydrate snack. Otherwise, there's no need to alter your activities. Of course, sexual intercourse is perfectly safe."

She tried to ignore the blush climbing her neck at his last piece of advice. "So the baby's okay?"

"No reason to suspect otherwise." He helped her sit up. "But your doctor will want to commence regular prenatal care, get you on a vitamin supplement . . . ."

"Vitamin supplement?"

"Yes. Folic acid is especially important in the early stages."

"*Spina bifida.*" She paled, laying a protective hand on her belly. She'd researched it once, for a feature article she'd wanted to write. "That's why I need the folic acid, to prevent birth defects?"

"Don't worry. The baby'll be fine. Just check in with your doctor when you get home."

"Okay."

"Well, congratulations and good luck."

"Thanks."

He turned to leave the tiny examining room, his mind clearly already on the next patient in the overflowing ER.

"Doctor?"

He glanced back inquiringly.

"It could be a few weeks before we get back to the States." She lowered her gaze. "Could you maybe recommend a supplement?"

"Of course." He pulled a prescription pad from his pocket and scribbled something on it. Tearing the sheet off, he handed it to her, smiling. "This is non-prescription, but you'll have to ask the pharmacist for it. They keep it behind the counter. Take care of yourself, now, Mrs. Graham."

She smiled back. "I will."

She dressed slowly, wishing there were some way to stave off the coming confrontation with Ray. Knowing she couldn't, she made her way out to the waiting room where he sat slouched watching the local headline news spool across a silent TV screen. He glanced up at her approach.

"Finished already?"

She nodded, not trusting her voice.

"Scans and everything?" He stood.

She drew a deep breath. "They didn't order any imaging."

His brows drew together. "Why the hell not?"

Not here, Ray. "Because they were sure I didn't need them."

"Dammit, I knew I should have stayed. Didn't you tell him anything? You *fainted*, for crying out loud. Not to mention woofing your cookies the other day ...."

She held up the folded bit of paper the doctor had given her. He looked a little mollified to see the prescription.

"He gave you something to stop the fainting business?"

Grace shoved the paper into the pocket of her hip-hugging jeans. "I think there's a pharmacy in the SuperStore we stopped at this morning. It's on the way back to the motel."

"The motel." He grimaced. "We should move on to another one. We don't want to hang around anywhere long enough to make too big an impression."

"We could go there first," she offered, seizing on the change of subject. "Check out tonight, if you like."

"No." He rubbed his chin, producing a scratchy noise from the stubble darkening his jaw. "No more late-night check-ins. I'll just pay for another night when we get back and we'll check out in the morning."

"You sure?"

"Yeah, I'm sure. If we check out at peak hours, they won't even look up at us. Come on, let's get out of here."

Grace was only too happy to oblige. When they reached the lobby, Ray instructed her to wait while he fetched the car. Which was all right with her. The less he asked her about the prescription she'd shoved into her pocket, the better.

He wasn't going to react well. Better to have it out in the dubious privacy of their thin-walled motel room than to get into it here.

Of course, maybe the doctor was way off base. Maybe she wasn't pregnant at all. If the test disproved that theory, there'd be no need to tell him anything.

But she was. She'd known it as soon as the doctor had mentioned the possibility. Now, alone in the vestibule between the inner and outer doors of the hospital entrance, she cupped her left breast experimentally. It was fuller, denser, and almost achingly tender to the touch.

But how had it happened? She was always so careful. After discovering early in their marriage that she tolerated oral contraceptives poorly, she'd switched to a diaphragm, which she used conscientiously. So how could she be pregnant? She'd used that damned thing *every* time.

Every time with Ray, she reminded herself. God knows what you did with ....

With who?

Dammit, why couldn't she retrieve a name, conjure the face of the man who'd dazzled her so completely that she'd left Ray for him?

Guess you can add that to the list of questions you never thought you'd ask yourself, Gracie girl. Who's the father of my baby? Right up there with, Who planted a pipe bomb in my house?

The automatic doors slid open with a whoosh. She glanced up to see Ray striding toward her, his gait purposeful, arms loose, hands free, gaze sweeping the area. Despite the spiky, unnaturally yellow hair and the hip-hop clothes, he looked just like what he was — a cop exuding the command presence that had been drilled into him.

"There you are!" he said, stopping several feet away.

Lord, he even *stood* like a cop. Quarter to quarter, his left shoulder facing her left shoulder rather than toe-to-toe. For some reason, she laughed. It rose in her chest, like an air bubble needing to escape.

"Dammit, Grace, are you okay?"

His sharp tone punctured her mirth. Pushing herself away from the support of the wall, she moved toward him. "I'm fine."

"You didn't see me pull up?" With a jerk of his head, he indicated the direction of the car parked immediately outside the doors. "When you didn't come right out, I thought ...." He broke off, shoving a hand through his hair. "Forget it. Let's go." He turned on his heel and strode out, the automatic doors sliding open just in time to prevent him from colliding with them.

Grace followed.

"I'm sorry," she said. "I must have been looking for a black Pathfinder instead of a blue Corolla."

He yanked her door open and stood there waiting for her to get in. She sought his gaze, perilously close to tears. It had been careless of her to scare him like that, but she couldn't handle his anger right now.

Oh, Lord, it must be hormones. And if she thought *this* was hard, just wait until they were finished at the druggists. "I must be tired, I guess."

His gaze seemed to soften a little, but the tension in his jaw didn't slacken. "Just get in the car, Grace."

They made the trip to the supermarket in silence. Just as well. The folded slip of paper felt like it was burning a hole in her back pocket. It wasn't until Ray parked the Toyota in the lot that he spoke.

"Why don't you wait here? I can run in and fill that prescription for you."

"No, I'll do it." She released her seatbelt and grabbed her purse from the floor by her feet. "Why don't *you* wait here?"

"Not a chance."

Just give me some damned privacy! she wanted to scream. But she couldn't. Not without arousing even more suspicion. *Think, Gracie.* Unfortunately, nothing inspired came to her, so she turned to him and said, "You've got to stop treating me like an invalid, Ray."

"Fine. You stop fainting, I'll stop treating you like an invalid." He scanned the parking lot around them, searching for danger, she supposed, then turned back to her. "If you insist on going in, we go together."

"Okay."

He released his seatbelt and patted his jacket pockets. Not feeling for his wallet like other men did, she realized. Feeling for his badge, his gun.

The thought made her throat close up. It was second nature to him. He loved being a cop and he could lose it all, because of her. Because of the damned mystery money she'd brought into their lives.

He popped his door open, unfolded his long legs and climbed out of the little car. Quickly, before Ray could get around to help her, Grace opened her own door and clambered out. He took her hand firmly in his and they crossed the parking lot. Their tattoos covered up by their jackets, they attracted very little attention.

Grace's heart thumped so hard as they entered the store, she feared Ray could hear it. "Why don't you buy us some snack food to take back to the hotel?" she suggested. "I'd kill for some yoghurt, or better still, some chocolate milk. Maybe some fresh fruit, too? I'm tired of fast food and hotel breakfasts."

He grunted an agreement. "Yeah, be nice to have some real food. We can use that cooler we bought, fill it with ice from the machine back at the motel." He eyed her. "You be okay on your own?"

She slanted him a wry look, hoping her relief didn't show. "For the few minutes this'll take? I think so."

He nodded once, then picked up a shopping basket and strode toward the grocery aisles. Grace exhaled, then headed straight for the drug counter. Catching a pharmacy aide, she said without preamble, "I need a pregnancy test kit. Quick."

The younger woman gave her a sympathetic look. "Sure thing. Let's just have a look at what we've got."

Grace knew she should ask for the pre-natal supplement, too, but couldn't quite bring herself to do it. While there was still a chance the doctor was wrong, she wanted to cling to denial.

"Try this one," the clerk said. "They're all very reliable, but this is probably the most economical."

Grace thanked her, paid for the purchase, shoved the small box into the depths of her bag and went in search of Ray.

She didn't get more than two aisles before her thoughts turned inward again. How often over the years had she thought about a baby?

Not often in the beginning, but more and more in the last year or so. But Ray had shown no sign that he shared similar ideas. Indeed, he'd seemed completely satisfied with the status quo. Reluctant, even, to change anything. Kids had always been something they both wanted 'later'.

Her steps slowed. Could she have taken the decision for him? Might she unconsciously have been less careful with the diaphragm? Removed it too soon?

Maybe.

Did she really hope she wasn't pregnant?

It'd be easier if she weren't. She wouldn't have to face Ray's anger and the inevitable suspicion about paternity. She wouldn't have to face her own doubts on that score.

But could she wish the baby away?

If she were pregnant with Ray's baby, it might be all she'd ever have of him after this was over. He'd never forgive her for what she'd done, for betraying him, for leaving him. And God knows, she didn't deserve for him to forgive her.

Answer the question, Gracie. Do you or do you not wish this possible pregnancy away?

She stopped dead in her tracks as the answer came to her. No, she didn't. An incredibly powerful wave of protectiveness washed over her, bringing the sting of tears to her eyes. She'd fight tooth and nail to keep her baby safe.

"Grace?"

She started. Ray, standing right beside her, his shopping basket full.

"You okay?" He laid a hand on her arm. "You've got that blank look again."

"Just tired."

"Get what you needed?"

She nodded.

"I guess we're all set, then." He gestured to his basket. "Anything else you wanted, or will that do it?"

The basket overflowed with fresh fruit, milk, yogurt and cheese. There was even a bag of those peeled baby carrots she liked to nibble on. His consideration made her want to cry all over again.

"No, that's great," she choked, turning away.

⁂

Ray narrowed his eyes as Grace bolted for the cashier. Following her, he plunked his shopping basket down on the conveyor belt.

Grace unloaded the stuff quickly while he dug the cash out of his wallet to pay for it.

Two minutes later, they were back in the car. Just as she had for the ride from the hospital, she sat rigidly in the passenger seat, staring straight ahead. Sighing, he slotted the key in the ignition and the Toyota sputtered to life.

She was hiding something. Something the doctor had said, no doubt. He thought about asking her flat out, but the uneasy feeling that she might come unglued if he forced the issue dissuaded him.

Checking his mirrors, he backed out of the parking spot. First chance he got, he was going to look at those prescriptions to make sure she really did get something to help.

Though he couldn't imagine what the doctor could prescribe for the after-effects of concussion. He'd had a couple of hard knocks himself over the years, and it didn't seem to him like something drugs could help, beyond painkillers. But Grace didn't complain of headaches anymore. All she'd mentioned was feeling tired.

Unless it wasn't from the concussion at all.

Ray mulled that idea over as he nudged the car into traffic. Maybe the doc was treating her for anxiety.

Damn! Bet that was it. Getting shot at, having to flee, seeing their house on the six o'clock news with cops and firemen tramping through it. Not to mention all the stuff that had come before. Was it just over nine days ago? The Gawd-awful scene in the kitchen when she'd told him she was leaving, the trauma of the car accident, the frustration of the memory loss . . . .

Now, *that* he could understand them medicating her for. Plenty of people turned to pharmaceutical help when things got hairy. He'd never done it himself, but he couldn't say he blamed anyone who did. He was all for whatever helped you cope, as long as it didn't get in the way of the job.

The job.

Braking for a stop sign, he fought off a burst of anxiety at what the guys back at the precinct must be thinking right about now.

Don't go there, Morgan.

His only job right now was to keep the two of them safe until Grace regained her missing memories. Easy assignment, compared to Grace's job, which was to remember.

Of course, being all twisted up with nerves probably wouldn't help her recollection any. He'd been trying his damndest to bury his own hurt and anger to help her relax, and he thought he'd been doing a pretty good job. He could have sworn she'd unwound pretty good at the seashore today. But then she up and fainted, scaring the bejesus out of him.

Maybe this was what she needed. Maybe a little Prozac or whatever they used these days would help her unbend enough to recover those missing days.

"Ray, you missed the Harbour bridge."

Damn. "No problem. We'll take Reversing Falls."

Back at the motel, he parked in front of the office, ran inside and paid cash for a second night. The clerk tonight was a new one, a young woman. A young woman who clearly liked men in baggy-assed pants, ragged jackets and girly jewelry. As she handed him his change, she took a second too long to let go of the bills.

For chrissakes. All he wanted was to yank the money out of her hand and get back to his room. Instead, he returned her appraisal. Not too much — he didn't want her thinking he was seriously coming on to her. But neither could he afford to let his genuine lack of interest show. She was a sweet young thing, all right. If he erred too much either way, she'd remember him.

"Workin' the graveyard shift tonight?" he asked.

She inclined her head, brushing her bangs back in a casual way she'd probably perfected in front of a mirror. "Get's pretty dull after midnight."

"I'll bet." He grinned. "If my old lady wasn't such a light sleeper, I'd bring you a coffee and keep you company."

With a wink, he turned and walked away. As he crossed the lobby, he strove for that cocky gait that came so naturally to the punks on the street. Feeling her wistful eyes on his back, or some part of his posterior anatomy, he strolled out.

As he approached the old Toyota sedan, he felt another pair of eyes on him. Grace's.

"Better," she said when he'd slid behind the wheel.

He turned to her blankly. "Huh?"

"The walk. I think you're finally getting it."

He blew out a breath. "I don't get it. What's with the whole baggy pants thing? And what's all this for?" He grabbed the fabric of the oversized t-shirt he wore and pulled it out a good eight inches. "I could get another friggin' person in here."

"Ah. Female clerk. She give you the eye?"

He glanced at her. Though she still looked drawn, the ghost of a smile played about her mouth.

"Can't imagine what's to look at. Certainly not my ass," he groused. "The crotch of these things is damn near to my knees."

The corners of her lips kicked up a little, but the half-smile faded quickly, leaving her expression tight again. No question about it, she was definitely worried about something.

When they got back to the room, Ray did a quick walk through, flicking on the lights, checking behind doors, sweeping back the shower curtain, checking windows. Well used to his routine by now, Grace waited for the all clear before entering.

Once inside, she headed straight for the bathroom, not even pausing to drop the small pharmacy bag. Damn. He'd have to wait until she vacated the bathroom before he could snoop. Or maybe he could slip in while the shower was running?

Nah, no hurry, he decided, picking up the TV remote. Flipping to the headline news channel, he sat on the edge of the bed to read the headlines as they scrolled across the screen to the accompaniment of soft rock from a local radio station. The stock report was followed by entertainment news, then sports. Top stories should be up next on the endless loop.

Blue Jays over the Yankees in a nail-biter. One piece of good news, anyway.

Recognizing the distinctive guitar of Jeff Healey in the background, he tapped the volume button on the remote a couple of times. Now that was music. Not that God-awful pseudo-R&B pop crap that clogged the airwaves these days —

A crash from the bathroom brought him to his feet.

"Grace?"

No answer. Had she fainted again? Dammit, he should have insisted on going in there with her and to hell with her modesty.

A second later, he was at the door. Twisting the knob, he tested it with his shoulder. Locked, but he could force it without breaking a sweat. Of course, then he'd have a broken lock to explain. Or he could take an extra fifteen seconds and jimmy it.

"Grace, you okay in there?"

"I'm fine," she said. "I just dropped something," but he heard the quaver in her voice.

"Open the door," he commanded.

"I told you, it's okay. I just knocked some makeup off the counter."

"Open the door *now*, Grace, or I'll force it."

"You wouldn't."

"I think you know I would, though it's not my first choice. It'd give them a reason to remember us."

Silence for a few seconds, then the knob turned under his hand. He released it, letting Grace draw the door inward.

He expected to see her looking pinched and pale as she had this afternoon, but her face was flushed.

He dropped his gaze to the floor. Well, she wasn't lying about the makeup. Her purse lay on the floor, much of its contents strewn on the ceramic tiles. Then he saw the box from the pharmacy.

He bent to retrieve it. Rotating it, he read the label. Willing his face blank, he lifted his gaze to meet hers.

"Grace, is there something you been meaning to tell me?"

Chapter 10

GRACE'S FACE BURNED AS she brought her right hand from behind her back. In it, she held the small test stick. Two pink lines glowed up at her.

Ray's face remained impassive, but a muscle leapt in his jaw. "What's that mean? Positive?"

Tears clogged her throat, so she just nodded.

"I see."

The complete lack of inflection in his tone betrayed the depth of his shock, as did his blank-faced expression. Something vital inside her felt as though it were tearing away.

"Ray ...."

"I'll go get us some supper."

She reached for him, motivated by the crazy idea that she could somehow draw his pain away. Like an electrical shock, maybe it would pass through him harmlessly and terminate in her chest, leaving ashes and dust where her aching heart now beat. But he pulled away, backing out of the bathroom.

"Pizza all right?"

Oh, God, he was doing it again, shutting her out, shutting down. Dropping the test stick, she followed him to the bedroom.

"Ray, we need to talk."

"Pizza it is, then."

He picked his wallet up off the nightstand where he'd dropped it and shoved it back into the pocket of his jeans.

"Please." She touched his arm, only to have him wrench away again. "Ray, we really need to talk about this."

Finally, his unnatural composure slipped.

"Not now, Grace. Now would be a very bad time to talk."

Her gaze flew to his face. For an instant, his brown eyes looked bleaker than she'd ever seen them. Then the mask was back again.

Nabbing the keys from the top of the TV, he strode to the door. With his hand on the doorknob, he paused. Hope rose in her chest that he might stay and hear her out, but his next words quashed it.

"Remember, let no one in." Then, almost as an afterthought, he lifted his t-shirt and drew his pistol out of its holster. Crossing to the nightstand, he deposited it beside the clock radio. "Don't touch it unless you need to," he warned. "It's loaded, there's a round in the chamber, and there's no safety."

She blanched. "I don't want it. You know I hate guns."

"You've got sixteen rounds," he said, as though he hadn't heard her. "One in the chamber, fifteen more in the clip."

He really was going to leave it. "I don't know how to use it."

"Just point it and squeeze the trigger," he said. "It's loaded with hollow-point ammunition. Aim for the center of mass and it'll do damage. Just don't shoot me when I come back."

With that he left, the door closing behind him with a quiet *snick*. Why couldn't he have slammed the damn thing? She'd rather his anger than this icy control.

Stifling a sob, she sat down on the bed. Outside, she heard the Toyota's engine leap to life, but he didn't peel out angrily. Rather, he reversed out of the parking space with careful control, then drove off. Misery a leaden lump in her belly, she curled up into a ball on the bed.

But there was something else in her belly.

A new life.

She put a hand on her flat stomach.

"It's okay, baby," she said, trying hard to believe her own words. "Everything's going to be just fine."

⋅⋟⋇⋞⋅

The crowd of teens hanging out in the pizzeria's parking lot fell silent at Ray's approach. He was used to that happening. Kids could smell a cop a mile away, even one in plain clothes. It took him a few seconds to register that he wasn't getting the hostility he usually got. He must be doing better at what Grace called 'the walk'.

"Dude, nice ink," said one of them, a male of seventeen or eighteen, with several tattoos of his own. Undoubtedly real ones, unlike Ray's, which had to be covered up in the shower and frequently retouched. Ray walked on.

The kid detached himself from the group and fell into step. "Hey, bro, you look like a man needs to take some edge off."

Ray raised an eyebrow. "Do I?"

"Got just the thing. Some quality bale."

Cripes. Seventeen years old and selling weed on the street corner. He forced his fisted hands to relax. "No, thanks."

"Sure? Thai stick, maybe?"

Ray gritted his teeth against the urge to put the kid facedown on the pavement. "No sale."

"Pharmaceuticals, then? Uppers, downers . . . ."

Losing patience, Ray aimed a hard look at the kid, who backed off immediately, raising his hands in a gesture of peace.

"Hey, you already hooked up? That's cool, man."

The boys melted away. Sighing, Ray went inside and placed his order. Twenty minutes, they told him, so he ordered a beer and sat in a booth to wait.

Pregnant.

What a goddamn disaster. He shoved a hand through his hair, then tipped the bottle up for a long haul. The beer, hardly colder than room temperature, tasted sharper than it should, yeasty. Still, it tasted like about eight more.

But getting drunk would be the height of stupidity, and he was done being stupid.

He laughed. Who was he kidding? He'd barely scratched the surface of stupid. Stupid was torturing himself with the idea of another man planting his seed in his wife's belly.

Ray tipped the bottle and took a fierce pull. God, he hated those images. Hated himself for having them.

Think, Morgan.

Okay, where did this leave him?

Somewhere along the way, he'd decided that once Grace got her memory back and they'd escaped this shit-storm they'd blundered into, he'd walk away, leaving her to her new man. But now, if she were pregnant, there'd be no quick break.

Hell, if the baby was his, there'd be no break at all. He'd be damned if he'd step back and let another man raise his child.

He put the near-empty beer down and pushed it away.

He'd been getting through the days and nights by telling himself Grace would get her memory back any time now. When that happened, they'd be able to go in. They'd be safe, free to go their separate ways. He'd be relieved of the daily torture of being so close to her. But this pregnancy pretty much killed his chances of being delivered from this hell any time soon.

So why, underneath all this anger, did he feel like a man who'd been granted a reprieve?

Cursing silently, he drained his beer, then got up to check on his order.

⚜

Grace woke to the sound of the lock turning.

"Just me."

Groggily, she pulled herself up to a sitting position on the rumpled bed and blinked as Ray came through the door. Lord, she'd actually fallen asleep. How'd that happen? Half an hour ago, she'd felt like she'd never sleep again.

The smell of pizza hit her as Ray closed the door, making her empty stomach churn.

"You should throw the security bolt when you're in here alone." He looked pointedly at the gun, which lay right where he'd left it, untouched.

"Sorry. I guess I dozed off."

She swung her legs over the edge of the bed as Ray deposited the pizza and a take-out bag on the room's tiny table. From the bag, he produced a Styrofoam container of Caesar salad, two small containers of homogenized milk and a two-litre bottle of Coke.

He handed her one of the cartons of milk and a straw. "The salad's for you," he said gruffly. "Figured you better have something green."

"Thank you," she managed around the sudden lump that had lodged itself in her throat. Damn these hormones. One considerate gesture on his part and she was on the verge of tears again.

He popped his soda can and flipped the box open. Helping himself to a piece of pizza, he flopped into a chair. She took a slice, too, but perched on the edge of one of the beds.

Silence reigned as they ate. She thought her stomach might be a little iffy about the very aromatic pizza, but, after the first bite, it settled down. Still, it might be just as well to get the business of eating out of the way before they talked.

"I shouldn't have run out on you like that."

She jumped at his words, causing a piece of pepperoni to slide off the slice she was poised to bite into. She plucked the greasy topping off her bosom and put it back on her slice. So much for her stomach.

"Don't worry about it," she said, putting the slice down on a paper napkin while she dabbed ineffectually at the grease spot on her shirt with another napkin. Then, because she couldn't hold it back any longer, she blurted out her fear. "I don't want to be a burden. Don't feel you have to .... I mean, I don't want you to think ...."

He crumpled the now empty aluminum can in his hand. "If you're carrying my baby, I'm not just gonna bow out and let you carry on."

She heart squeezed in her chest. "I don't want you to."

A muscle leapt in his neck, but his tone when he spoke was carefully bland. "Better reserve judgment on that until you recover your memories." He leaned forward to toss the flattened can into the plastic-lined wastebasket. "Whatever happens, if that baby's mine, I intend to be part of its life."

He came over to stand by the bed, his nearness and sheer size intimidating. "Are we absolutely clear on that point?"

At his softly-voiced question, she lifted her gaze to meet his. "I'd never deprive you of your child."

"You made a damn good try."

"But I didn't know I was pregnant!"

She saw doubt in his eyes, but he didn't voice it.

"Now you do," was all he said.

She refused to flinch. After all, she'd earned his distrust, hadn't she? She deserved it.

"Now I do." Balling her napkin up in her fist, she stood.

Ray took an immediate step back. Grace told herself it was nothing personal, just his natural cop instincts to preserve his personal safety zone. Believing it was a little harder.

"Try not to worry about anything, okay?" he said. "I intend to take care of you."

For now, she mentally finished his sentence. *Until we know whose baby we're talking about.*

Blinking rapidly, she picked up the uneaten remnants of her meal and dropped them in the waste paper basket. "I think I'm going to have a soak in the tub."

Grace decided to use the bath as an opportunity to regroup. Reclining in the hot water, she closed her eyes and willed the heat to leach the deep, muscle-knotting tension from her limbs.

Ah, there. She rolled her shoulders to relax them. Things weren't that bad.

Yeah, not bad. *You screwed around on Ray, dumped him, crashed the car. Now, because of that suitcase full of money you were heading out of town with, the source of which you've forgotten — forgotten! — Ray is now under suspicion for God knows what.*

Had she left anything out? Oh, yeah, someone had tapped their phone, probably the same person who'd shot at them. The whole house was likely bugged, by some mob types, no less.

So, to recap, despite the fact that someone out there wanted to kill them, they couldn't turn to the cops for fear they'd get whacked while the business of the mystery money was sorted out.

Neither could they go home . . . .

Home. In her mind, she saw her house, door hanging off its hinges, vinyl siding blackened and melted. She opened her eyes, focusing fiercely on the blue tiles of the tub surround.

Come on, Grace, she scolded herself. *You're a natural optimist. You can do better than that.* Taking a deep breath, she tried again to look on the bright side.

Things really *could* be worse. They weren't in any immediate peril. Nobody had shot at them or tried to blow them up for ... well, *days.*

Of course, I'm pregnant and can't say for sure who the father is ....

"Arrgh!"

Grace heard the volume on the television dip. A second later, she heard Ray from the other side of the door.

"You okay in there?"

Ray looking out for her, as always.

"I'm fine." She heard him move away from the door.

He'd protect her and the baby she carried, no matter whose child it was. But dammit, the baby was *his.* Ray's. The certainty moved through her now just as it had done earlier at the hospital. If only he had the same faith ....

She let her breath out. That was never going to happen. She'd given him no reason to trust her. Come to that, she didn't even trust herself. How could she, with that big chunk of memory missing?

Sitting up, she flipped the toggle to open the drain. Heedless of the water sloshing everywhere, she clambered out of the tub and grabbed a towel. Enough was enough.

As a therapeutic, the soak in the tub had bombed, but it did seem to revive her appetite. Ten minutes later, dressed in boxers and t-shirt, she sat on the bed polishing off a piece of pizza. Ray reclined on the other bed, watching a ball game. She'd even been able to eat the Caesar salad without fear of food poisoning because Ray had thought to stick it in the mini-bar fridge.

"That was good. Thanks."

A grunt from the other bed was her only acknowledgment.

"I think I'll turn in now."

He glanced up at her. "Want me turn the TV off?"

"No, it's fine."

She felt his gaze on her as she prepared for bed, but when she settled on her side under the covers, he turned back toward the baseball game. She studied his face for a moment. In the flickering light cast by the muted television, the grooves bracketing his mouth looked deeper than ever. Lord, she'd loved that face at first sight. Still loved it.

How could she have betrayed him?

"I'll get them to do a paternity test when the baby comes."

Her words fell into the silence.

For a moment, she wondered if he'd heard her. Then he turned toward her, the glitter of his eyes unreadable in the darkened room. "Okay."

Grace rolled away, pulling the covers up to her chin. *Don't think, don't think. Just sleep.*

⁂

Ray came awake, suddenly and completely, to the sound of harsh breathing, but he didn't move a muscle. These few days on the run had taught him as much about stealth as all his years on the force. Eyes still closed so their glitter couldn't give him away, he reached slowly over the edge of the bed. Unerringly, his hand found the gun, which he'd left jutting out of his hightop runners. Only then did he open his eyes a sliver.

The darkness inside the room was almost total, but he didn't need to see to know where the sound was coming from. The far end of the room, near the chair in the corner. Slowly, he curled up until he could reach the lamp on the night table. Leveling his weapon in the direction of the heavy breather, he hit the switch.

In the instant of illumination, he saw it was Grace in the chair, her knees drawn up to her chin, the picture of misery.

Grace. Not an intruder.

Whether from the unexpected flood of light or from the gun he was brandishing, she shrank deeper into the chair. He lowered the gun.

"Sorry. I thought we had ourselves a visitor."

He saw a shudder pass through her at his words and cursed himself. *Atta boy, Einstein. Terrify her a little more, why don't you? That oughta help speed the old memory back.*

"Sorry, it was just reflex. I must be wound a little too tight. We're safe in here. Really."

Which they were. Probably. But she didn't look especially convinced. In fact, she looked pretty scared still, her gaze wide and frozen on him.

Of course. He still held the damned gun, though he no longer pointed it in her direction. He leaned over the edge of the bed and shoved the weapon back into his shoe. Rolling back, he pulled himself to a sitting position, propped against the headboard.

"So, what are you doing up?" he asked, as the ferocious *jerk, jerking* of his heart finally subsided to a mere pounding.

She bit her lip, then released it. He watched the color flood back into the delicate tissue.

"The money ...."

His slowing pulse leapt again. "What about it?"

"It came out of our account."

Holy hell. "You remembered about the money?"

"A little bit. Not enough."

She looked so miserable, his initial excitement ebbed. What had she remembered to make her look so unhappy?

"Tell me what you *do* remember."

She'd shifted forward in the chair, perched now on the edge, her upper body hunching forward. He noted her posture, elbows on her thighs, hands clenched between her knees, head down.

"I don't know where it came from, but it was in our account. I remember standing there in the bank, smiling at the teller. I asked her how much I could take out and felt the sweat running down between my breasts while I waited for her to check."

"What'd she say?"

Grace continued to look down at her hands. He could see how tightly they were clenched from the whites of her knuckles.

"She told me there are no holds on cash deposits and I could have as much of it as I wanted."

Cash deposit. Cripes. "Which account?"

"Savings."

That explained why he hadn't seen the deposit. He looked in on their modest savings account infrequently.

"Nothing about where the deposit came from?"

She swiped moisture from her cheek with the back of her hand, then looked up at him. "Nothing."

Damn. "What about how you felt? You said you were sweating. Hot sweating or nervous sweating?"

"Nervous sweating. My hands were shaking." She unclasped her hands at last and extended one. "Like this."

Aw, Grace. He wanted to go to her, hold her until the shaking stopped, tell her not to torture herself anymore. Instead, he forced himself to sit there and wait for her to continue.

"I kept them clamped on my purse so Patty — that's the teller's name who waited on me — wouldn't notice how bad they were shaking." She paused to inhale a calming breath. "I was scared that if I showed how twitchy I was, I wouldn't be able to get the money."

That surprised him, but he kept his face carefully blank. It was a joint account. Had she imagined the teller would refuse to give her the money out of some sort of morality judgment? Protecting the matrimonial assets? "You thought she might change her mind about letting you have the money?"

"Yeah, I guess I did."

"Why?"

"I don't know." She shook her head. "I don't know that it was a totally rational reaction. I just remember thinking I needed it right then. If she wouldn't give it to me ...." She swallowed. "I just had to have it that minute, to get away."

Get away. Interesting choice of words. "Anything else?"

"I remember Patty counting the cash out. She put it in a big envelope for me. I folded it and stuffed if in my purse."

"You must have been relieved." He swung his legs over the edge of the bed to face her more fully.

"Relieved?" She blew out a breath. "I thought my knees were going to buckle right there."

Relieved to get away from him.

Easy, Morgan. Leave your emotions out of this.

He hunched forward, resting his arms on his knees, purposely mirroring Grace's posture.

She straightened, folding her hands in her lap. He waited a beat and did the same. She didn't notice. Nobody ever did, unless it was another cop. Or maybe a car salesman. The good ones knew how to use mirroring to silently say, *I like you; you should like me. You should* trust *me.* Just as he was doing.

"So, now you've got the cash in your bag. What then?"

"I left." She stared straight ahead, but he knew she was looking inward, remembering. "You wouldn't believe it, Ray, the way I felt . . . . The twenty steps to the door felt like a mile. I felt like all eyes were on me. Like alarms would go off when I walked out the door."

Ray's stomach lurched. Her words, her intensity, pointed to a guilty mind. Guilty of more than just planning to jettison a husband? Where had the damned money come from?

"And from the bank you went where?"

She met his gaze. "I don't know. The car, I guess. It's blank after that. The next thing I remember is the hospital room. I don't recall the confrontation you say I had with you, the accident, the paramedics, the emergency room . . . nothing."

Damn. He'd hoped for more.

"That's okay. You did good. It's starting to come back. That's progress."

"I guess," she said dully.

He turned his hands over and let them rest together in his lap, palms up in a receptive gesture and leaned forward a little. "You were crying just now. Was it because you were reliving the anxiety of being in the bank, thinking about whether or not they'd make a fuss about the money?"

"Partly, maybe."

"What was the other part?"

"I don't know. I guess I hoped I was acting as some kind of courier. You know, taking the money from point A to point B for someone else, in which case it would really be nothing to do with me. Until I remembered actually taking it out of our account, I just assumed someone had given it to me to . . . ."

She broke off suddenly, sat back in the chair and crossed her legs, but his mind was busy dissecting her words.

What did she mean by *courier?* When they talked on the beach, his random questions had teased a memory out of her about planning to go to Mexico. Could she be acting as a mule?

Casually, he leaned back on the bed and crossed his ankles in a subtle echo of her new posture. "Courier as in doing a favor for someone? Or courier as in —"

"You bastard!"

Her vehemence caught him by surprise. "Huh?"

"You're *working* me."

"What are you talking about?"

She leapt up. "Do you think you're the only one who's ever conducted an interview? I can't believe you're *working* me!"

He felt a guilty flush climb his neck. "Grace ...."

"Don't *Grace* me, Raymond Morgan. I know what you're doing. You're *mirroring* me."

Dammit. No one ever caught on. Let alone got in his face about it. He scowled. "Was I? I didn't notice."

She snorted. "My foot, you didn't notice. It *had* to be deliberate; you never pay that much attention to me. What do you think tipped me off?"

"Hey, wait a minute. That's not true. I'm always conscious of you when you're in the room."

"Yeah, so you can take the appropriate tactical defense posture."

That did it. He surged to his feet. "That's a load of crap!"

"Is it? Then why are you presenting your weak side to me right now?"

He looked down at himself. Jesus, she was right. He *was* standing in such a way as to protect his sidearm from being captured, if he'd been wearing one .... Wait a minute. How'd she know 'weak side'? And why the hell was she so mad at him? He was just trying to help her extract the memories.

She stepped closer and he automatically moved sideways. "See?" she accused. "Protecting your personal space. And look at your stance. Feet apart, one in front of the other ...."

"All right, all right, dammit, I get your point. "But there's a reason for that. It's a little thing we like to call *officer safety.* It has to be automatic, ingrained. Dammit, Grace, it's what keeps a cop alive."

"And in control of your environment. *All the time.*"

He narrowed his eyes. "What's that supposed to mean."

"What do you think it means?"

"You think I try to control you?" How had this escalated?

"*Us,*" she corrected. "I think you use your damned self-control and your damned command presence and all your other little cop tricks to control how things are between us."

"That's crazy."

"Is it?"

She took a step closer and this time he managed to control the urge to step back to preserve his safety zone. Barely. He felt sweat break out on his brow.

"Why don't you ever come home after a really good shift?"

He knew what she meant by 'good'. Anything a civilian would call bad. Adrenaline-pumping, mouth-drying, exhilarating action. A car accident or a chase or a drug bust. Never failed to leave a guy horny.

"I do come home. *Did.* I always came home to you."

"Not right away, you didn't. And you sure as heck never came home like the other guys."

He scowled. "What would you know about the other guys?"

"Oh, for heaven's sake, wives talk, Ray. I think some of them look forward to the busts and the raids more than you guys do. Best sex they ever get, to hear them talk about it."

"Grace, listen —"

"They exchange their little notes, then turn to me expectantly," she continued. "I just duck my head, and they laugh. *Poor Grace. Too shy to talk about that stuff.* But you and I know the truth, don't we, Ray? The truth is, I don't have anything to talk about." She emphasized her point by jabbing him in the chest with her finger. "Do I?"

Ego smarting, he grabbed her wrist and pulled her close to his face so she could read the anger in his eyes.

"Think you were missing out on something?" he ground out. "Is that it, Grace? Is that why you found yourself another man? To get laid good and proper?"

He expected her to recoil from his deliberately ugly words, but she held her ground.

"Yes!" she hissed, her eyes shooting fire at him.

His hand slackened on her wrist. "So, you remember."

"No, I don't remember anything."

"But you said —"

She glared at him. "I meant yes, maybe I *did* feel like I was missing out on something. And if I couldn't get it from you, then maybe it stands to reason —"

Before he knew his intent, he grabbed her, pulling her hard up against his chest. "You wanna know what you've been missing? Is that what you're telling me?"

She lifted her chin, her eyes glittering. "What if I do?"

"Then I guess I'll have to show you."

He had time to see a brief flare of alarm in her eyes before he took her lips in a crushing kiss.

Chapter 11

Grace's heart, already pounding from their charged exchange, took a crazy leap when Ray crushed her against his chest. Alarm stiffened her limbs when his mouth crashed down on hers, but only for a few seconds. Only as long as it took for his tongue to push past her teeth and sweep into her mouth.

Hot and fierce and impossibly arousing, it was like that day in the car outside the motel. Elemental.

Yes, he was angry; she could feel it in his coiled muscles, taste it in the demand of his mouth and the bite of the hand cupping her head. But it didn't matter. Anger was honest. Anger was real. Right now, she'd take it.

Ray's hand raked up under the hem of her loose boxers to squeeze her bottom and she arched into him. Oh, yes, she'd definitely take it!

For long moments the only sound in the room was their ragged breathing as they strained together. Then something changed. The hands roaming her body became a little less fevered, the mouth a little more deliberate. It wasn't a softening of his anger. It was more of a subtle shift, a distancing.

She tried to pull back to search his face, but he pushed her down on the bed and came down on top of her. Under his weight, her disquiet was forgotten in a surge of raw lust.

Ray, sweetheart, it's been so long.

Then his hands were at her waist. The t-shirt came over her head. A second later, he dragged her boxers off. Feeling exposed by the rapid stripping, she sought reassurance in his eyes but found only hard-edged hunger. Then he came down on her again, crushing her doubts.

His clothes had come off somehow, too, because she felt his erection pressing into her belly and the crisp hairs of his chest abrading her breasts. She wanted to cradle his hardness against her softness a while, savor the anticipation while they took each other higher with lips and mouths and tongues. But when she tried to pull his mouth back to hers, he levered himself higher. She found herself looking up into the face of a man who might be a stranger for all the emotion she read in those carved planes.

She shivered. "Ray?"

His answer was to nudge her legs apart with his knee. Then she felt his hand on her sex, shocking in its sudden insistence.

She seriously thought about stopping him then. And he *would* stop if she told him to. She was utterly certain of it. But she'd deliberately goaded him in an effort to finally crack that damned self-control of his. She couldn't turn coward now, couldn't retreat to the safety of their old roles.

Besides, if she put on a display of maidenly vapors at this juncture, it would only serve to prove the problem was hers, and she refused to accept sole responsibility.

He slid two fingers inside her and she shuddered.

"Is this what you like, Grace?"

He stroked her deeply while using his thumb to stimulate the nub of nerves buried in her slick folds. The pleasure was almost unbearable, but it was tainted. His talented hands were too deliberate, too calculating, as he ruthlessly propelled her toward physical release. Heaven and hell met, merged.

"Is this what you wanted?"

She dragged in a breath, which seared her throat. "I want *you*."

It was a cry from the heart, a plea for him to join with her in real intimacy. For a fleeting second, she saw her husband, the man she knew, a man who understood her plea. Then the stranger's face was back, a man who chose to construe her appeal on a more literal plane.

With an alarming speed and economy, he covered her body again, urging her legs apart. One powerful thrust and he was home. Pleasure warred with shock. Then he was moving inside her, establishing an insistent rhythm. Inexorably, despairingly, her excitement rose.

Propped on his arms, he seemed more focused on the way her breasts bobbed with each rocking thrust than on her face. Again, she tried to pull him down, face to face, heart to heart, but he closed his eyes and plunged on. She heard his breathing grow harsher, felt his climax approaching.

Why, then, did she feel so alone? Like she could be any woman under his straining body. A faceless partner. An inflatable goddamn doll.

He slipped a hand between them, his fingers sliding into her folds. Helpless, she convulsed around him, contracting, coming apart in a violent orgasm. He followed, pumping his seed deep into her.

Seconds later, he rolled away to collapse on the mattress beside her.

Limbs trembling, she lay there, feeling the aftershocks of her orgasm shudder through her. She glanced over at him to see that he lay with one arm cast over his eyes. She watched the heaving of his chest recede to a normal rise and fall, but still he didn't speak.

Damn him.

⁂

Ray wished he could take it back. He wished he'd held onto that stupid temper of his. He wished he never had to open his eyes again.

Dear God, she'd all but begged him to love her and he'd *banged* her.

After a couple of minutes, he heard Grace move away. Lifting his arm, he glanced at her. She was staring at the ceiling, her face unreadable in profile.

"You okay?"

"Fine."

Aw, hell. Her voice was tight and she didn't even look sideways at him, which made him feel lower than the worst skell. Dammit, she'd *asked* for it. *Literally.*

Except you didn't have to be so ... impersonal. Hell, he'd viewed porn performances that were less insultingly clinical.

He blocked that train of thought. What he needed here was a good defense. Unfortunately, he couldn't think of one. So he said, "Don't get all huffy. You're the one wanted to know what you were missing."

She turned her head toward him, her gaze liquid, blue and withering. Then she looked back to the ceiling. She made no effort to cover herself, either. Her flushed, naked body lay there like an accusation. His face burned.

Levering himself up on one elbow, he said, "Hey, don't take it out on me, you don't feel so great about it after the fact. I just gave you what you flat out said you wanted."

Her gaze seemed to be trained on a stained tile on the ceiling. "You gave me nothing."

Nothing? *Nothing?*

Okay, he'd been a bastard about it. But what about *his* feelings? He'd vowed to stay out of her bed for his own peace of mind — hell, for his sanity — and then she comes along and goads him right into it. Then she says it was nothing?

But you didn't have to humiliate her just because she handed you the means.

Flopping back on the pillow, Ray pressed a hand to his forehead as though he could hold the voice in his head back, but there was no stemming it. To drown it out, he spoke, though his voice sounded funny coming from a chest gone tight. "I'm sorry you feel that way."

She said nothing for a moment. He lifted his hand to see that she'd turned those eyes on him again.

"I feel," she said, "exactly like you wanted me to feel."

"Yeah?" Again, he closed his eyes to escape her cool gaze, pressing a thumb and forefinger into his lids. "How's that?"

At her silence, he lifted his head, reading the answer in her eyes. The answer, unfortunately, was a word a woman like Grace would never say aloud.

She rolled off the bed. Scooping her nightclothes from the floor, she stalked naked to the bathroom, her head held high.

Ah, hell. *Way to go, Morgan. Aren't you just the man?*

He heard the shower come on. Trying to wash away the traces of him, no doubt. Too bad a shower couldn't wash him clean. *There's not enough hot water in the world for that, buddy.*

He crawled out of Grace's bed and re-made it. It was the least he could do to wipe out the reminder of what they'd done, what *he'd* done. Then he retreated to his own bed. Punching the pillow into shape, he lay back, closed his eyes and let the self-loathing wash over him.

⊹

The room was in darkness when Grace finally emerged from the bathroom. She'd stood under the stinging spray until her skin protested the scrubbing and the motel's seemingly-endless supply of hot water started to wane. Now there was nothing for it but to try to escape into sleep.

She stood there a moment, letting her vision get acclimatized. There he was in his own bed, a dark shape looming under the blankets. Thank you, Lord. It would be hard enough to face him in the morning. She sure didn't want to do it now, tired and achy and tearful.

She crept to her bed, fumbling with the bedding a few seconds before realizing Ray had re-made it. That made tears sting her eyes. Blinking rapidly, she peeled the covers back and slid in.

"Grace?"

Her heart lurched. In the gloom, she could see he was sitting up, the covers pooled in his lap. "What?"

"Can I come over there?"

She tried to say something, but her throat closed up.

"I just want to hold you."

God, it hurt. Her throat. Her heart.

"There's such a howling in my head. If I could just hold you … if you'd just hold onto me …."

Unable to speak, she threw the covers back. He covered the distance to her bed in seconds.

The arms that came around her were strong and urgent, but she felt a tremor run through him as he gathered her close, tucking her head into his chest.

"I'm sorry."

Fresh tears welled. "It's okay."

"No it's not," he rasped, his ragged breath stirring her hair. "I'm so sorry ...."

"Hush." Her tears spilled then, falling hot between them. "Don't lets talk about it now."

He tipped her head up, using his thumb to dry her cheek. Then he kissed her forehead, her eyelids, her nose, and then, very gently, her lips. His tenderness pierced her, opening the floodgates anew.

"Ah, Grace." He kissed her wet face, then pulled her close again.

She went blindly, one hand pressed against his chest, palm open, the other sliding around his back to draw him closer.

Oh, the warm musk smell of him, so familiar. And the wide expanse of his chest, smooth here, hair-roughened there, the breadth of his shoulders, the thrum of his pulse beneath her ear. Lord, she'd missed it all. But most of all, she'd missed the absolute and complete security she felt in his arms.

"Don't let go." His words were muffled by her hair.

As if she could. She tightened her grip on his back. "I won't."

He drew the covers up over them, settling her more comfortably against him.

Though her face was still wet, Grace smiled in the darkness. With his shoulder for a pillow, she closed her eyes. Not that she was going to sleep. Not with this unexpected gift of genuine closeness to be inhaled, savored, memorized ....

❧

When Grace awoke, someone was showering in the unit next door and the grey tinge of dawn had begun to invade the room. But it wasn't the sound of the running water that woke her. Nor was it the fingers of light creeping under the drapes that caused her to stir in her sleepy, warm cocoon.

It was the hand on her breast. It was the wanting in her belly, so fierce she thought she might die of it.

Ray.

She opened her eyes slowly. With her head tucked into his shoulder, she had an excellent view of his hand, which shaped and kneaded her left breast through the thin t-shirt she wore. The sight of his tanned, blunt fingers moving so cleverly on the white fabric was almost as stimulating as the actual feel. Almost. He dragged a thumb across her tightening nipple. She moaned, then moaned again when his fingers came back to pinch the small crest into a hard point.

She tipped her head back to find him waiting for her. In the rapidly lightening room, she could read the hunger in his eyes. Not that the impressive erection jutting against her belly left much doubt about the matter.

"Let me make love to you." His voice was thick, with need. "Please, Grace. Let me do it right this time. I'll make it good."

She swallowed a lump in her throat. "You always made it good."

He held her gaze. "I hear a but in there."

But what? His lovemaking had always been considerate, tender and oh-so-skilled. She knew women who'd crawl over broken glass for what Ray gave her.

"Grace?"

She grimaced, searching for the best way to express it. "I guess I wished you'd let me climb down from my pedestal once in a while."

His fingers closed around her breast. "You're my wife. I just wanted to treat you with respect."

"The highest respect you could pay me would be to share yourself with me. Your *whole* self."

She saw something stir in his eyes and held her breath, but he dropped his eyelids, his hands going still.

"I don't think I'm any good at this."

"I just want you to let me in. Here." She touched his temple. "And here," she added softly, touching his chest.

He opened his eyes, and they burned with uncertainty. "Oh, Grace, honey, you don't know what you're asking. There are ugly parts, so many of them. Parts I don't even want to think about, parts I wish I didn't have."

"We all have those parts." She touched his face then, smoothing his brow, then trailing her fingers down his beard-roughened face. "You think I imagined I'd married a saint?"

He caught her hand. "What do you want from me, Grace?"

That was easy. "Everything." She wanted to touch his chest, but since he held her hand prisoner, she insinuated one leg between his legs, delighting in what it did to his breathing. "I don't want you to hold anything back. I don't want you to be so careful with me all the time."

"Grace ...."

"I want you to give me as much as I can take, and then I want you to give me more."

"Like I did last night?"

His voice was rough, laced with self-disgust. God help her, she'd never loved him more.

"Last night could have been wonderful, if you'd been there with me. Really there."

Desire blazed in his eyes again, hot enough to singe her. She pulled her hand free from his, sliding it beneath the covers to encircle his erection. His flesh leapt at her touch and he surged against her hand, but again he checked himself.

"I don't want to hurt you," he gritted.

"You won't." She stroked him, delighting in the contradiction. Steel and velvet. "I'm not a doll. I won't break."

"The baby ...."

The baby. She'd forgotten. Then she remembered the ER doctor's advice. "Sex is perfectly safe. The doctor said so."

He needed no further prompting. One wrench and the blankets were gone. Then they were rolling on the sheets, hands tugging at each other's nightclothes, baring skin. As soon as they were naked, he rolled her under him. She would have slid her arms around him to welcome him, but he captured them, lifting them over her head. Pinning them there, he kissed her, deep and thrilling. Too soon, he pulled away, rolling off her. She tried to follow to preserve the friction of his moist skin on hers, but he held her fast.

"Wait, sweetheart. I want to look at you."

She thought the wanting couldn't get any worse, but she was wrong. Watching his eyes turn hotter as he surveyed her trembling body, she felt everything liquify.

"I love your breasts."

"They're too big," she said automatically.

"They're perfect. Look at them."

She looked down and had to concede they looked different like this, with her body stretched like a bowstring, arms uplifted. Their rosy tips tightened instantly, as though his gaze had brushed them. Couldn't he see they needed touching? "Please ...."

"Please what?"

"Please touch me."

And he did. One hand holding her arms above her head, he touched her with the other hand. Beside him, she twisted, burning, dying, as he tweaked first one nipple, then the other, pinching, shaping, squeezing. She hardly recognized her own voice begging for more, asking for his mouth, his lips, his teeth. Then, in one swift move, he straddled her.

The length of his erection rested in the seam between her closed thighs, inciting a sharp new need. Moaning, she tried to pull him down, desperate to have him inside her. But he pushed her arms back, using his hands to weigh them down as he swooped to catch the up-turned tip of one breast with his mouth.

Oh, God! He'd pleasured her breasts before, taken long, leisurely delight there. But this was different. He came at her with hot, rough, frantic need, first one breast, then the other. She arched against him, sensations ripping through her like lightning.

"Please, Ray!"

He answered her plea by sliding down her body, his mouth racing over wildly sensitized skin, biting, sucking, kissing, his hands streaking over the wet path his mouth left. The swell of her rib cage, the slight curve of her belly. Onward to the curve of her hip, the smooth length of her thigh, the sensitive backs of her knees, down to her slender ankles. Then back up, up, up ....

"Ray!" She clamped her legs together, more from reflex than conscious decision.

"Let me, Grace. I want to taste you."

Her ingrained inhibition warred with profound excitement. The latter would have won, but he didn't wait for the outcome of the bout. Parting her thighs, he pressed his open mouth to the heart of her femininity. The shock went straight to her core.

"Oh, God, Ray! Ray. Ray?"

He turned his head and bit her thigh gently. "Ray what?"

"Don't stop!"

He didn't. With lips and tongue and fingers, he pleasured her until she flew apart, trembling, shaking, crying. Only then did he slide back up her perspiration-dewed skin to cover her mouth with his, letting her taste her own fulfillment.

At last, she was able to slide her arms around him, pull him down. She'd already found her release, but she was mindful that he hadn't. Catching his engorged member, she guided him to her entrance. The feel of him pushing into her even as her muscles contracted and pulsed with her dying orgasm felt like nothing she'd ever experienced. He felt huge. He was invading her. Oh, God, she'd never be able to take him. Yet she'd die if she didn't have him now, this minute.

"Ray ...."

He covered her mouth again and sank into her, burying himself to the hilt. She gasped. He lifted his head and looked into her eyes.

"Okay?"

She let her breath escape. "Okay. Better than okay."

"Good enough to come again?"

Again? Impossible. "I can't."

"You can. For me, you can."

And so saying, he set about proving her completely, totally, deliciously wrong. He filled her. He completed her. And he brought her to another sobbing climax before he took the same leap.

Afterward, Grace cradled his crushing weight in her arms, savoring every inch, every ounce of him. Dear Lord, she loved him so much. No wonder she'd sacrificed her own happiness to keep him safe from that lunatic, Landis. She'd die before she let that murderous bastard get at Ray.

Landis. Viktor Landis.

Her body went still as it came back to her in a rush.

Human smuggling, forced labor and Lord knew what else. She'd stumbled on it, trying to research what was to have been a comprehensive piece for the newspaper on integrating landed immigrants into the local community.

Oh, God. Oh, no.

That's why she'd been leaving town.

That's where the money came from.

She was supposed to leave for good. If she did, Landis said he'd let her live. If she didn't go and stay gone, he'd kill her.

But not before he killed Ray.

And just in case she had any ideas about going to the cops for help, he'd feed the get-away money into Ray's account, leaving a trail the shallowest of investigations would disclose. People loved to think the worst of each other when it came right down to it, Landis had smirked. Especially if he, Landis, confirmed it with just the right degree of sheepishness. There'd be no difficulty convincing them Ray was dirty, he'd assured her. If she didn't comply, not only would her handsome husband die, he'd die marked as a corrupt cop.

"I love you, Grace." Ray's voice was gravel, guttural, pulling her back. "Whatever happened, I don't care." His arms tightened around her, cutting off her breath. "I just want you back. I want *us* back."

Grace returned his crushing bear hug with a desperation of her own.

He lifted his head and looked deep in her eyes. "You hear me, Grace? I don't goddamn care. You're *mine*. I love you."

Tears spurted. "I love you, too."

"We'll work it out, about the baby. Okay? I'll take care of you, no matter what."

The baby. It was his, of course. There'd never been another man. She'd made it up to keep him from following her. *Mother of God.* Her heart was breaking.

"Okay," she agreed.

He rolled off her, pulling her into another fierce hug. She returned the pressure, wishing she could hold on to him like this forever. Wishing she could enjoy the security of his embrace tomorrow and the day after and the day after that. Except she knew she couldn't. She had to leave him again. But this time, it wouldn't be good enough just to get out of town. It was far too late for that. This time, she had to do something about Landis, before he did something about Ray.

⋅⊱⋆⊰⋅

Ray woke with a sense of foreboding in his gut. Lying there with his eyes partially opened, he tried to analyze the source of his unease. The air conditioner hummed as usual, and the traffic on the highway sounded right for the time — almost 9:00 a.m. according to the digital clock on the night stand.

Grace.

He sat up, scanning the room. Where was she? The door to the bathroom stood ajar, but there were no sounds issuing from it. She'd left the room. He felt her absence in his very marrow. But she wasn't long gone; he could almost feel the echo of her.

Panic blossomed in his chest. Dammit, what was she doing, going out there all alone?

Calm down, Morgan. She'd probably just run across the parking lot to the café for her beloved coffee. He'd wander over there and give her an escort back. He grabbed his jeans and hauled them on.

Man, oh, man, she was something last night. As he pulled an enormous black t-shirt over his head, he thought about what they'd done together. Hell, he was half-hard again, he realized, and laughed.

Hard to believe, especially after that last time. In the full light of morning, she'd shed her shyness to climb astride him, taking his aching need into her warm woman's body. He'd let her control their union that time, and she'd rewarded him by making slow, sweet, mind-blinding love to him.

Half-hard, hell. Looking down at the decided tent pole effect he'd achieved, he laughed. Okay, score one for the baggy-assed pants.

To give things a minute to settle down, he brushed his teeth quickly and ran a comb through his hair, grinning at his reflection. He looked years younger, and it had little to do with the damned yellow hair.

Nor was it just the sex, though that had been great.

No, correction — it had been *fantastic*.

But the biggest kick of all was that he loved her more now than ever, and she loved him right back. She'd said so.

He'd had another epiphany, too, one that put him on top of the world. The baby Grace carried was his. It had to be. This guy she'd met might have mesmerized his Gracie, but she wouldn't have slept with him. Not yet.

No matter how wrongheaded Ray had been in trying to keep her ... what? ... *pure?* ... she wouldn't have done it. No matter how sexually stifled she might have felt, she'd need to make the break with him before she'd consummate the other relationship. That was just how she was made. If he hadn't been so eaten up with jealousy, he'd have seen it sooner.

Yeah, they had some challenges ahead of them, all right, like staying alive until they could clear themselves. But as far as their marriage was concerned, they'd work things out. Anything was possible this morning.

Whistling, he found his wallet and shoved it in his pocket, then poked his feet into the hightop runners. He was halfway to the door when it struck him — his gun. It should have been in his shoe.

Going back, he lifted the bed skirting and peered under the bed. Nothing. Likewise nothing in the drawer of the night stand, behind the night stand, under the night stand.

How could he have lost his service weapon? Christ, they'd have his badge for this. He wasn't even supposed to have it on him when he was off duty. Not to mention its disappearance would leave them unarmed.

Think, Morgan.

Would Grace have taken his weapon?

Not likely. She hated guns. And she sure wouldn't take it for a quick skip across the parking lot.

Unless ....

No, she wouldn't leave him. Not again. Not after last night.

Still, his heart thundered in his throat as he yanked the shaving kit out of his gym bag and unzipped it.

Though most of the cash remained, he saw instantly that a couple of bundles of bills were missing.

Numbly, he walked to the window and pulled the drapes back. The Toyota was gone.

Chapter 12

GRACE DIDN'T BREAK ANY speed limits this time as she drove the highway between Saint John and Fredericton. Nor were her eyes blinded by tears. She couldn't afford another accident.

She was past tears now, anyway. Not even picturing Ray waking up in that dismal motel room to the realization that she'd left him again could make her cry. Since she'd made her decision this morning, an eerie calm had descended on her. A calm she was going to need if she were going to make this desperate plan work.

She grimaced. Not that it was much of a plan. It pretty much just involved getting close enough to the Russian to kill him with Ray's gun. What had Ray said? Aim for the center of mass.

Landis's thugs would probably kill her. She knew that, accepted it, though she couldn't dwell on the knowledge that her baby would die with her. She shied away from the thought, knowing instinctively that it carried the power to destroy the protective layer of ice her mind had laid down.

What if, by some miracle, she survived the confrontation? The police would arrest her, of course, and she'd go to prison. But she'd get to have her baby ....

She jerked her thoughts back. Either way, Ray'd be safe, and that's all that mattered. She'd gotten him into this when she blundered into Landis's operations. Now, she'd get him out.

She chewed her lip. Removing the Russian was only part of the equation. She'd need to explain about the money, how Landis wanted to neutralize Ray, the most persistent threat to his empire, by destroying Ray's credibility. God willing, she'd be able to do it in person, but she couldn't take that for granted. She'd write a note for the police. And another note for Ray.

Ray. Though he'd be safe, and cleared of corruption allegations, he'd still be in plenty of hot water, particularly since she planned to use his gun in the commission of a homicide. But there was no help for it. An investigation would clear him. They'd see it was all her doing.

She flicked on the radio and tuned in a rock station. *Nickelback.* Cranking the volume up, she willed the music to blow all thought from her mind. There was nothing left to think about.

⁕

Back in Fredericton, Ray sat on the patio at the deli across the street from the cop shop, drinking his third cup of coffee. He'd paid for a full meal that he'd barely touched and tipped the lone waiter handsomely, so no one objected to his lingering on a Tuesday morning. Though he pretended to read a newspaper, his gaze behind tinted glasses was trained on one of the station's exits.

At four minutes after twelve, Sergeant John Quigley emerged, looked up and down the sidewalk. Ray felt Quigg's glance brush over him, hesitating ever so slightly. Probably noting him as a potential dirtball. Then Quigg started off down Cumberland on foot.

With a wave to the waiter, Ray headed east on Cumberland behind his Sergeant. He didn't bother crossing the street. Quigg would cross to this side on the next block.

Sure enough, at the next crosswalk, right behind a pair of suits, Quigg crossed the street. But instead of turning right as Ray expected, he continued east. No longer confident of Quigg's destination, Ray picked up the pace. He'd closed to within half a half block when Quigg turned right, into an alley. Anxious not to lose him, Ray put on a burst of speed. He rounded the corner of the alley and almost slammed into Quigg.

"About time you showed."

Ray swore. "I can't believe this. You *made* me?"

"Only because I've been looking for you every day for the last two weeks. Let me tell you, Razor, I was getting tired of leaving my doors unlocked, waiting for you to show up."

"You knew I'd come?"

"Eventually. 'Course everyone else is thinking the same way. There's a tap on my phone, I'm pretty sure."

"That's why I didn't call." Ray glanced up as a group of teens passed the mouth of the alley, but he needn't have worried. They didn't even look sideways to check for possible vehicle traffic.

He turned back to Quigg. "Aren't you going to ask me why I didn't come in?"

Quigg shrugged. "I figured you had your reasons. Now, what do you need?"

No lectures, no long-winded discourse on how Quigg was putting his career on the line to even talk to him. Just, *What do you need?* Ray swallowed hard.

"To find Grace."

Quigg's eyebrows shot up, something that didn't happen too often. "I thought she was with you."

"She was. She left me again."

"Again?"

"It's a long story."

"I can't wait to hear it. Listen, I'll go get a vehicle. Give me ten minutes, I'll cruise this alley and pick you up."

Eight minutes later, Ray slid into the backseat of the blue-and-white, staying down.

"Okay, start talking, Razor," Quigg said without turning his head. "Make me understand what's going on here."

Ray talked. Quigg listened. And drove.

Some ten minutes later, Quigg pulled the cruiser to a stop.

"Okay, you can sit up now."

Ray eased himself up and glanced around the parking lot of the Delta Hotel. "Good choice."

"So, to recap, you think Grace's memory returned this morning? That's why she flitted?"

"Yes."

"And finding out where the money came from is key to finding Grace?"

"Yes."

"You don't think she just took off again for parts unknown to meet this guy?"

"No."

"Why not?"

Because she loves me.

He cleared his throat. "Because she'd have cleaned out the rest of the cash if that's what she had in mind. She only took enough to keep her on the road a couple of days."

Quigg digested that. "So, what now? To the bank, to see what you can find out from the teller?"

"That's what I had in mind."

"Okay. I'll drop you off in the parking garage and wait for you there. Then we'll see what we can figure out with the information you're able to glean. Now let's get you up front. We don't need to attract any more attention than we need to."

"Thanks, buddy. I owe you one."

"I'll say. I'm thinking your first born should take care of it." Quigg got out of the car and opened the rear door.

Ray climbed out. "Yeah, well, there's actually one more detail I didn't mention."

Quigg raised an eyebrow. "What's that?"

"Your chosen method of payment? Gracie's incubating it."

"Oh, *hell.*"

⚜

Forty minutes later, Ray strode out of the bank and into the parkade. Quigg was right where he'd said he'd be, second aisle. His friend held up four fingers in a gesture Ray understood. *Ten-Four. Everything's okay.* After one last glance around, Ray returned the four-fingered salute.

Moving quickly, he crossed the parking garage to Quigg's cruiser, his brisk footfalls echoing inside the enclosed structure. Ray slid into the passenger seat.

"Well? Find anything?"

The radio crackled. Dispatch with a barking-dog call on the north side. Ray tuned it out. "Cash deposit made the same day Grace split. Ninety-five hundred dollars, in hundred-dollar bills. The teller remembers the transaction very well."

"Did you get a description?"

"I got better than that. I got a name. Aleksei Fyodorov."

Quigg's eyes widened at the mention of Viktor Landis's henchmen. "Are you sure?"

"Very sure. And Grace withdrew it the same day it was deposited, the day of her accident."

"How do you know who made the deposit? Did he sign the deposit slip?"

"Davine, the teller, remembered him. Seems our boy Aleksei was smitten by her, invited her for dinner. Splashed out for a real nice meal at an expensive restaurant."

"Davine McLaughlin?"

Ray nodded.

"She the one with the salt-and-pepper hair? Kinda plain, kinda middle-aged?"

"That's her."

Quigg shrugged. "She must have been to Aleksei's taste."

"Not for long, apparently. Davine's still waiting for the phone to ring again."

They sat silently for a minute. Ray's brain raced. One of Landis's goons deposited the money to his and Grace's joint savings account. Grace withdrew the money the very same day. This was not good. It meant Grace had to have known the deposit was going to be made, and when.

Could Landis be the bastard who lured her away?

No. Grace'd see through that superficial charm to his ruthless heart. Wouldn't she?

Besides, Landis wasn't going anywhere, not with the little empire he was building here. And Grace was so sure she'd been leaving the country . . . .

Realization hit him with the force of a fist in the gut.

"Dammit, Quigg, she wasn't running into some man's arms. She was just *running*. That bastard has something on her."

"Something on Grace?"

"Or maybe she has something on him. Something he didn't want to come to light."

"And Landis, being such a gentleman, just hands her the money to get out of Dodge?" Quigg's expression was skeptical. "Excuse the indelicacy, but why wouldn't he just whack her? The cost-benefit analysis doesn't compute."

Ray swore viciously.

"What?"

"It computes, all right. Christ, I can't believe I didn't see it sooner. It lets Landis kill two birds with one stone."

"How so?"

"He has Aleksei put the money into my account, then makes damn good and sure the teller remembers him so she can recount the details for inquiring minds at IAD."

"Okay, I'll buy that. No better way to make a woman remember you than wine her, dine her, and drop her without explanation."

"And he threatens Grace, giving her a powerful reason to take the money and run. Without which, the scheme wouldn't have worked. Any other time, a deposit like that shows up in my account, I'm gonna march right down to the bank and sort it out. That would have led me to our man Aleksei, after which I'd be covering my ass six ways to Sunday."

"Jesus."

Ray barely heard Quigg's expletive. "This way, they get Grace in a situation where she feels like she needs to take the money and split, and wham! They got me." He slammed a fist into his palm. "In one move, he completely destroys my credibility, putting into question everything I've done."

Quigg whistled. "Smooth. Landis gets rid of Grace, plus he finds a way to make the mud stick to you. Then he leaves a trail a blind man could follow."

Ray massaged his throbbing temple. "Bastard's probably still patting himself on the back for this one."

"Except Grace didn't leave town. She crashed her car, took a knock on the head and promptly forgot that she was supposed to be running."

"Christ, Quigg, I really botched this. I shoulda figured it out days ago." Ray dug his fingernails into his palms until it hurt. "I just wasn't thinking straight. That damned story about a boyfriend … I was sure this mystery man gave Grace the money. You know, to show her he could take care of her better than I could. Pathetic, huh?"

"Don't beat yourself up."

They were both silent for a moment. The radio crackled a TA at Dunsmuir and Main.

"So, what are you going to do now?" asked Quigg.

Ray blinked. "Find Grace and stop her before she puts a hole in someone with my service weapon."

"*Oh, Lord.* Gracie is walking the streets with a loaded 9mm semi-auto in her purse? With no safety?"

"No, my *other* service weapon," Ray growled.

"Hey, take it easy."

Ray blew out a frustrated breath, then rubbed his temple. "Sorry. Yes, she's got my gun."

Quigg's brow furrowed with worry. "I think we better call in the troops, Razor. We can find Grace faster, take her into protective custody before she does something crazy."

"No, Grace'll be okay," he said, his mind racing. "I've got plenty of time to scoop her up. Remember, I've watched Landis for months now. He could be a bloody vampire, the hours he keeps. Grace'll most likely be sitting on that night club he runs, waiting for him to show, which he's not going to do for a couple of hours yet. I'll have lots of time to round her up and take her back into hiding while we figure something out."

"Let us help. You've got friends, Razor. Lots of them."

Ray shook his head grimly. "Thanks, man, but I can't take the chance. If Grace has something on Landis, you know he won't let her live to testify. It'd just be a matter of how many of us he has to wade through before he can get to her."

"We could slide her right into witness protection."

"Can you guarantee you'll be able to do that fast enough? Or that he won't find her? He's got eyes and ears everywhere. Man, he had my phone tapped, my house bugged." Ray shoved a hand through his hair, making it stand up even more. "You've heard the rumors, too. I know you have. We talked about it way back when, remember? I didn't really believe it then, but I do now. He's already made three attempts to erase us."

Quigg sighed. "So what are you going to do?"

Whatever I have to do to protect Gracie. "I think we're both better off if I don't answer that question."

"Damn, I knew you'd say that. Okay, anything I can do?"

"Thanks, but you've done enough. I've already dragged you deeper than I should have. Suzannah'll skin me, she finds out I involved you."

"You must need wheels, at least till you catch up to Grace. I think my dad still has that old Ford …."

Of course! Ray clapped his friend on the back. "Quigg, I do believe you *can* help me after all, ol' buddy."

"It's a an old Focus wagon, but it'll get you around, I guess."

"I don't want the car. I want your Hog."

"My Harley?"

Under other circumstances, Ray would have laughed at the way his friend blanched. "Still store it in your dad's garage?"

"Well yeah, but …."

"Then let's roll. Daylight's burning."

"Ray, that motorcycle is my *baby*."

"I'll treat her good."

"You sure the Focus won't do?" Quigg asked mournfully.

"Sorry. I need the bike."

Quigg sighed. "Okay, buddy. Only for you." He extracted a heavy ring of keys from his pocket and detached a set. "You'll treat her right?"

Ray accepted the keys. "Like a princess. Can we roll now?"

⚜

Ray spotted the old Toyota less than a block from Landis's club. Guiding the Harley into an adjacent parking space, he killed the bike's motor and swung off it. His legs felt like rubber, but not from the unfamiliar vibration of the powerful machine between his thighs. No, his legs felt like rubber because, dammit, Grace wasn't in the car.

She must be inside.

Cursing, he turned up the collar on the leather jacket Quigg had loaned him and checked his reflection in the bike's mirror. Well, at least nobody would make him in this get-up, and they certainly wouldn't approach him. Tooled out in leather, do-rag tied over his hair and looking grim around the mouth, Biker Thug Ray looked like an infinitely scarier prospect than Rapper Thug Ray.

The interior of the club was cool and dark, creating an atmosphere of night for the early patrons, most of whom sat alone nursing drinks. Watered drinks, he knew, and the contents of the bottles probably not the premium brands claimed by their labels.

It took a few seconds for his eyes to adjust, and another few seconds to find Grace. She sat alone at a booth along the room's east wall. While he watched, she lifted her glass with a quick, jerky motion, took a large gulp, then put it down again.

Christmas, she was screwing up her courage to pull a gun out and shoot a man in cold blood. And knowing Grace, the beverage probably wasn't even alcoholic, on account of the baby.

The mix of emotions that lodged in his chest was too complicated to name. Incredulity. Fear. Helpless rage at the man who'd put her in this position. And yes, admiration.

Though he couldn't sanction what he suspected she planned to do, it humbled him that she was prepared to do it. She could have just taken what remained of the money and run when her memory came back. Instead, she chose to do this for him.

Pushing the knot of emotion back down, he strode over to her table. She flicked a quick glance at him, then lowered her gaze to her drink again. Incredibly, she didn't recognize him.

"You're wasting your time," she clipped. "I bat from the other side of the plate, if you take my meaning."

Ray slid into the booth. "Coulda fooled me last night."

⁂

Grace's head snapped up to look at the owner of the voice she'd know anywhere. "Ray!"

"Sssh, keep it down."

Grace shot a glance around the room. No one seemed to take particular notice of them.

Ray. Here.

For a moment, relief overwhelmed her. Then she remembered. "You have to get out of here."

His eyes narrowed. "Is that all you can say after the trouble I took to track you down?"

Belatedly, she wondered how he had managed to do it. "How *did* you find me?"

"I followed the money. Nine times out of ten, it'll lead you to the answer. This time it led me to Viktor Landis."

Landis. The mere mention of his name sent a shiver through her. "But so fast … how?"

He shrugged. "Wasn't hard, now that we know the money went through our savings account. Our Russian friend left a trail a mile wide at our bank to make good and sure someone found it."

Her tongue came out to wet her dry lips. "You don't look surprised to find me here."

"I'm not."

She dropped her gaze to her drink. How much had he figured out? Could she convince him Landis was her lover? If so, he'd leave. Even after last night, he'd leave. If she could sell it. If she could make him believe that's what she truly wanted.

"Don't even think about it."

She blinked rapidly. "Think about what?"

"You're fabricating another story. Don't bother to deny it; I can see it in your eyes. But I'm not buying this time, so you can just forget it. Besides, we have to get out of here."

Her heart skipped a few beats. "Another story?"

"Yeah, another story. Like the first one." He leaned toward her, a menacing stranger in black leather, but she didn't flinch from him. He'd never looked dearer to her. "I know there wasn't another man. I know you didn't want to leave me."

Lord, she couldn't do this anymore. Tears stung her eyes.

"Come on." He took her hand, pulling her out of the booth.

"I can't see," she said.

"Just follow my lead."

A moment later, they stepped outside. The sun was sinking but it was still bright enough outside to make her blink after the darkness of the bar.

As Ray led her to the Toyota, she turned her head toward the west where the sunset had stained the sky a dusky pink over the tops of concrete buildings. The lump in her throat expanded. It was so beautiful and Ray was here, really here, and he knew she hadn't cheated on him and it was all coming apart and they were both going to die.

"Why'd you have to find me?"

He glanced up from unlocking the Toyota. "To keep you from committing murder."

Her mouth fell open. "How'd you know?"

"I followed the heart." He opened the door and waited for her to get in.

Stunned, shaking, she slid behind the wheel.

"As soon as I learned where the money came from, I put it together," he continued. "You ran because you had to, because you learned something Landis couldn't afford to have you repeat. You took the money because you had to. And you concocted that boyfriend story to keep me from coming after you."

With that he closed her door, circled the car and got in the passenger side. "Right so far?"

Fresh tears sprang to her eyes. She nodded blindly.

"And then you stole my gun and abandoned me again because you thought you had to take care of Landis by yourself."

"Ray, I wish you hadn't come. I'd have dealt with this."

"They'd kill you, sweetheart."

A shiver skated over her skin. "Maybe not."

"Maybe not," he agreed. "In which case the Crown Prosecutor would send you up for pre-meditated murder."

"I wouldn't care. I *don't* care." She flung the words out. "I can still do it!"

His response was equally fierce. "I won't have it. You're my wife, my *pregnant* wife. I won't lose you."

He grabbed her purse from the floor of the car where she'd deposited it and retrieved the 9mm, holstering it quickly.

"You'll lose me anyway." She laid a hand on his tensely corded forearm. She had to make him see sense. "I saw his eyes, Ray. He's not going to let us live, either one of us."

"You're preaching to the converted, honey. But you don't have to risk life or liberty. There's a better way."

"No!" Her voice was sharp with panic. "You were right all along, refusing to go in. The police can't protect us, or not for long, anyway. He told me about other times, other witnesses. He said witnesses are easy to find, easy to kill, if you have enough money and if you inspire enough fear. That's why he let me go."

"That, and to give him a handy way to dirty me."

"I'm sorry about that. I had to take the money."

"I know."

"But we can't turn ourselves in to the police. You see that, don't you?"

"Who said anything about going in?"

Her eyes widened. He meant to kill Landis himself! "No, Ray, you can't. You're a police officer. Your oath . . . ."

"Relax. I'm not going kill him, much as I'd like to. I'm just going to get him to make that mistake we haven't been able to get him to make." He looked away to scan the area in front of the night club. "You know, maybe we should take this around the block, out of sight." He turned concerned eyes back on her. "You okay to drive, or would you like me to?"

"I can do it." She started the car, flipped on her signal light and moved into light early-evening traffic. She took the first right, then a left, and pulled into a parking space.

"Okay," she said, killing the engine. "How are you going to get Landis?"

"We've got a ton of intelligence on him, but as long as we play by the rules, he's too careful, too cagey to get caught. But the way he's jammed us up, I got no trouble coloring outside the lines. I'll make him so mad he'll screw up and the boys'll nail him."

Grace's jaw dropped. "You think you can *convict* him in a court of law? Who's going to testify against him? I just told you what he said."

"His own men will, to avoid deportation. According to Interpol, some of them could be facing pretty grim odds if we were to ship them back home. That's the downside of exploiting your own people."

Another memory reached up to pull her down. "They're using them like slaves."

"Huh?"

"Illegal immigrants. Forced labor. Prostitution, too."

She broke off, remembering the sea of surprised faces turned up from crowded workstations when she'd literally stumbled into the warehouse's back room. Row upon row of women and children, bent over their labors as they turned out authentic hand-crafted 'imports'. Here illegally, unable to speak English, terrified of discovery as they worked to pay off their 'fares'.

Ray's hand under her chin tipped her head toward him. Once again she saw his warm eyes, not the sea of frightened faces.

"You've seen this? You can show me where?"

She shook her head. "They're gone. That's the first place I stopped when I got back into town, the warehouse in Industrial Park. He must have moved shop after I blundered into it."

He blanched. "Today? You went there by yourself? Did anyone see you?"

"No. And even if they did, they'd never recognize me as the woman who was there before." She lifted a lock of red hair to emphasize her point.

"Don't ever take a risk like that again. You hear me, Gracie?"

His words were harsh, but his voice vibrated with emotion. With fear. She covered his hand with hers.

"I had to. This was all my fault. I put us in this trouble and I wanted to get us out."

"It's not your fault."

"It is. I was digging around for a story, something that would make Katie sit up and take notice."

"Grace, honey, Katie loves you. Everybody loves you."

"Yeah, like they love a three-year-old with ringlets." She drew her hand back, closing it on the steering wheel. "They pat me on the head and give me those stupid fluff pieces to do. All I wanted was a crack at general assignments, but I couldn't get anyone to take me seriously. The biggest thing they ever let me tackle was the court briefs, and then only because the regular guy was out with the flu."

That's how she'd met Ray, that week covering the courts. "I figured if I could turn in a really good story, they'd see me in a different light and throw more serious things my way."

"So you thought you'd start by going after the frigging *Russian mob?*"

She colored. "I did *not* go after the Russian mob. I was working on a feature story on immigrant populations in our community. For your information, it was going to be a really good piece. It's just that one thing led to another and another, and there I was, stumbling onto that sweatshop. I just blundered along, following the trail without thinking about the consequences. And because I didn't think, here we are."

She closed her eyes, waiting for his censure. The hand that closed warmly on her thigh caused her to jerk in the bucket seat.

"Don't apologize for bringing this home. I ran the same risk every day I was out there dogging Landis, but I didn't think twice about it." He grimaced. "How's that for arrogant?"

Her gaze flew to his, finding his eyes warm.

"Pretty good piece of investigative work, all in all."

She let out her breath. "Really?"

"Really. Hell, Grace, *we* didn't know about the sweatshop. I mean, it's not a surprise. That's how most ethnic gangs get a foothold, by exploiting their own people. Then they branch out into other criminal activity as opportunity allows. But Landis is so far into the latter – drugs, money laundering and whatnot – that we figured he'd graduated beyond that stuff."

She smiled tremulously. "Thanks."

"You're welcome." He leaned across the console, grasped the back of her head and pressed a quick, hard kiss to her mouth. "Now you've got to get moving so I can do a little bear baiting."

Bear baiting. Oh, Dear Lord, he was going to deliberately provoke Landis. What had he said? *Color outside the lines.* Fear leapt anew, making her heart thud against her ribs.

"You think I'm going to leave you here alone? It's my fault we're in this mess."

"No, it's Landis's fault. And I absolutely do expect you to leave me to take care of business. In fact, I want you to go right now, check into a motel and wait for me."

"Ray—"

"The Fredericton Inn on Ellis Road, or the Day's Inn on Delancey if there are no vacancies at the Fredericton. Park the car right outside the unit so I'll know which one you're in. I'll knock, but don't open until you're sure it's me. Got it?"

"How can you expect me to sit around twiddling my thumbs in a motel room while you're out here risking . . . risking . . . ." She couldn't say it.

"I can't afford the distraction of worrying about you. This next part is going to be delicate. Nothing I can't handle," he hastened to assure her, "but I'll need to keep a clear head. It'll be easier knowing you and the baby are safe. Please, Grace."

She dropped her head, gripped the wheel hard again. "Okay. I'll do it."

"Good girl."

He leaned over and kissed her again, this time with impossible tenderness. Abandoning her death grip on the steering wheel, she captured his head with one hand, holding him to her for long minutes. Her other hand she pressed to his chest, feeling the powerful thudding of his heart under her palm. When he lifted his head, his eyes burned through to her soul.

"Promise me you'll come for me," she said.

"I will."

"The baby's yours. You know that, right?" As soon as she blurted the words, she felt stupid. Of course he knew that. He'd already said he figured out there was no other man.

"I know." He smiled, pushing a stray strand of hair behind her left ear with a gentle finger. "I figured that out this morning when I woke up in that motel room."

This morning? "But how? You didn't know about Landis then."

"Don't take this the wrong way." He lifted her hand and carried it to his mouth, brushing the backs of her knuckles with his lips. "It's not that I don't think other men want you. Hell, I think they *all* want you. How could they not?"

He lowered her hand but didn't release it. Instead, he traced patterns on the back of it with his thumb, his gaze downcast. Grace dropped her own gaze so she could see what he saw, his big calloused hand surrounding her smaller, whiter one.

"And it's not that I don't think there are better men out there," he continued. "Men who'd be better *for* you, better *to* you. Better jobs, better financial position, better social position, and Lord knows, better looking."

She felt his hand tighten on hers.

"But it finally sank in that even if you were planning to run away with Russell-friggin'-Crowe, you couldn't have slept with him until after you'd broken off with me. Not you, Grace."

She looked up to find his gaze hot on her face.

She swallowed. "Thank you."

"Thank you? Hell, you should be kicking my butt for being so slow. I shoulda figured that out weeks ago." He released her hand. Then, gruffly, "You okay to drive?"

She nodded.

"You sure? 'Cuz now would not be the time to be pulled over for erratic driving. We're not fugitives, but the authorities are very interested in talking to us at this time."

"Hey, I'll get there okay," she said. "Just make sure *you* do, too."

"Give me two hours." He checked his watch. "If I'm not there by ten, drive to Quigg's. Don't check out, just get in the car and go. And don't call ahead. Quigg's phone is bugged, and I'm not sure who put the tap on, the good guys or the bad guys."

Fear churned in her stomach. She forced it back, struggling to keep a clear head. "You've talked to John?"

"Briefly. Now pay attention, Grace. If I'm not there by ten, drive right over to Quigg's and ring the bell. He'll be at the station, but Suzannah will call him and get him home on some pretext. Tell him everything, including what Landis said about witnesses. Quigg can help you disappear until it's safe."

Fear churned her stomach. "Ray, let's go to John right now. He can help both of us disappear."

"What kind of a life would that be, looking over our shoulders all the time? And what would we do? I could never take another job on a police force, or you at a newspaper. That's exactly where they'd start looking for us."

"But Ray —"

He took both her hands this time and squeezed them. "We've got a good chance to put this guy away for a long, long time. Think about those people in that sweatshop, the young women he's pressed into prostitution. Who's going to help them?"

"The police, dammit."

"He's never going to make a mistake unless we goad him into it, but it's never going to happen as long as we have to play by the rules. Right now, I'm just the man to get at him. My career is probably down the toilet anyway, unless we can bring him down."

Her heart constricted. "You're not going to kill him, are you?"

"That's not my plan."

Grace didn't miss the judicious wording of his reply. "Be careful. Don't do anything you can't live with."

He lifted an eyebrow. "Trying to save my soul, Grace?"

And why not? He'd come to save hers. She felt tears well, but no way would she surrender to them. She had to be strong now, for Ray, for the baby.

"Among other things."

He smiled. "Don't worry. I've got a plan."

She leaned across the console and kissed him, the same kind of quick, hard kiss he'd given her. Then she pulled back. With trembling fingers, she turned the key in the ignition. The Toyota sputtered to life. "Just make sure you make it back to me, okay?"

He grinned his old cocky grin. "Count on it."

Then he opened the passenger door, climbed out and strode back toward Landis's club. Before she could succumb to the desire to run after him, she found first gear and pulled away.

She'd wait at the damned motel. She'd wait for two hours, just as she'd promised. Then, if he didn't show, she was coming back, weapon or no weapon. She'd kill Landis with her bare hands if he hurt Ray.

Chapter 13

Ray sat in the booth near the men's washroom for an hour before he got his chance.

He'd already killed two shots of vodka and sat nursing a third. Not that he'd imbibed much. He'd long ago learned how to throw the hard stuff back, then spit it into the beer 'chaser'. His breath would reek of vodka and no one would be the wiser.

When one of Landis's key henchmen finally went to take a leak, Ray slid out of the booth and followed him.

So secure was Vladimir Rusakevitch, he didn't spare more than a glance when Ray entered the washroom behind him. A quick check of the stalls confirmed what Ray already knew — he and the big Russian were alone, and there were no security cameras.

Drawing his weapon, he strode up behind Rusakevitch. Pressing the barrel of his pistol to the base of Rusakevitch's skull, he shoved the man into the wall.

"Hey! What the hell?"

"Shut up. You're job is to listen. You got me?"

The other man dragged in a breath, seeming to grow in girth and height, but he responded appropriately. "Got it."

"Okay, turn around."

"Do you mind if I ....?" The Russian gestured to his pants, which were still undone.

"Yes, I do mind. In fact, I want you to drop them around your ankles. Then I want you to turn, keeping your hands on top of your head where I can see them."

Rusakevitch cursed fluently, in a mixture of Russian and English, but complied, his dark eyes spitting hatred. "You'll die for this, dirt bag."

Ray brought the barrel of his gun around and pressed it into the goon's lips. "I think I said your job is to listen. Understand? Or do you need to suck on this a while?"

A slight tremor passed through the big man. "Understood."

"Okay, tell your boss Landis to keep his hands off the illegal drug trade. No smack, no crack, no blow, no nothing. Nada. Not a single, sorry goddamn-skinny reefer. Got that?"

Rusakevitch roared.

"Shut up." Ray held the man's chin and pressed the barrel of the gun against his now clenched teeth.

"He'll kill you," the Russian ground out.

"I really don't like to repeat myself." Ray applied the barrel of the gun to his captive's teeth more forcefully. "From now on, you red fellas are gonna stay away from the drug trade. Keep your underfed whores, keep your illegal cigarettes, keep all your other scams. Hell, make a buck any way you can. Knock yourselves out. But stay away from the drugs. That's *our* territory. Got it?"

"Got it," Rusakevitch muttered though closed teeth.

"Good."

Giving Rusakevitch a good, hard shove, Ray turned and left. Counting on the other man having to recover his balance and yank his pants up before raising the alarm, Ray strode through the bar. He encountered no opposition.

Once outside, he broke and ran. He leapt onto the Harley, which started on the first try. God bless Quigg for his devotion to the old relic. Revving the engine, Ray waited until a knot of men burst out of the club's door. Then, he peeled out. Giving them a good look at him, he roared past the club, blew the red light to the accompaniment of blaring horns and disappeared into the night.

꧁꧂

Fifteen minutes later, he rolled into the parking lot of an apartment building on Greenfield Drive, parked the bike then set off on foot toward the Fredericton Inn. Five minutes later, he spotted the Toyota. A minute after that, he raised his hand to rap on the door of unit 116, but Grace opened it before he could knock.

"Oh, thank God!"

She closed the door again to throw the chain, then ripped it open and pulled him into the room.

"You're okay?" Her hands moved over his arms, his shoulders, his chest, as though to assure herself he was intact. "Omigod, you're okay."

"I'm fine."

"What took you so long?"

He checked his watch. "Hell, there's still twenty minutes to spare —"

She launched herself at him, the force of her momentum knocking him back a step. A split second later, he was crushing her against his chest, devouring her mouth with his.

As they kissed, she dragged him deeper into the room until he felt his legs collide with the edge of the bed. They both went down, hands streaking everywhere, mouths seeking. Desire ripped through him, fierce and hot and wild.

Man, he had to get a grip. Grasping her arms, he pushed her away.

"No, don't stop. Oh, please, Ray, don't tame it. I want you like this."

Her plea fogged his brain with fresh lust, but he beat it back.

"No, it's not that. I have to call Quigg. If I don't set things in motion, we'll have a *real* gang war on our hands, not just a potential one."

He sat up and grabbed the phone from the nightstand, punching in Quigg's number at the station.

She came to her knees beside him, her eyes worried. "Gang war? Ray, what did you do?"

Before he could respond, John Quigley answered.

"Quigley here."

"Sergeant Quigley, this is your lucky day. I've got an anonymous tip for you."

"Anonymous, eh?"

Ray grinned. Quigg's tone told him he knew just who he was talking to. "Yeah, just call me Deep Throat. Here's the scoop, Sergeant. The Red Fellas are girding for a battle with the Disciples tonight."

A short pause.

"Landis's boys making war on our local motorcycle gang? You sure about that?"

"Yeah, I'd say it's a good bet. Seems like a lone rider went into Landis's nightclub a short while ago and warned him in pretty explicit terms away from the illegal drug trade."

"That so? And this rider walked away in one piece after delivering a message like that?"

Ray's grin widened. "The rider was very careful."

"I'm glad to hear it."

"Anyway, I'm thinking if you were to stake out the Disciple's den real quick-like, you might just net yourself some highly illegal automatic weapons among Landis's crew when they show. Maybe even some incendiary devices," he added, thinking about his own house. "Enough to put some folks away for a very long time. A fella could even get deported over something like that, I would imagine."

"I don't suppose there's any chance you could describe this lone rider?"

Ray almost choked. "Um, let me see. Mean-looking white guy, about six feet tall, maybe one-ninety. Lots of leather, a tattoo or two, wearing one of those do-rags over his hair."

"Gee, we should be able to pick him out of a crowd of bikers, no problem."

"You know how it is. These dirtballs all look alike."

"I s'pose he was riding a Harley?"

"You got it."

"Well, thanks for the tip. We'll get right on it."

"Good. And Sergeant? Tell your boys to be careful."

"My boys are always careful."

Ray heard Quigg break the connection and hung up the phone. Beside him, Grace's laugh rang out.

"Brilliant! Landis's men get caught with a cache of illegal weapons and agree to rat their boss out to avoid deportation."

"Simple but elegant," he said smugly.

Her smile dimmed. "But what if Landis's men try to shoot their way out when they realize they're being pinched?"

"They're pros. When they realize what's happened, they'll cut their losses."

"Are you sure?"

"Sure as I can be." He put the phone back. "But even if it doesn't go down that way, without a shot being fired, the guys know the score. Believe me, Grace, they'll welcome a chance to break Landis's back once and for all. They're trained for this, equipped for it. Hell, they've been dying for a chance like this."

The last of her smile faded. He knew she was contemplating the things he was trained to do, the risks he assumed every day.

"Ray."

She said his name on an exhalation of breath. To Ray, it sounded like a plea, or maybe a prayer. She leaned toward him and he met her. As soon as their bodies touched, the moment their mouths fused, that elemental need blossomed again.

He pulled her down. Over and over they tumbled on the queen-sized bed, hands sliding under clothing, bodies straining together, mouths ravenous. A few moments later, she reared up.

"Get this off!" she demanded, tugging on his leather jacket.

Ray sat up, shrugged out of the jacket, dragging his holster off with it. While he was at it, he tore his t-shirt over his head.

Grace pulled at her own clothing. Skimpy, navel-baring shirt, those athletic pants he'd come to find so sexy, bra, panties — it all hit the floor.

Breathing like he'd just run a 10k race, he tore off the leather chaps and shucked out of his jeans. He barely had time to kick free of his underwear before Grace fell on him. Then her hands were everywhere, small, fierce, gloriously demanding. And her mouth.

He closed his eyes. *Oh, God, her mouth.* It was burning a hot, wet path of fire along his neck, down his chest, across his belly. Her breath against his skin the most erotic caress he'd ever experienced. For a wild second, he allowed himself to imagine what it would feel like for her to kiss him intimately, to close her mouth around him and ....

"Grace!"

At his cry, she glanced up.

"Do you want me to stop?"

He squeezed his eyes shut against the erotic picture she made at his groin. "Yes! No."

"Am I hurting you?"

Oh, Lord, she was killing him. "God, no."

"I'm too clumsy?"

Clumsy? Her untutored mouth was just about the sexist thing he'd ever felt. *Ever.* "No."

"Then what?"

What, indeed? "Grace, you don't have to do this."

"What if I want to do it?"

His erection jerked beneath her hands, but evidently she didn't think that was answer enough.

"What if I told you I've fantasized about doing this for a long time? What if I told you how often I wished I dared suggest it? How my insides just sort of liquify thinking about it? How my breath catches in my lungs and …."

"Grace!"

She stroked his member lightly. "Is that a yes?"

God help him, yes. He guided her back to him.

For the next minutes, his world narrowed to the wet warmth of her mouth, the teasing play of her tongue. When he could stand no more of the torment, he dragged her up beside him.

Her breath came in ragged pants through flared nostrils. "I wasn't finished."

"Well, you almost finished me, sweetheart. And that, my love, I don't think you're quite ready for."

"Oh. Oh!"

She laughed, and Ray grinned at the sound. This was new, this easiness, an unexpected product of laying himself bare, letting her in. Lord God, he loved her.

Suddenly, the humor was gone. There was nothing left now but need.

"I hope you're ready for me," he rasped, rolling her under him, "'cuz in about five seconds, I'm gonna be inside you."

"Ray Morgan, I was born ready for you," she breathed against his ear, even as she guided him to her entrance.

He slid home with one strong thrust. Both of them froze.

"Ray?"

"Yes?"

"Do that again. Pull out all the way and do it again."

Her words excited him. Words she never would have dared say a month ago, a week ago.

It struck him then, what he'd deprived her of. The right to express her sexuality, explore it. He'd rectify that, he vowed, even if it killed him. Starting now.

He pulled out of her body, then buried himself in her slick heat again. She stifled a sob. Bracing himself on his arms, he looked down at her. Her face was flushed, her eyelashes lying sooty against her white skin, her lush lips parted.

"Open your eyes, Grace. Look at me."

She lifted her lids, her blue gaze meeting his, and the sheer desire reflected there jolted him to the bone. *Grace, I'm so sorry. I didn't mean to take this from you.*

"What's it feel like?" he managed to say.

"Good." The word came out on a sob.

"No, *tell* me. What's it feel like when I'm inside you?"

Her fingernails bit into his shoulders. "Ray ...."

"Talk to me. Tell me how it feels. Tell me everything. Tell me what you want."

He felt the shudder that rippled through her. Once more, his arms trembling, he pulled almost completely out, then thrust strongly into her again, sheathing himself to the hilt.

She moaned. "It feels like ... oh, God, like I'm being impaled. Like if you were any bigger, I'd be able to taste you in my throat."

He surged into her again, unable to control his response to her words.

She picked up his urgency. "It feels like you're never going to fit, but then you do."

He withdrew and plunged into her again.

"Oh, God, Ray, you fit so good."

He felt her words slam into him. *Slow down, Morgan. Slow down.* "What do you want, Gracie?"

"Everything. Anything." She clutched at him with her hands, digging her fingernails in. "As long as you're right here with me, like this."

"I want what you want." He thrust into her again. "Just tell me, Gracie. Anything. Whatever you want."

She whimpered.

"Grace?"

"Fast. I want it fast, Ray. Hard."

He looked into her eyes. The need he saw there electrified him, but he made one last grab for control. "The baby . . . ."

"The baby's safe. The doctor said." Her words emerged on short, pants breaths. "Please, Ray."

Thrusting hard into her, he bent to bite her shoulder.

"Oh, yes! Like that."

The rest was a haze. Beyond all thought, beyond reason, he pounded himself into her. There were no more words, at least not intelligible ones. Just broken sobs — his, hers, theirs — as they plunged closer and closer to completion.

Then, suddenly, she was convulsing around him, shimmering, flying apart. Seconds later, he followed, his own release ripping the lid right off his world.

Slowly, like a feather on the breeze, he felt his spirit lilt back and forth until finally it settled to earth again.

Incredible. He'd just had the hottest sex of his life, and he'd had it with his wife of almost five years.

He rolled, taking Grace with him. She went easily, happily, nuzzling into his neck. Her left hand settled on his chest, right over his heart, right where the new thing uncurled.

Happiness so pure it was pain. Love.

Ah, hell, forget the mind-blowing sex. The question he should be asking himself was this: how could it take a man five years — *five frickin' years* — to finally learn to love his wife? To really see her, know her, appreciate her?

She curled into him, practically purring. He responded by wrapping himself around her.

Morgan, you are one slow sonofabitch.

Grace lay looking at the ceiling in dazed pleasure.

They'd made love again, with her astride him, her eyes locked on his, communicating silently as she rode him to a triumphant orgasm. He'd grasped her hips and surged into her for another minute, finding his own release in a hot surge of semen.

"You know what I'd like right now?" she asked, when their heart rates had returned to normal and they lay together in blissful exhaustion.

His breath whooshed out, half laugh, half groan. "Grace, honey, if this is going to require an erection on my part, I should warn you it may not be within my power to grant."

She laughed. "Nothing quite that hard, if you'll pardon the pun. What I'd really like is a cup of coffee. A decaf, double cream would be heaven."

"Now, that I can do." He pressed a kiss to the top of her head and rolled away. "There's a Tim Horton's just down the street. I'll run over and get us some coffee."

She lay back, watching him drag on his jeans and pull his t-shirt over his head.

"A honey cruller, too. And maybe a Boston Cream."

"Heck, I'll spring for a dozen. Be right back. Remember . . . ."

"Don't open the door for anyone but you," she finished.

"And throw the bolt as soon as I've gone."

"I will." She got up, wrapping the sheet around her, and followed him to the door.

He pressed a kiss to her mouth, then left. Smiling, she threw the security bolt.

Life was good, she thought as she headed to the bathroom. She had her husband back. *Better* than back.

In the mirror, she watched her lips curve upward in a satisfied smile. She had Ray's baby growing inside her. And thanks to Ray, there was every chance they'd get their lives back, literally.

And soon, she would have coffee and doughnuts.

Grinning, she turned away from her reflection and started the shower. When the temperature was regulated, she dropped the sheet and stepped under the spray. Five minutes later, as she toweled herself off, she heard a rap on the door.

"Just a sec, Ray," she called.

Quickly, she tossed the wet towel into the tub, re-fastened the sheet sarong-like around her. Hairbrush in hand, she strode to the door. At the last minute, she remembered Ray's caution and pressed her eye to the viewer.

Landis.

The hair brush fell to the floor with a clatter.

"Open up, Mrs. Morgan."

Mrs. Morgan? She was registered under a false name. How had he found her?

"We have your husband."

Oh, God! Her heart thundered so loud in her chest, she could barely think. What would Ray have her do? He'd told her not to open for anyone but him. If he were really out there, surely he'd call out, tell her what to do.

"Mrs. Morgan? Are you going to open this door?"

"I don't believe you," she croaked.

"He'd confirm it for himself, but I'm afraid he's bleeding rather a lot —"

"Don't hurt him!"

"That's entirely up to you, Mrs. Morgan."

Grace dragged the bolt back and opened the door. Landis shouldered his way in, pushing her backward with a grip on her arm, his other hand brandishing a deadly-looking handgun. She glimpsed another man in the parking lot, but no sign of Ray.

"Where's Ray? What have you done to him?"

Still grasping her arm, he dragged her to the bathroom to satisfy himself she was alone.

"Yes, well, I'm afraid I lied about that part," he said, his tone politely civil. "I don't have him . . . yet. But it's good to know you're expecting him soon. I've got a charter to catch."

Grace tried to wrench away from him, but he tightened his grip on her elbow so hard it felt like bones were rubbing together. Tears sprang to her eyes, blurring her vision.

"And thank you, by the way, for letting me in. It'll be so much easier, catching him unawares like this."

"Bastard."

"Quite. Now let's get you settled."

Before she knew what his intent was, he released her elbow, grasped the sheet knotted between her breasts and yanked it off. A shove sent her sprawling onto the bed. Panic clawing her insides, she rolled away but he grabbed her foot and dragged her back, this time pinning her leg to the mattress with his foot.

"No need for hysterics, Mrs. Morgan," he drawled. "As tempting a package as you might present, I'm a little pressed for time at the moment. I merely need the sheet to tie you up."

Tie her up? She couldn't let him do that. If she were tied, she'd be no use to Ray.

Landis's shoe bit deeply into her calf, effectively tethering her face-down on the bed as he tore a strip from the sheet.

Think.

She could scream, but that would surely bring the thug from outside, and they'd subdue her twice as fast, twice as easily. As she heard Landis rip a second strip, she knew she had to act.

Dragging in a deep breath, she kicked with her free foot at the leg that pinned her. Lying face down, she couldn't get much power behind the kick, but somehow the sideways blow managed to dislodge his foot. It also hurt like hell as his leather-shod foot slid off, since he'd been applying considerable weight to her leg.

Ignoring the pain, she rolled away, this time gaining her feet. She'd almost reached the door when he caught her arm.

He yanked her back, almost tearing her arm from its socket. "I think I mentioned I don't have time for this."

Then he struck her — a casual, measured clip to the side of her face with the butt of the pistol. White-hot pain exploded in her head. She crumpled. Though her vision grayed, she didn't pass out.

"There's a good girl." He shoved her back down on the bed.

Grace's vision wobbled. The whole side of her head felt like it was on fire, and something warm dripped down her cheek. Blood. Her blood.

Her stomach wanted to revolt. She closed her eyes against the nausea, but opened them again seconds later as she felt Landis binding her wrists. She should struggle, do something, but she couldn't make her trembling limbs obey. Besides, there seemed to be two of everything, including Landis.

I'm so sorry, Ray.

She lay there limply as he bound her ankles. Then he produced a length of the cotton sheet, dangling it in front of her.

"Just one more. I hate to have to do this to a lady, but I'm going to have to gag you."

She peered up at him. Her left eye had begun to swell shut, but at least she was seeing only one version of Landis.

Too bad her mind didn't seem to be clearing as fast. If she were thinking clearly, she'd understand why he was doing this. As it was, she couldn't fathom it out. When he stepped closer with his makeshift gag, she blurted it out.

"Why are you doing this? I know you're going to kill me anyway."

"I'm afraid I am," he admitted. "But to be perfectly fair, I told you as much when I gave you the opportunity to disappear. I would have sworn you were smart enough to take it."

"I understand why you did that now," she said, trying to keep her terror from making her voice waver. "You wanted to set my husband up, make it look like he took money from you."

Landis smiled, a chilling thing. "A definite bonus," he conceded. "Now, enough talk. Let's get this gag on you."

She had to keep him talking. Ray could be back any minute. If she could avoid the gag, she might be able to warn him.

"Why not kill me now?" she blurted.

His eyes widened, and she was struck by what a handsome sonofabitch he was. How could evil disguise itself so effectively behind that urbane mask?

"Such a hurry, Mrs. Morgan. You know, most people prefer later rather than sooner."

"I just want to understand. You've said you're going to kill me anyway. You also said you were in a hurry. So why all this trouble?"

"Why? Because your husband has proven just a touch hard to kill. If he gets difficult tonight, you'll be my ace in the hole."

Landis squatted by the bed, drawing the cold muzzle of the gun across Grace's midriff. Unable to control her revulsion, she shrank away.

"How many seconds do you think it's going to take him to throw down his weapon, Mrs. Morgan, when he assesses this situation? Hmmm? How long?"

Ray's weapon! He hadn't taken it. She was sure of it.

She glanced furtively around the room. Not on the night table, not on the TV. Maybe it was still in the holster, inside his jacket, which was on the floor on the other side of the bed. He'd shrugged out of it, when they'd made love.

It didn't matter, though, did it? Gloom descended on her as she remembered that Ray would walk into this trap unarmed. He'd probably never know what hit him. And she'd never be able to get to his gun in time to stop it, even if her hands weren't bound.

"So he walks in, you shoot him, and when you're sure he's dead, you shoot me," she said dully.

"Right again, Miss Hotshot Reporter. But then I guess it didn't tax those keen deductive powers of yours too much, hmmm? Now I really do need you to shut up so I can get this gag on."

Don't let him do it.

Her heart pounded in her throat as he bent closer, and her breath came in ragged, panicked gulps. So hard to think. Terror was making her brain sluggish.

Not knowing what else to do, she rolled, trying to evade him, but with her bound limbs she couldn't wriggle away fast enough. He caught her easily.

Scream. She'd rejected the idea before, but now there was nothing else for it. Maybe she'd bought Ray enough time. Maybe he'd be close enough to hear her cry before Landis silenced her. Maybe she could give him that little edge.

Filling her lungs, she opened her mouth and screamed — for all of about a tenth of a second.

Anticipating her again, Landis shoved a pillow over her face almost before the first sound broke. Unable to breathe, she panicked, thrashing and bucking.

This was it. She was going to die. Even as she fought, she knew it was useless. In a remarkably short time, her consciousness started to dim. So, too, did the panic. All that was left was a piercing regret.

I'm so sorry, Ray.

Chapter 14

RAY HAD BEEN WAITING on the coffee and doughnuts when it hit him, that dull feeling low in his gut.

He shouldn't have left Grace.

For a moment, he argued with it, using logic to try to beat back that ominous feeling. No one knew where they were. No one knew *who* they were. No one had followed him on the bike; he'd made damn sure of that. Even if they'd found the Harley, he'd left it in the parking lot of an apartment complex blocks away. There were at least three other motorcycles in the apartment lot, so it wouldn't draw undue attention.

And Landis was otherwise occupied dealing with the perceived challenge from the Disciples. There was absolutely nothing to worry about.

The leaden sensation in his gut wouldn't lift. Dammit, he shouldn't have left her.

"That'll be six eighty-five."

He threw a twenty at the startled server and left without his purchase.

He hit the pavement running. A minute later, he'd reached the edge of the motel's parking lot. He could see their unit's door from here, see that the drapes were pulled just as she'd left them.

A thin shaft of yellow light was visible where the curtains just met. It looked just the same as he'd left it, but somehow he knew it wasn't. His instinct was to rush the door of the unit, to pound on it until Grace answered. But that would be rash, stupid, and he couldn't afford any mistakes here. Not with Grace.

Melting deeper into the shadows, he paused a moment to bring his breathing under control. Then he crept closer to the west side of the building, keeping to the cover of the cars until he had a good view of Room 116. He forced himself to be still and just watch. No small feat when his heart pounded like a jackhammer and his muscles screamed for action.

His hard-won caution was rewarded a moment later when he spied the man standing motionless beside a dark SUV, scanning the parking lot with slow and thorough deliberateness. Then the man lifted his hand and drew on a cigarette. He'd cupped the cigarette to shield the light, but from where Ray crouched, the dim, fleeting illumination was all he needed to ID the guy.

Vladimir Rusakevitch. Landis's man.

Ray's heart slammed against his ribs. If he hadn't forced himself to slow down, he'd have caught a bullet in the back before he ever reached Grace's door.

And what were Landis's thugs doing here? How had they found them? Had something gone wrong with his ploy to lure out Landis's men? Did Landis have someone inside the station? Someone who'd listened in on Ray's conversation with Quigg and put the pieces together?

With that thought came another adrenaline jolt, but this time he embraced it. This time it fueled muscles already cramped from crouching as he worked his way closer to Rusakevitch, ghosting from the cover of one car to the next.

Damn, he wished he had his weapon.

Of course, he wouldn't use it anyway. Not yet. And not because he had any compunction about shooting Rusakevitch. He'd kill him in a heartbeat. But if anyone got a shot off, it could be curtains for Grace.

If she were still alive.

Grace, at the mercy of Landis's thugs . . . .

He choked off that thought. One thing at a time, and right now, his task was to take out the sentry.

Ray crept up to the rear bumper of the Russian's vehicle, a shiny Mercedes. Carefully, he drew the keys to the motorcycle out of his pocket. Holding his breath, he lobbed them softly into the air. They landed with a *chink* several yards to the right.

Rusakevitch's arm came up instantly and Ray caught the dull gleam of a deadly-looking assault rifle. Cautiously, Rusakevitch started toward the spot where the keys had landed.

Ray made his move then. From behind, he darted in, striking the Russian's arm with all his might. The rifle went skidding across the pavement. Rusakevitch's yelp of pain and surprise was cut off as Ray locked his arm around the other man's neck.

"One move, one sound, and I'll snap your neck."

"Okay."

"Where's your other weapon?"

"What other weapon?"

Ray tightened his grip, applying a little more torque to the big man's neck.

"Waistband, small of my back."

With his free hand, Ray fished under the Russian's jacket and extracted a Glock. He hefted the 10mm in his hand. It'd do, he decided. Without wasting another second, he brought the butt of the pistol down behind Rusakevitch's ear. Hard. The man hit the ground without so much as a grunt.

Quickly, Ray ran his hands over the unconscious man, determining that a) he was still alive, and b) he'd been packing a third weapon, a Beretta .22 short semiautomatic. He shoved the second pistol into his hightops, grateful for the baggy pants that all but concealed his feet.

Standing, he examined the rifle he'd knocked from Rusakevitch's hands. Kalashnikov AK-47. Good weapon, but unwieldy. He kicked it under the shadows of a parked tour bus.

Okay, job one was done. Now, how to play this next act?

In his mind's eye, he saw the room key atop the TV stand. Dammit, if he'd just stopped to pick it up, he might have been able to open the door soundlessly enough to gain the element of surprise. But he hadn't. He'd been too sated, too happy, too complacent about finally emerging from this nightmare.

Okay, no point beating himself up now. There'd be plenty of time for that later. *If there was a later.*

Okay, so what were his options?

He could ask for another key, but that could prove sticky. Grace had checked in alone. They'd need her permission to give out a second key, especially to a man. Even one claiming to be her husband. Maybe *especially* to a man claiming to be her husband, given awareness of domestic violence.

He imagined trying to explain to the night clerk the danger Grace was in and quickly discarded the idea. Too time consuming, and even then the night clerk would insist on accompanying him, knocking on the door and announcing the intrusion.

He could kick the door in, go in like gangbusters. Of course, that was always presuming he *could* knock the door down. He'd never tried anything like that. That's what they had ERT units and battering rams for.

That's it! He could call the Emergency Response Team.

Of course, if Landis's men hadn't stormed out to do battle with the Disciples tonight, he and Grace would be right back to square one. They'd potentially be sitting ducks for Landis. But right now, with Grace's life on the line this very minute, he didn't see any other option.

Yes, dammit, he'd call in the troops and take his chances with Landis tomorrow. If he didn't act now, Grace wouldn't have a tomorrow to worry about.

The whole process of analysis had taken less than thirty seconds, but now that the decision was made, he felt like he'd wasted too much time. Turning on his heel, he started toward the lobby to commandeer the front desk phone. He hadn't gotten five paces when he heard a sound that froze him in his tracks.

A scream. Grace's scream. Muffled, then quickly cut off.

Primal rage blasted away his reason. Gun held high, he raced back toward Grace's unit. He'd tear the door off its hinges, then he'd take Landis's goon apart. He'd tear the bastard's heart out with his bare hands and feed it to him.

But what if the door didn't give? What if righteous fury wasn't enough?

Fear curdled in his stomach, fear for Grace. With it came a return of rationality. How many times would Landis's thug listen to him batter the door before he put a bullet in Grace's brain?

If he hadn't already killed her with a silenced weapon ....
Dammit, Morgan, use your head! There has to be a way in.
There was, he realized, drawing his lips back in a fierce, tooth-baring smile. He'd just knock on the door and ask.

⚜

Grace inhaled shallowly through her nose and let her breath shudder out again. Not dead after all.

If she were dead, her head wouldn't be throbbing like this with every pulse. If she were dead, the bindings cutting into her wrists and ankles wouldn't hurt. If she were dead, she wouldn't be fighting the nausea created by the gag in her mouth.

She lifted her head to find Landis sitting in the chair in the corner.

"Good, you're awake," he said. "I didn't want your husband to think you were already gone."

She dropped her head back to the pillow. That's right. He didn't want to kill her ... yet. Not until he was sure Ray was dead. She was his pawn, his tool to make sure Ray took his medicine, after which he'd execute her without so much as a frown disturbing his smooth, handsome brow.

Maybe she should play dead when Ray came. That would serve Landis right—

A knock sounded at door, Ray's bare-knuckled, happy tap. "Grace, sweetheart, open up."

Her gaze flew to Landis, who pushed to his feet. Pistol raised, he crossed to the door. Standing to the side, he turned the knob and let the door fall inward.

Grace gathered herself to scream, knowing the gag would muffle her efforts. Before she could make even that small alarm, the door burst wide and Ray charged in, gun leveled. In seconds, he'd taken a bead on a surprised Landis, who also had Ray in his sights.

Ray had a gun.

The significance sank in. But where had he gotten it?

Unless he had taken his service weapon with him after all. No, she didn't think so. He had on just his t-shirt ....

"I guess you must have overpowered Vlady," said Landis.

"It wasn't hard. But then, good help is hard to find, isn't it, Landis? Which I guess is why you're in here terrorizing my wife instead of having one of your henchmen do it."

Grace watched in amazement. She knew Ray had taken in her situation in his first sweep of the room, but you'd never know he had anything on the line from the easy tone of his voice.

"My *henchmen*, as you call them, are unfortunately otherwise engaged." For the first time, Grace saw the first flicker of emotion cross Landis's face.

"Oh, yes, that's right. I heard something about that. Man's got to protect his turf, I guess."

"Except the challenge was a fiction, wasn't it, Detective?"

"Was it?"

Landis's face darkened. "You tell me. After all, you're the one who carried the message, Detective."

Ray's service weapon, thought Grace. If she could slip off the bed, she might be able to fish it out of its holster in that tangle of clothing. Even with her wrists tied, she should be able to grasp it two-handed. Thank God Landis hadn't thought her a sufficient threat to bind her hands behind her back.

She shot a look at the Russian. His polite, urbane mask was gone.

"Me?" Ray raised an eyebrow. "What makes you think I'd spread a nasty rumor like that?"

"I don't think, I *know*. Vlad fingered you. We picked you out on the security tapes from earlier in the evening. Even then we wouldn't have made you as anything but a low-life Disciple if we hadn't seen you with this bitch."

Landis indicated Grace with a jerk of his head. She'd been scooting closer to the other edge of the bed, but froze at his words.

"You must have known I'd figure it out if I saw you two together."

"So how'd you find us here at this motel?"

"To borrow your phrase, it wasn't hard. External cameras showed you getting into that disreputable-looking vehicle. This was just the second motel we checked."

Grace turned her head to scan the floor. Their clothes were strewn on the carpet but had been kicked almost under the bed.

"So, you made me," said Ray, his voice finally sounding a little stiff to Grace. "I guess this means you smelled a setup and called your boys off?"

"Not soon enough, unfortunately." Landis's voice was pure icy rage. "They're all guests of Her Majesty tonight, thanks to you, Morgan."

"Cheer up, Landis. They'll probably all be out tomorrow and it'll be business as usual."

"Enough!" Landis roared. "We both know they'll turn on me like the stinking sewer rats they are. Now put that gun down."

Ray's arm didn't waver. "You know I can't."

"I know you *will*." In one quick, smooth motion, Landis trained his weapon on Grace. "Now put down the gun."

⁂

Ray heard the muffled sounds of protest that Grace was making against her gag. He couldn't make out a word she said but he understood anyway.

Don't do it. He's still going to kill us. He'll kill us both. Save yourself. Don't put the gun down.

He put the gun down.

If he hadn't had the second gun biting into his ankle, he would never have done it. He knew Grace was right, that Landis intended to kill them both. If he didn't have the second weapon, he'd have tried for the perfect takedown shot. He'd have tried to hit that two-inch band circling Landis's head, right at eye level. If he hit it just right, Landis might go down without squeezing his fingers in reflex, sending a round of automatic fire into Grace's unprotected body.

A big *if*. Too big.

Holding both hands out in plain view, he bent and placed the Glock carefully on the carpeted floor.

"Now kick it over here."

Ray obliged.

"That's better." Landis retrieved the Glock, jammed it into his waistband, then started to swing his gun back toward Ray. This was it. He had to go for the pistol. Now or never.

A sudden thump dragged Landis's attention back toward the bed. Ray shot a quick glance in that direction, too.

Oh, Lord! Grace had rolled right off it onto the floor. Landis's strode back toward the bed. Ray went for the Beretta in his hightop. Without hesitation, he aimed and squeezed the trigger.

Nothing.

Oh, Jesus. Landis was standing over Grace now, bringing the pistol's muzzle down . . . .

"No!" Ray cried, lunging toward Landis, impotently squeezing the trigger of the little .22.

A sudden explosion of sound shocked his eardrums in the small room, followed by another.

Incredibly, Landis reeled back, slamming into the wall between a pair of motel art pictures. Then he sank slowly to the floor, an obscenely-wide crimson streak on the white wall tracking his descent.

Ray vaulted over the bed, kicking the pistol away from Landis's lax grip. One look at the man and he knew he needn't have bothered. Hollow-point bullets at near point-blank range rarely left any doubt, but he pressed a hand to Landis's carotid artery automatically to confirm it.

No pulse, and no possibility of resuscitation.

Immediate threat eliminated, he turned to check on Grace. His heart stumbled in his chest.

Even in the confusion of the moment, he'd known the killing shots had to have been fired by Grace, but somehow he wasn't prepared for the sight of her, lying there on the carpet.

Naked, bound and gagged, she clutched his service weapon between trembling hands, her arms still stiffly extended.

"Oh, Grace, honey." He dropped beside her, gingerly prying the gun from her tight grip. Placing the weapon on the night table, he dealt swiftly with the gag by dragging it down around her neck, then pulled her into his arms.

She shuddered, dragging in a shaky breath. "Is he dead?"

"Very." His voice shook just as badly as Grace's had. Damn, that was close. Too close.

Scooping the bedspread off the floor, he wrapped it around her. He tried to untie the binding at her wrists, but he couldn't budge them. Swearing, he dug his Swiss Army knife out of his pocket and started sawing through the material. He worked carefully but quickly, anxious to restore circulation to her poor fingers.

"Did he hurt you?"

"Not much. Just a tap on the head."

He jerked his gaze up from her discolored hands, which he'd been massaging back to life. Now that the gag had been removed, he could see she'd taken a blow to the face. The skin beneath her eye was already turning blue and the flesh was torn over her cheekbone. The eye area itself was swollen, too.

"If the sonofabitch wasn't already dead, I'd kill him for that," he said matter-of-factly.

"I killed him." She looked past him to where Landis lay slumped against the wall. "I killed a man."

Her gaze was blank, her voice devoid of emotion. That would come later, after the shock passed. She'd have nightmares about it. All that blood, the smell of death, the vacant look in the eyes after life was extinguished. It was hard to deal with even when it was part of your job.

"You saved us, Grace." He turned her away from the grisly sight, leading her to the other bed where he gently urged her down. "He'd have killed us both."

She blinked. "We better call the police."

"No need. Hear that?" She nodded that she could hear the sirens. "Someone must have called 911 after shots were fired." He quickly cut the bindings at her ankles. "In about two minutes, this parking lot's going to be lit up like Christmas."

He was wrong. The cavalry arrived in under a minute.

Instructing Grace to stay put, Ray stepped outside. He raised his arms high in the air as two patrol cars converged in the parking lot, their red-and-blue bar lights bouncing crazily off buildings and cars. He recognized the first officer out of his car, Corporal Jake Hartland.

"Jake, it's me. Ray Morgan."

Hartland tipped the weapon he'd leveled at Ray's chest upward a fraction of an inch. "Razor?"

"Yep."

"What's going on?"

"You got a DOA inside, Room 116. And to your left, beside that black Mercedes SUV, you'll find a man down. He's a hospital case, too, unless he's crawled off. Probable fractured skull."

"Detective Morgan?"

Ray glanced at the second officer, a new recruit. "Crowly."

The youngster lowered his weapon and Ray lowered his arms.

"Holy hell, Ray, what'd you do to yourself?" Jake again. "I wouldn't have recognized you, man."

He grinned. "Long story. You should see Grace."

"Grace is here?"

Ray's face sobered. "Grace is the shooter."

If Jake had been wearing his hat as policy preferred, his eyebrows would have disappeared under it. "This *is* going to be a long story." He shook his head. "Okay, where's the guy with the cracked melon? We better see to him before he *does* crawl off."

Ray led them to the black Mercedes behind which the Russian still sprawled unconscious. Jake knelt to check him out.

"You gonna tell me Grace did this, too?"

"No, that was me," he said. "I might have hit him a little hard."

"Nah. He's still breathing." Jake stood. "Don't suppose you can tell me who it is?"

"Vladimir Rusakevitch."

"Cripes, another one of Landis's men?"

"Yep."

"Jeez, we've been processing these guys all night. Holding cells are full of them."

"So I heard," Ray said.

"Yeah? From who?"

"Landis."

"Don't tell me — Landis is our DOA?"

"Yep."

Jake whistled admiringly. "And Grace shot him?"

"Yes."

"Damn, I can't wait to hear this."

The ambulance arrived just then, followed by another squad car.

"Our sergeant," Jake said, as the female officer climbed out of her car. Jake waved for the EMTs who had piled out of the ambulance with a gurney.

"Over here," he called, then turned to the other patrolman. "Dennis, you stay with our friend, Vlad." Then he turned to Ray. "Razor, buddy, I'm gonna have to put you in my car while Sergeant Copeland and I secure the scene."

"But Grace needs me —"

"Grace needs to give us an independent statement."

Standard operating procedure to separate witnesses for questioning. Ray knew it, but it didn't make it any easier to accept. She'd looked so blank, so stunned. He wanted to be with her, help her through this. But it was out of the question and he knew it. He was going to have to give his own statement, too. Dammit, it would likely be hours before he could wrap his arms around her again.

"Okay, Jake." He forced his fisted hands to relax. "Okay."

❧

It was almost six hours later before Grace saw Ray again.

In those hours, she'd held an ice pack to her cheek while she told the bare bones of her story to Sergeant Roberta Copeland. She'd then been taken to hospital where the ER doctor had checked her over thoroughly, closed the gash on her cheek, and pronounced her fine.

Then she'd gone to the station and repeated her story in greater depth for Detective Dave Samsel, a colleague of Ray's from Major Crime, and Jake Hartland.

She'd written out a full statement and answered what felt like a thousand questions from Samsel and Hartland. Finally, *finally*, they told her she was free to go.

Thank God. She was so tired, her head was beginning to spin, which did nothing for her stomach. She needed a dark room, a soft pillow and the blessed escape sleep would grant.

"Where's Ray?"

"Right outside this door, I expect," Jake said dryly. "At least, that's where he's been this last hour or so."

He was right. He was at her side the moment the door opened.

"Grace, you okay?"

She looked up at his face as he took her hands. He looked dog-tired, too, but she could see the watchfulness in his eyes, the concern that softened them.

"I'm fine." She smiled wanly. "Just tired. Can we go home?"

He grimaced. "I think a hotel would be a better bet."

Her stomach roiled violently.

"Are you saying it's not over? We're *still* not safe to go home?"

"Oh, no, sweetheart. It's not that." He pushed a strand of her hopelessly tangled hair back behind her ear. "We're out of danger. Landis is dead and his thugs are rounded up. There's nothing to worry about."

Despite his reassurance, fear gripped her exhausted mind. "How can you be sure? How do you know there won't be reprisals? He must have had connections …."

"Listen to me, baby. Landis was the boss. His organization is broken. Yes, he had connections. All gangs do, especially these new ones. They'll partner with the devil himself to make a buck, but their affiliations tend to be very fluid, very *ad hoc*. Those loose partners aren't going to charge in to avenge Landis, believe me."

"Ray's right," Dave Samsel said, and Grace turned toward the detective. "Makes it damned hard for us to catch them when relationships form and dissolve so quickly, but it'll work to your advantage here. No one cares enough about Landis to do anything, except maybe to try to fill the void he leaves."

She turned back to Ray. "Then why can't we go home?"

"The explosion," he reminded her. "The house is secure enough — Quigg says they boarded it up in our absence — but it's not pretty." He rubbed a thumb along the line of her jaw. "The door, the siding, shutters, eavestroughing…it's still a mess."

She looked into Ray's eyes, looked deep into those warm brown depths, and let go of the fear.

"Okay." She let her breath out. "A hotel it is. But I want to stay at a *nice* one. And I want to register as Grace and Ray Morgan and pay with our credit card, and I want to look the desk clerk square in the eye when we check out. All right?"

Ray grinned back at her. "All right."

⁂

Ray lay on his back in the king-sized bed as the watery light of dawn seeped into their fifth-floor room. If he got up and stood at the window, he knew he'd be treated to a spectacular view of the sun rising over Fredericton, but he didn't budge.

Grace was sprawled beside him, her face pressed into his shoulder, hand on his chest. He watched her sleep, counted her soft respirations.

Lord, he was so lucky. Lucky to be alive. Lucky to have Grace. Lucky to have a second chance to learn to love this woman the way she deserved.

Was it only two weeks and change since she'd walked into their kitchen and dropped that bombshell?

He'd been devastated, unable to imagine how he would go on. But the damnable thing was, he hadn't even begun to love her then. Not really. Not for the woman she was. He'd loved an idea, the image he'd imposed on her.

But he loved her now. She was smart and brave and she loved him extravagantly. If he lived to be a hundred, he'd never forget the way she'd looked in that club, nursing a soda and waiting for Landis, the weight of Ray's gun in her purse.

His hand tightened on her hip. If anything had happened to her, if he lost her now ....

She stirred in his arms. "Ray?"

He pulled her to him, crushing her against him. "Don't ever scare me like that again."

She returned the pressure of his embrace with her own slim arms. "I'll try not to."

He stroked the silky skin of her back. "I can't lose you now. It'd kill me, Gracie."

She pulled back to look at him and his heart stuttered at the expression in her pale blue eyes. *Troubled.* Then she dropped her gaze to his chest. She lifted a hand to stroke the hairs there, her touch incredibly soft.

"I can't go back, Ray."

His heart started hammering. "You're not coming home with me?"

"No, that's not what I'm saying. At least, I hope not." She pulled out of his arms and sat up, tucking the sheet across her breasts. "I'm saying I don't want our relationship to go back the way it was. I don't want to go back to the way *I* was."

He laid a hand on her bare back. "Sweetheart, I'm so sorry about that —"

"I'm not like your mother," she interrupted. "I tried to be, but I can't. I'm not really that much of a lady, I guess."

He felt the words welling up in him, then. Words he'd never said to another living soul. Reflexively, he tried to push them back down, choke them back, drown them.

Grace was still talking. "I can't be that woman you wanted," she said. "I mean, I wasn't *un*happy exactly. But now, after this past week, I can't go back to —"

He opened his mouth to say again that he was sorry, but what came out were the words he'd tried to swallow down.

"My mother was a whore."

⁂

The words exploded in Grace's head. *My mother was a whore.* She gripped the sheet in her fingers. What was he talking about? Gladys Morgan had been a paragon.

"Say again?"

"My mother was a drug-addicted prostitute."

His words were expressionless.

"But you said ...."

"Yeah, *I said.*" He laughed harshly. "I said a lot of things about my mother. I said she was a saint. And of course, devoted to the memory of my dear departed father."

"She wasn't those things?"

"She was a hooker in Montreal and I'm her bastard child. I don't know who my father was. I grew up with her turning tricks in our lousy little two-room apartment. The things I saw .... Then she'd use most of the money getting wasted. Sometimes, she'd even send me out to score for her."

"Oh, Ray."

"When I was old enough to leave school without bringing the social workers down on us, I got a job. I figured if I could provide for us, she wouldn't have to turn tricks."

She squeezed his leg in a wordless encouragement.

"But see, it wasn't about the money. I finally figured that out. It was about self-destruction. She was on some kind of twisted journey and she wasn't interested in any detours."

"What'd you do then?"

"I left. Went to Toronto. Supported myself for a couple of years working for a courier company, then got admitted to U of T as a mature student. I invented what I thought was a nice, normal childhood, dated nice, normal college girls, and planned a nice, normal life as a mechanical engineer."

Grace blinked. "You were going to be an *engineer*?"

"I only did one year."

God, he'd lied to her, about his entire background, for their whole marriage. That's what it amounted to, didn't it? A lie?

No, not a lie, she realized. Survival. He'd created his own personal witness protection program to disappear into, a cover under which he could shed his pain and shame. He hadn't set out to deceive her. He'd just gone about living the new identity he'd created for himself.

She swallowed a lump in her throat. "What happened? Why didn't you finish your degree?"

"My mother died. Strangled to death. One of her johns, they thought, though they never found the guy. Hell, they never even tried very hard. Just one less hooker walking the track. One less junkie."

Her heart contracted. No matter what else she'd been, she'd been his mother. "Is that what made you decide to be a cop?"

"Went straight into the academy. The rest you know."

"I'm so sorry." She slid back down beside him but he didn't close his arm around her as before. Undaunted, she curled close against him. "I wish I'd known. It all makes sense now."

He closed a hand on her upper arm, holding her away. His eyes glinted with suspicious moisture. "You gotta believe I didn't understand what I was doing, how I was hurting you."

"Sssh," she put a finger to his lips. "You didn't hurt me."

"I did." He caught her hand. "I tried to arrest your development."

"You were very tender. Very sweet."

"I stifled your sexuality."

"Are you planning to do it again?"

He shook his head solemnly.

She grinned. In a swift move, she pulled herself astride him. "Then you're forgiven."

He curled up to wrap his arms around her for a fierce hug. She returned his embrace with equal fervor. Then his hands were in her hair, angling her head so he could kiss her feverishly.

Desire pulsed to life again, along with the conviction that she would never, ever get enough of this man, not if they grew old and grey together.

Sighing, she rubbed her breasts against his chest, shivering at the glorious friction. Ray's hands dropped away from her shoulders to cup the sides of her breasts. She gave herself up to the sensation, groaning when the caressing heat of his hands was withdrawn. But then he was lifting her, shifting her. A second later, he joined them. Grace gasped, throwing her head back, clinging to his shoulders. Ray shuddered.

"I love you, Gracie." He muttered the words into her neck. "I really, truly, *finally* love you the way you deserve to be loved."

A shaft of sweetness, so poignant it was painful, pierced her.

"I love you, too. You're never gonna get rid of me now, Ray Morgan."

He covered her mouth in a kiss of overwhelming, chaste tenderness. She wanted that sweetness to go on and on without end, but the desire thrumming through her veins wouldn't be denied.

Almost unconsciously, she began moving against him, over him, her urgency growing.

"Slow, sweetheart. Let's make it last this time."

They did. Beneath her, he set an exquisitely slow pace, all the while whispering to her. His words alternatively soothed and inflamed her, as did the hands that roamed her back, her neck, her buttocks.

Finally, when her need outgrew the languorous tempo he'd imposed, she cried out her need. In answer, he rolled her under him and brought them both to a swift release.

Afterward, she rested her head on his chest as they lay tangled, listening to his pounding heart gradually slow.

"Oh, Lord, this is nice," she said eventually.

"Nice? It's perfect."

Perfect? Almost. She pulled back far enough so she could look at his face, propping her head on one hand. She rested the other hand on his chest, not ready to break their connection.

His expression changed. He didn't tense, but his hooded eyes suddenly looked less slumberous. "What?"

She shifted her gaze to his chest where her white fingers contrasted with his darker skin. *Just say it.* She lifted her gaze to meet his worried one.

"When I said I couldn't go back to how it was before, I meant more than just this."

His heart kicked beneath her hand. "What do you mean?"

"My job. Ray, I can't go back to the way it was at the paper, covering the IODE house tours and writing fluff pieces. With the story I'm going to turn in, Katie will let me do other assignments. She'll *have* to. This is my chance."

He regarded her for a moment. She could see he was thinking of all the reasons why she shouldn't pursue investigative reporting. Heaven knew she'd heard them often enough before, from Katie and from others.

You're a woman. You're not tough enough.

Now she had more to add to the list: You're pregnant. You botched your last effort royally, putting lives in danger.

Lifting her chin, she waited for him to enumerate these and more. Instead, he drew a deep breath and closed his eyes. When he opened them a few seconds later, they were clear again.

"Okay."

She blinked. "Okay?"

He caught her hand, grazing her knuckles with a kiss. "If it's what you really want to do, you should do it."

She grinned. "I can't believe this. I thought you'd say it was too dangerous. That it was okay for you to go out and face down criminals every day, but that no wife of yours blah, blah, blah."

"I *do* think it can be dangerous." He returned her hand to his chest, pinning it there with his own. "We've just seen exactly how dangerous it can be. But other times, I imagine it's just hard work, routine slogging. Just like police work."

"Exactly! But I still can't believe you're not going to fight me on this."

He shrugged. "I trust you not to take unnecessary risks. And you're pretty good at it."

Tears, sudden and unexpected, stung her eyes. "Thank you."

Ray felt emotion threaten to close his own throat as he watched his Gracie blink back tears. "Don't thank me yet," he said, his voice gruff. "I'll probably hound you every day to find out what you're working on so I can assess the risks."

She smiled. "Fair enough."

"And I'll teach you every trick I know, for self-defense, for keeping command, for defusing situations."

"Good idea."

"Not that you'll need to use it, 'cuz you're going to tell me about anything that remotely looks like it might get sticky."

"Of course."

"I'll worry about you," he warned, smoothing her hair, the silky texture under his hand both a comfort and a sensual pleasure. "I can't shut that off, so don't ask me to."

She stretched up and kissed him, their lips clinging for minutes.

"So," he said when he lifted his head, "that leaves just one thing."

"Yeah? What's that?"

He brushed a tendril of fiery hair back behind her ear. "Can I please, *please*, go back to wearing jeans with the crotch where it's supposed to be?"

Her laughter rang out, clear and joyous, until he reached up and caught it for himself, absorbing it.

Gracie. He sighed against her lush, kiss-swollen lips. *My Grace.*

Thank you for investing your time — that most precious of commodities — in my book! If you enjoyed *Saving Grace*, I would be thrilled if you could help me buzz it. You can do this by:

Recommending it. Help other readers find this book by recommending it to friends, readers' groups and discussion boards.

Reviewing it. Please share with other readers what you liked about this book by reviewing it wherever you purchased it, or at readers' sites such as Goodreads. If you do choose to review it, I would be delighted to gift you with an electronic copy of your choice of any of my other titles. Simply email me to alert me to your review and let me know which of my books you would like to have and in what electronic format. My email address is norahwilsonwrites@gmail.com.

Read on for an excerpt from *Protecting Paige*, the next book in my Serve and Protect Series.

Also available from Norah Wilson:

Sensual Romantic Suspense
GUARDING SUZANNAH, Book 1 in the Serve and Protect Series
PROTECTING PAIGE, Book 3 in the Serve and Protect Series
NEEDING NITA, a novella in the Serve and Protect Series

Sensual Romantic Suspense w/ Paranormal Element
EVERY BREATH SHE TAKES
(coming soon from Montlake Romance)

Sensual Paranormal Romance
THE MERZETTI EFFECT: A Vampire Romance
NIGHTFALL: A Vampire Romance

As N.L. Wilson
(writing partnership of Norah Wilson and Heather Doherty)
Dix Dodd mysteries (humorous)
THE CASE OF THE FLASHING FASHION QUEEN:
FAMILY JEWELS
DEATH BY CUDDLE CLUB (coming soon)

As Wilson Doherty
(writing partnership of Norah Wilson and Heather Doherty)
YA Paranormal
THE SUMMONING: Book 1 in the Gatekeepers Series
ASHLYN'S RADIO

About the Author

Norah Wilson lives in Fredericton, New Brunswick with her husband, two adult children, her beloved Rotti-Lab mix Chloe, and numerous rats (the pet kind). Norah has had three of her romantic suspense stories final in the Romance Writers of America's Golden Heart® contest until she sold her first story in 2004. She was also the winner of Dorchester Publishing's New Voice in Romance contest in 2003.

Norah loves to hear from readers!

Connect with Her Online:

Twitter: http://twitter.com/norah_wilson
Facebook: http://www.facebook.com/#!/profile.php?id=1053773212
Goodreads:
http://www.goodreads.com/author/show/1361508.Norah_Wilson
Norah's Website: http://www.norahwilsonwrites.com
Wilson Doherty's Website: http://www.writersgrimoire.com

Excerpt from Protecting Paige
(Book 3 in the *Serve and Protect Series*)

Single parent Paige Harmer is at her wits end about her son. Dillon's a good kid, but he's fallen in with a bad crowd. She's determined to enlist the help of her next door neighbor, the extremely handsome and much younger Tommy Godsoe. Tommy is a local cop, and up until he got shot recently in a police raid, was a dog handler. His injury is such that he can never go back to field work, and he refuses to be a desk jockey. All he wants is to nurse his wounds in solitude, and he's done a great job driving his friends and colleagues away. But Paige is an unstoppable force. Before he knows it, he's drawn into their lives. As it turns out, Paige and Dillon are going to need a cop in their corner. And Tommy needs Paige to drag him out of his self-pity and back to life.

Protecting Paige

C ONSTABLE TOMMY GODSOE'S BLOOD sang.

His breath rasped harshly in his ears as he pelted along the concrete sidewalk, but he wasn't winded. Not yet. Not even close. Max, the four-year-old Belgian Malinois straining at the business end of the thirty-foot lead, lent Tommy extra speed. Even now, backup was falling further and further behind, but Tommy couldn't check Max's momentum or the dog would think he was being corrected.

Suddenly, at the mouth of an alleyway, Max slowed. Without conscious thought, Tommy took up the slack in the lead even as he studied the dog nosing the asphalt. The dog wheeled in a tight semi-circle, then turned away from the alley and shot off again down the sidewalk. Tommy fixed the location in his mind. Max had eliminated the alleyway as a direction of travel. Always had to remember the last negative sign. If they lost the trail further on up ahead, they could come back to this spot, so Max could pick up the scent again.

At the next alleyway, Max did the same check, but this time he bounded off down the narrow passageway. Tommy raced after him, his heart rate kicking up another notch.

Fence!

Max cleared it in one leap, and Tommy vaulted over it right behind him. Over the sound of his own breathing, he heard backup in the mouth of the alley now. Good. No need to radio his location. He could save his breath for —

Ding-*dong.*

What the hell?

Tommy jerked awake, struggling up into a sitting position. The sheets, cool with sweat, pooled in his lap, and his heart pounded against his ribs as though he'd run a marathon.

Ah, Jesus wept. A dream. It was just a dream. He wasn't a cop anymore. He wasn't a dog handler. Bitterness, familiar as the pain in his hip, curdled his stomach.

A light tapping at his door.

"All right, all right, keep your shirt on."

Throwing off the sheet, he swung his legs gingerly over the edge of the bed. He thought about scooping up the blue sweat pants from the floor and hauling them on over his boxers, but another peel of the doorbell dissuaded him. Grabbing his cane, he lurched to his feet and hobbled toward the living room, grimacing with every step.

Ding-*dong.*

Cripes, that's what his doorbell sounded like? Something from a '50s Avon commercial? He'd lived here four years and couldn't remember ever hearing his own doorbell. No doubt the 'Beware of Dog' sign had something to do with that. He and Max never stayed indoors when they could be outside, and they sure as hell never waited around for life to come to them.

Until now.

The doorbell sounded again, and he wished he still had his service weapon. He'd happily put a round into that little speaker by the front door.

Reaching the door at last, he tore it open. *"What?"*

⁂

Paige Harmer took an instinctive step backward.

When she'd moved into this duplex last month, the other side had been vacant. The landlady'd said its occupant was in hospital recovering from surgery. But even after her neighbor had come home nearly two weeks ago, the unit next door had been unnaturally quiet. No visitors came or went, and no music thrummed through those walls. If it weren't for the small bag of garbage that materialized at the curb beside hers every Tuesday morning, and the occasional muted sound of a television deep in the night, she'd have sworn the other apartment was deserted. Now, her neighbor stood framed in the doorway, wearing a pair of white boxers and a thunderous expression.

And oh, Christmas, he was most gorgeous thing she'd clapped eyes on in years, outside of a Calvin Klein ad.

Despite their current storminess, his eyes were as blue as the July sky. Black hair, a startling contrast to his pale complexion, stood up in all directions, all the sexier for its dishevelment. Thick, black eyebrows slanted over those killer eyes. More dark hair crowned his chest in a liberal thatch, tapering to a thin line that arrowed out of sight beneath his boxers.

Runner, she thought. *Endurance athlete.* Just a hair over average height, with a leanness that shaded toward too thin. Yet the conformation of arms and chest disclosed enough wiry muscle to give the impression of power.

"Can I help you?"

Mister, if you can't, there's no help for me.

The thought barely had a chance to form before her internal censor roared to life. He was way too young for her to be ogling, for goodness sake. *Hardly much older than Dillon, by the look of him.*

There, that did it. Though he was clearly nowhere near as young as her son, the mental association was enough to clamp a firm leash on her imagination.

Unfortunately, the extra seconds it took to channel her thoughts in more pure directions didn't go unnoticed. One thick eyebrow arched inquiringly, reminding her she hadn't yet stated her purpose.

She felt a flush begin to climb her neck. No chance he'd miss that, either. Her skin was almost translucent, at least the stuff between the freckles. She lifted the foil-wrapped plate she held. "I thought you might like some dinner."

He looked at the plate. "Thanks, but I'm not a big eater."

"I can see that," she said, injecting her tone with the same censorious note she might use with her son when he ignored his body's nutritional needs. He shifted, and she finally noticed the cane, which he appeared to be leaning on pretty heavily. "Don't worry. It'll freeze nicely if you can't handle it all right now."

"Look, lady, that's real nice of you, but —"

"I'll just put it in the refrigerator for you, shall I?"

She angled sideways and slipped right past him before he could finish brushing her off. No way was she going back to her lonely unit to worry about Dillon. Not tonight.

"That way, I presume?" She indicated the direction the kitchen must be, if the place were laid out in the mirror image of hers.

"Uh … yeah."

Seconds later, Paige stood in front of a white dinosaur of a refrigerator, a twin to the one that rattled and hummed in her own kitchen, right beside the commercial refrigeration unit she'd installed for her business. That's where the similarity ended, she discovered, as she opened the refrigerator's door.

Five bottles of beer, domestic. Some Chinese takeout cartons that bulged ominously as though approaching an explosive state. A drying chunk of cheddar cheese, circa 2008. A few bottles of condiments. No eggs, no dairy, no vegetables, no fruit.

Hearing him arrive at the kitchen door — the thumping of the cane on the linoleum-covered floor announced his progress — she glanced over at him.

"Is this the part where you tell me you're really one of the undead and have no need of sustenance beyond human blood?"

He didn't smile. If anything, he scowled more fiercely. "I've been meaning to get to the grocery store."

"It must be hard."

He followed the drift of her gaze. She could tell by the way his hand tightened on the cane's handle.

His jaw hardened even further, if possible. "I manage."

"Are you hungry? The food's still hot." She waggled the foil-wrapped plate temptingly. "Stuffed pork chops with mashed potatoes, glazed carrots and gingered parsnips."

"It's okay," he said, after a split-second hesitation. "You can just put it in the fridge."

Fat chance. She'd caught the fleeting look of indecision in his eye as she'd described what was under the foil. He was hungry, all right. "Aw, come on, sit down and eat. I need the distraction."

Those cigar-thick eyebrows soared. "You want to stay and watch me *eat*?"

"Relax, fella. Nothing kinky. I just don't want to go back over there yet. I've done two loads of laundry, vacuumed the carpet within an inch of its life, baked three cheesecakes and seven pies. I have nowhere to put any more baking and nothing left to clean. So if I go home now, I've got nothing left to do but worry about Dillon."

"Who's Dillon?"

Ah! A question. And she hadn't even dragged it out of him. That was an improvement. "My son."

"Where is he?"

She blew out her breath, lifting a strand of auburn hair off her face. "If I knew that, I wouldn't be worried, would I? Or maybe I would, at that," she amended, thinking about the hard-looking young man Dillon had been hanging with lately.

"He's missing?"

The sharpness of his tone drew her glance to his face. His eyebrows were drawn together again in a frown.

She shrugged. "He's seventeen, almost eighteen. I can hardly describe him as missing every time he slams out of the house in a foul mood."

That surprised him. She could see him doing the mental arithmetic, calculating her minimum age. *That's right, son. Old enough to be your mother, even if I don't look it.*

Okay, that was an exaggeration. A huge exaggeration. But older than him by quite a few years, she'd wager.

"Sit." She pulled a tea towel off the oven door handle where it had been hung to dry after its last use and flopped it on the table as an impromptu place mat, then plunked the plate down on it. "I nuked the ceramic plate before dishing up the food so it would stay nice and warm."

"I don't even know your name."

Way to go, Paige. Barge in and take over the man's life without an introduction.

"Sorry." She wiped her right hand on her jeans and extended it. "Paige Harmer. Your new neighbor."

She regretted her gesture immediately, as he had to lurch forward to grasp her hand. He didn't grimace, but she could feel the tension in his grip. Pain.

"Tom Godsoe."

"I know." At his enquiring look, she hastened to add, "Mrs. Graham mentioned your name."

Paige had been impressed at how close-mouthed her landlady had been about her tenant's private life. As a prospective new tenant, all Paige had needed to know was that her neighbor wasn't a creepazoid. She'd found her landlady's discretion commendable at the time, but now she couldn't help but wish the other woman had been a little less discreet. For instance, what did Tom Godsoe do for a living? How had he sustained the injury that made crossing a room the grueling ordeal it appeared to be?

"Okay," he said at last, "if I'm going to have an audience, I think I'd better get dressed."

Not on my account.

Before something like that escaped her mouth, she averted her eyes from those square shoulders and lightly-muscled expanse of chest. "Take your time. I think I spotted some coffee beans and a grinder. I'll just brew us a pot of java."

"Be my guest," he drawled, then turned and thumped away.

A smile tugging at her lips, Paige reached for the gourmet coffee beans.

⚜

A film of perspiration slicked Tommy's brow before he'd made it halfway to his bedroom. Damned useless leg. He paused by the couch and leaned on the back of the hulking piece of furniture for a few seconds. Gritting his teeth against the white-hot shards of pain he knew would explode in his hip and lower back with each step, he resumed the trek to the bedroom.

Why hadn't he given that crazy, wild-haired woman the boot? He wasn't *that* hungry. He still had waffles in the freezer, and dry Fruit Loops were a perfectly adequate source of nutrition.

Yeah, right. The hospital food he'd subsisted on for so long was better than anything he had left in the cupboards. A pork chop and actual vegetables sounded like heaven. He only hoped the price of dinner wouldn't be too high. She had the look of a hard customer to move along, if she wasn't of a mind to go.

Of course, she'd never experienced Tommy's post-injury brand of hospitality. He'd managed to chase off friends and fellow officers — no, make that ex-fellow officers — even before he'd checked out early from the rehab center. Getting rid of one slip of a woman shouldn't be too hard.

When he reached his bedroom, he sank down on the edge of the bed and cursed his trembling leg. Weak as a damn baby. It took another few minutes to drag the sweat pants on. By the time he'd located a t-shirt and pulled it over his head, his whole body was slicked with sweat. Pitiful. Completely done in by a twenty-foot walk.

He grabbed the pill bottle off the night stand, dumped two tablets into his palm and dry-swallowed them. His hip was gonna kill him tonight, for all this activity. Already, he pictured himself lying on the mattress in the dead of night, going quietly crazy while the pain radiated down to the soles of his feet.

Kitchen, he reminded himself. If he was going to sell his soul, or at least his privacy, for a home-cooked meal, he'd better get there before the food fossilized on the plate.

By the time he made it back to the kitchen, the crazy woman — Paige? — not only had a pot of coffee brewed, but she'd cleaned out his refrigerator as evidenced by the armload of inedible stuff she was dumping in the garbage can when he hobbled in.

She glanced up at him. "I hope you weren't too attached to any of that stuff."

"You cleaned my refrigerator?"

She grinned. "Couple more days, that stuff would have walked off on its own, anyway."

As he lowered himself onto a chair, a laborious proposition in itself, she washed her hands under the tap and dried them on a clean towel she must have found in a drawer. Then she zoomed in on him again, removed the foil covering from his meal and rotated the plate so the meat was within easy reach. The delicious aroma that rose up from the hot meal was almost enough to take the edge off his irritation at her hovering solicitousness.

Almost.

"I swear to God, if you pick up those utensils to cut my meat for me, I won't be responsible for my actions."

She started at his tone, and although she didn't evacuate the physical space she occupied by his left shoulder, he felt her take a mental step backward. And she looked at him, really looked, which she'd managed not to do since she'd inventoried him in the doorway earlier. He met her gaze, keeping his expression flat. Best way to discourage sympathy, he'd found.

"I'm sorry," she said.

He picked up his fork. "If I detect the merest whiff of pity from you, you'll be taking that coffee to go, good deeds notwithstanding. Understood?"

"Pity?"

She blinked at him in what appeared to be genuine disbelief. Her eyes were green, he noticed. Not the improbable green of those tinted contacts women wore, but a soft, mossy green.

"Mr. Godsoe, I assure you it hadn't occurred to me to pity you. It was just the mother in me coming out."

He stabbed a parsnip. "I don't need a mother."

"That's going around, I guess. Neither does Dillon."

She turned away to grab a mug, but not before he caught a glimpse of the worry lines creasing her forehead.

He went back to eating as she fixed her coffee. By the time she plunked down opposite him at the small pedestal table, her brow was smooth once more. He'd also devoured half the pork chop.

"This is wonderful," he said around his food. "Where'd you learn to cook like this?"

"My fourth and final foster home. I finally figured out you had to bring value-added if you wanted to stay put."

His question had been rhetorical; he certainly hadn't expected an answer, let alone one like that. With her wide, inviting face, freckled complexion and burnished hair, she looked like apple pie and picket fences, not the product of an underfunded and overburdened child protection system.

Dammit. It was no concern of his who she was and where she came from. He had more than enough of his own problems to worry about. Instead of uttering one of the half-dozen questions that sprang to mind, he nodded and went back to his meal.

"Actually, I make my living cooking," she said. "Desserts, specifically, for some of the nicer restaurants around town. Cheesecakes, pies, flans, tarts, you name it. Speaking of which, would you like a piece of lemon meringue pie? I could run home and get you one."

Homemade lemon pie sounded great, but he wouldn't send her out for it. "No, this is good."

"Coffee?"

He felt her gaze on him as he used the last morsel of meat to mop up any lingering traces of juice from his plate.

"Please." God, it felt good to have a hot meal inside him. He could almost forget the insistent throb of pain that was his constant companion.

Once again, *almost.*

She put a mug of steaming black coffee before him, along with a half-pint of cream and the bowl of lumpy sugar she must have found in his cupboard.

He shot her a look. "Where'd the cream come from?"

"I ran home and got it while you were changing. Eggs, too, and whole-wheat bread. Some dry cereal. A couple of bananas. Wish I'd thought of the pie."

It was his turn to blink in disbelief. Until twenty minutes ago, he'd never laid eyes on her. Since then, she'd pushed her way into his home, fed him, cleaned his kitchen and done her level best to restock his cupboards.

"Okay, this must be the part where you smile disarmingly and tell me you're some kind of *Pacific Heights*-type psycho and I'm never gonna get you to leave."

A smile lifted the corner of her lips, making a dimple flash on the right side of her mouth. "I guess this wouldn't be the time to confess that I really loved Michael Keaton's tenant-from-hell character in that movie?"

Irritated with himself for noticing her mouth, he grated, "Dammit, I told you, I don't want your pity, or your groceries. I let you in the door, and now you're making yourself at home, digging through my cupboards —"

"Look, Tom — can I call you Tom? Tommy?" Without bothering to wait for a reply, she forged on. "I can see you don't get around very well, whereas I do. Your cupboards were bare. Mine aren't. No biggie. Heck, you can replace the groceries, if you feel that strongly about it."

He scowled at her reasonable tone. "I just don't want anyone feeling sorry for me. I'm doing fine, dammit."

"I didn't mean to imply you weren't." Her green eyes narrowed. "Do you have some tragic story I should know about?"

"Hardly." He said it without hesitation, and just to prove how tragedy-free he was feeling, he lifted his coffee cup to his lips and took a sip.

"Good, because now wouldn't be a good time to talk about it. It'd just ruin your digestion. Let's talk about me instead."

He choked on his coffee.

She turned those big eyes on him. "What? I thought we'd established you don't want to talk about your accident or your surgery or whatever, so why not me? Or my suddenly difficult son."

Why talk at all? He could plead a bone-deep agony in his hip and leg, which would be no lie. The pain pills hadn't kicked in yet. Then he remembered the look on her face when she'd first mentioned her son.

"Dillon, right?"

She brightened. "Yes, Dillon."

"What's his problem?"

She shrugged, but it wasn't the same nonchalant gesture she'd displayed before. This shrug spoke of helplessness.

"I wish I knew. We used to be really close, but now … his moods are so … changeable."

"He's eighteen."

"Not for another couple of weeks."

"My point is, being surly and uncommunicative is par for the course."

"I know. But he's always been such a sweet kid."

He watched her absently stroke her coffee mug. "Boys grow up."

She shook her head. "That's part of it, for sure. Maybe even the biggest part of it," she allowed. "But he really didn't want to make this move, or at least not as fast as we did. Consciously or not, he's punishing me for disrupting our lives." She chewed the inside of her lip a moment. "Maybe I should have postponed the move. But I'd already held off until he finished high school, and he'd have had to move *somewhere* in the fall anyway, for university, so I figured why not here, right?"

He realized she was looking at him as though she expected some kind of reaction. "UNB's a good school. He'll like it."

She looked down into the depths of her coffee mug again. "Besides, I'd won a major contract that pretty much required me to relocate here. Not that he had to pick *this* university just because I was coming here. He'd been accepted by three different schools, and we could have stretched the budget to pay for residence, but this one really does have the best computer science program."

What was he supposed to say? "I've heard very good things about it."

"I know it was a wrench to leave his friends so soon after graduation, but I figured he could use the time to get to know the city, make a few friends here."

Man, she'd obviously been over this ground a few times, rationalizing, regretting, second-guessing. He knew all about that. "His father around?"

Another shake of the head. "Not since Dillon was little."

"Maybe he needs to connect with his dad."

As soon as the words were out of his mouth, he recognized that he'd slipped into problem-solving mode. Dammit, he wasn't a cop anymore. And he sure as hell wasn't a social worker.

"That's not in the cards."

He pushed back his own too-raw emotions. She clearly needed to talk to someone, and he'd been elected. What had she said? Oh, yeah. The kid's dad was out of the picture. "Dead? Dillon's father, I mean."

"Dead*beat*," she corrected, lifting her gaze from her mug.

"What about Big Brothers?" He found himself looking away.

"It's a good program. A lot of kids from single-parent families benefit from the influence of a male role —"

She held up a hand to stop him. "You're preaching to the converted, here. We were in the program for four years, until Dillon's Big Brother moved to Halifax. Now, he thinks he's too old for that kind of stuff."

Tommy gingerly shifted in his chair. "Again, he's nearly eighteen. It's natural for him to look to his peers rather than an adult."

"I think he found something else to fill the void."

Of course. "Girl, eh?"

She grimaced. "I wish."

Whoops. "I see."

"Oh, no! It's not like that. Dillon dates girls. There's just no one special."

"You know, a lot of mothers might be glad there was no one special. I seem to remember my mother getting uneasy when I was that age and stuck on a girl."

That drew a weak smile from her.

"Afraid one of those sweet young things was going to whisk her son off to the altar, was she?"

Shotgun marriage? There'd never been much chance of that. Not that an accidental pregnancy had been out of the question. He'd just been far too immature and self-involved for marriage, as had the girls he'd run with. His father would have just pulled out his checkbook. Of course, his father also would have given him a hearty thump on the back as though he'd finally done something praiseworthy. *Well, at least this proves you're not a queer.*

"Something like that," he muttered, taking a sip of his coffee. Lord, even her coffee was incredible. "So, if it's not a girl, he must be hanging with a bad crowd."

Her hand tightened on the handle of her mug. "Bingo."

"It's probably not that bad," he offered. "Kids that age talk a good line of trash, but they're not nearly as bad as they'd have the world believe. I've seen 'em fold pretty quick when —" Damn. Talking like a cop again. "What I mean is, it's usually just posturing. He'll grow out of it."

She slanted him a look. "You don't have kids, do you?"

"No, I don't."

"Adults." She sighed and pushed back in her chair.

"Huh?"

"He's hanging around with adults. I only got a good look at one of them. He was relatively young, I suppose, but still a lot older than Dillon. Mid-twenties, probably, and way, way harder than my son, from the look of him."

Tommy frowned. That kind of age differential usually spelled bad news. He could too easily picture unscrupulous adults feeding a troubled kid's ego and thirst for attention until the kid was ripe for exploitation. Drug-dealing, auto theft, pornography, prostitution .... All the ugly possibilities flashed through his mind.

"And you think they're up to ... what?"

"No good," she said darkly. "Although since I haven't had an actual conversation with any of these men, I have to admit I'm basing that judgment entirely on prejudice and stereotypes. Which makes me feel like a total hypocrite, since it's exactly the kind of thing I've tried to teach Dillon not to do."

"Let me guess — shaved heads, baggy pants, shirts buttoned at the neck and open at the bottom, tattoos?"

"Not to mention the cold eyes. Oh, yes, and the chopped pick-up with the tinted windows, and the kind of stereo that sets off minor earthquakes with the bass notes when it drives by."

The cynic in him said she'd probably nailed the demographic accurately, but he stayed silent.

"So?" She looked at him expectantly.

"So, what?" He shifted again, just a few millimeters, to ease the ache in his leg. The relief was exquisite. Unfortunately, it lasted about a tenth of a second, then started throbbing again.

"So, are you going to pat me on the head and tell me I'm being a paranoid, over-protective mother?"

"No," he said. "No, I won't do that."

She sagged. "Damn. I was hoping you would. Hoping even harder that you could make me believe it."

"Sorry."

Their gazes locked for a few seconds, and Tommy felt an unexpected surge of sexual awareness rocket through him.

His first reaction was relief; he'd begun to think of his libido as KIA. Then the inappropriateness struck him. This was a distraught woman, a worried mother. A mother whose son, technically speaking, was old enough to make her a *grandmother*.

She jumped up and carried her cup to the sink, where she rinsed it and set it on the draining board. "Look," she said, turning back to him. "I can see you're in pain. You probably need to lie down or something. I'll get out of your hair."

"The leg's gonna hurt no matter what. You don't have to rush off, if you don't want to."

Christ, was that him talking? Had he just invited the original Velcro woman to stay?

Her green gaze caught and held his again. "Really?"

"Really," he heard himself say. Oh, Lord, he must have taken too many of those pain pills.

"That's very generous of you, especially after I pushed my way in here."

"You *did* feed me."

She tilted her head in an attitude of listening. "Looks like you're off the hook. That must be Dillon now."

He heard it too, the sound of a car's engine. At the end of this cul-de-sac just barely inside the city limits, they didn't get much drive-by traffic. Good. The kid was home where he belonged, and now he could have his solitude back.

"Thanks for holding my hand," she said, turning to pick up her plate. "No offense, but I hope it'll be the last time."

The latter was delivered with a wide smile, but he could see the tension and worry beneath it.

"Look, do you want me to talk to him or something?"

Oh, hell, where had *that* come from? She looked just as stunned by the offer as he was about making it.

"Thanks, but I don't think so. I know my son. If I just spring you on him, it'll be worse than if I just leave it alone."

"Well, if you change your mind …."

She smiled at him again, and he was struck once more by a pang of desire, this one even stronger than the last.

"Thanks, Tommy."

She let herself out, and the sound of the door closing echoed behind her. For a split second, her absence felt like a hollowness, in his house and in his chest.

Damned lust. Now that the relief had passed, he almost wished he'd stayed dead that way. Didn't he have enough aches without adding another?

Pulling himself to his feet, mainly by dint of his upper-body strength, he picked up his cane and clumped toward the bedroom. He'd almost reached his customary resting spot by the sofa when he heard the scream — shrill, female and clearly terrified.

Paige.

Adrenaline ripped through his system like a shot of juice from a live electrical wire. He covered the distance to the door in a flash, with no sensation of pain. Endorphins. He'd pay for it later. Tearing the door open, he lurched out onto the step.

"Paige?"

⁂

A hand still clamped to her mouth to stifle the scream she'd been unable to suppress, she swiveled her head toward Tommy's voice. He stood on the steps outside his unit, looking like he was ready, willing and able to use his cane as a weapon, if need be.

"What it is? What's the matter?"

She pointed to her doorstep.

"Jesus. What's *that?*"

"I don't know." Her stomach did a sick little flip, but her voice was surprisingly steady. "But it's dead and it seems to be minus its fur."

He swore, then hobbled a few feet closer. "I take it that the car we heard wasn't Dillon coming home?"

"Dillon's car's not home," she replied, choosing her words carefully. These days, she couldn't rule out anything where her son was concerned, even his participation in something as ugly as this. He'd closed himself off so completely from her. Not that she thought he'd *lead* something as gruesome as this, but he might go along for the ride, especially if he didn't know in advance what the plan was.

"You're welcome to call it in from my place," he said, gesturing toward his unit. "Phone's on the wall just inside the kitchen."

Call the police? Without talking to Dillon?

"Ah, that's okay." She took a step backward, closer to her own doorstep. "Thanks for the offer, but I think I'll just deal with this myself."

"You're making a mistake, Paige."

His tone was quiet, without any detectable inflection, but it arrested her retreat in a way a forceful command might not have.

"What do you mean?"

"By not reporting this. You think you're protecting your son, but if his new friends did this, with or without his involvement, you'd do better to tackle it head on. He needs to know that his choices have repercussions."

He was right and she knew it, but it wasn't that simple. Dillon was her *son*. He was all she had, and getting further away from her every day. She didn't know how to guide him toward a better path without driving him to worse rebellion. Her frustration boiled up into anger.

"Who said I thought this has anything to do with Dillon?"

"So, you think it was what? Random sicko? Or maybe a customer who didn't like your Tiramisu?"

She glared at him. "There's no need for sarcasm."

He sighed. "Okay, let's say it has nothing to do with your son. All the more reason to call the cops right now. They might be able to get impressions from the car's tires. Presuming somebody carried it to your doorstep, there could be footprint evidence. But that stuff is transitory. You have to act fast."

She snorted. "You sound like a cop."

"That's because I am."

Oh, shit.

Printed in Great Britain
by Amazon

19074642R00130